D0182386

Dear Reader,

I am very pleased and honored to be part of Harlequin American Romance's 20th anniversary. I was privileged to have one of my love stories, *Touch of Fire*, selected for publication that first year. To date, I have published seventy-one novels. Fifty-nine of them have been Harlequin American Romance titles.

And the reason for that is simple. Harlequin American Romance novels embody everything I hold dear about family and friends, love and commitment. The stories can by funny, serious, sad and happy. They are a slice of real life with a dollop of romance and fantasy thrown in. And they end happily—every time.

My heartfelt thanks to the wonderful editors I have worked with over the years, including and especially my editor for the past eight years, the supremely talented Denise O'Sullivan.

To the readers who have read and loved my books and shared them with family and friends— you make it all worthwhile.

My very best to you all.

Cathy Gillen Thacker

Dear Reader,

What a spectacular lineup of love stories Harlequin American Romance has for you this month as we continue to celebrate our 20th anniversary. Start off with another wonderful title in Cathy Gillen Thacker's DEVERAUX LEGACY series, *Taking Over the Tycoon*. Sexy millionaire Connor Templeton is used to getting whatever—whomever—he wants! But has he finally met his match in one beguiling single mother?

Next, *Fortune's Twins* by Kara Lennox is the latest installment in the MILLIONAIRE, MONTANA continuity series. In this book, a night of passion leaves a "Main Street Millionaire" expecting twins—and has the whole town wondering "Who's the daddy?" After catching a bridal bouquet and opening an heirloom hope chest, a shy virgin dreams about asking her secret crush to father the baby she yearns for, in *Have Bouquet, Need Boyfriend*, part of Rita Herron's HARTWELL HOPE CHESTS series. And don't miss *Inherited: One Baby!* by Laura Marie Altom, in which a handsome bachelor must convince his ex-wife to remarry him in order to keep custody of the adorable orphaned baby left in his care.

Enjoy this month's offerings, and be sure to return each and every month to Harlequin American Romance!

Melissa Jeglinski
Associate Senior Editor
Harlequin American Romance

Cathy Gillen Thacker

TAKING OVER THE TYCOON

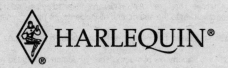

TORONTO • NEW YORK • LONDON
AMSTERDAM • PARIS • SYDNEY • HAMBURG
STOCKHOLM • ATHENS • TOKYO • MILAN • MADRID
PRAGUE • WARSAW • BUDAPEST • AUCKLAND

If you purchased this book without a cover you should be aware
that this book is stolen property. It was reported as "unsold and
destroyed" to the publisher, and neither the author nor the
publisher has received any payment for this "stripped book."

ISBN 0-373-16973-6

TAKING OVER THE TYCOON

Copyright © 2003 by Cathy Gillen Thacker.

All rights reserved. Except for use in any review, the reproduction or
utilization of this work in whole or in part in any form by any electronic,
mechanical or other means, now known or hereafter invented, including
xerography, photocopying and recording, or in any information storage
or retrieval system, is forbidden without the written permission of the
publisher, Harlequin Enterprises Limited, 225 Duncan Mill Road,
Don Mills, Ontario, Canada M3B 3K9.

All characters in this book have no existence outside the imagination of
the author and have no relation whatsoever to anyone bearing the same
name or names. They are not even distantly inspired by any individual
known or unknown to the author, and all incidents are pure invention.

This edition published by arrangement with Harlequin Books S.A.

® and TM are trademarks of the publisher. Trademarks indicated with
® are registered in the United States Patent and Trademark Office, the
Canadian Trade Marks Office and in other countries.

Visit us at www.eHarlequin.com

Printed in U.S.A.

ABOUT THE AUTHOR

Cathy Gillen Thacker married her high school sweetheart and hasn't had a dull moment since. Why, you ask? Well, there were three kids, various pets, any number of automobiles, several moves across the country, his and her careers and sundry other experiences (some of which were exciting and some of which weren't). But mostly, there was love and friendship and laughter, and lots of experiences she wouldn't trade for the world.

Books by Cathy Gillen Thacker

HARLEQUIN AMERICAN ROMANCE

HARLEQUIN BOOKS

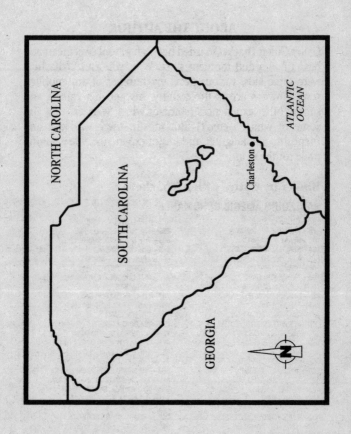

Chapter One

Kristy Neumeyer waited until the tall, sexy man in front of her finished his silky-smooth spiel before she put her paintbrush down and wiped her hands on the rag looped into the belt of her jeans. Turning back to him, she decided not to mince words this time, and she gave him her most stubborn smile. "I've got just three words for your proposition."

He waited, hope shining in his gorgeous gray eyes, as Kristy tightened her lips and continued. "Not. Gonna. Happen." Not ever, no matter what he did. No matter how attractive Connor Templeton looked standing there with his neatly cut, dark blond hair, the hint of autumn tan on his handsome face. No matter how easily his confident and commanding presence could take her breath away. And it was high time the ultrasuccessful real estate tycoon realized that, Kristy determined. His development projects might attract gold, not just in Charleston, South Carolina, but all up and down the East Coast of the United States, but they did not interest her. Not for a red-hot second.

For the briefest moment, Connor Templeton's chiseled jaw dropped, and he regarded her in stunned amazement, as if unable to believe she was going to pass on the oh-so-lucrative proposition he had just politely and painstakingly laid out for her. His own smile fading, he watched as she

finished painting one of the shutters beside the double
lobby doors a deep pine-green. "You obviously haven't
fully calculated my offer," he stated finally.

As the warm October breeze ruffled her hair, Kristy
picked up her bucket and brush and moved a little farther
down the covered porch that faced the Atlantic Ocean, to
the next double hung window. Ignoring his frank perusal
of her, she took a tranquilizing breath and continued painting. She'd had the outside of the 1950s lodge painted a
snowy white by a professional crew, but to save money,
had left the trim work around the first floor doors and windows for herself. "And I don't intend to, either, Mr. Big
Business," she said. If he had his way, he'd swiftly have
her leading the life of the rich and idle, instead of bringing
life back to the resort she had inherited from her beloved
aunt Ida.

Connor followed her, being careful not to get paint on
his casually elegant clothes as he leaned against one of the
square posts that supported the porch roof. He thrust his
hands into the pockets of his khaki slacks. "The name's
Connor," he reminded her cordially. "Connor Templeton."

Kristy slanted him a glance, ignoring the way his broad
shoulders filled out his classic navy blazer and patterned
shirt. "Daisy Templeton Granger's older brother, I know."
Daisy was a good friend of hers. They had gotten to know
each other through mutual friends the previous spring.

"Then you should also know," Connor insisted, "if
you're friends with my baby sister, that I am a nice guy."

Who wouldn't hurt a flea? "I don't care if you're the
king of England, Mr. Templeton," Kristy told him firmly.
"I'm staying put. So take that back to your business partner
and all the investors you and Skip Wakefield have rounded
up." She stopped what she was doing and marched forward
until they were standing nose to nose. Refusing to let that

slow, sexy smile of his turn her knees to jelly, she continued, "Because I am not selling Paradise Resort. Not now. Not ever."

The oceanfront lodge, twelve cottages and a stretch of beautiful private beach that comprised the Folly Beach, South Carolina resort, was not just Kristy's inheritance, it was her future and long-held dream. And she was not parting with it. Not even for the five million dollars purchase price Connor Templeton and his partner, Skip Wakefield, were waving in front of her nose. Money that would more than obliterate both mortgages on the resort and Kristy's own mountain of debt.

She knew she still had a lot of work to do on the interior of the lodge, particularly in the individual guest rooms. But thanks to the grueling work she had put in all summer, the rest of it, including all the common areas, were shaping up nicely. Plus the resort had old-fashioned charm, reminiscent of relaxing family vacations of a bygone era. There were no tennis courts here, no golf courses or video arcades, just the lodge, the dunes and the beach. It was quiet and low-key and appealing, a place where people who simply wanted to spend time together could come. The two-story, white clapboard lodge had a dramatically pitched gable roof over the lobby, club and dining rooms, kitchen, reservation desk and private office, all located in the central part of the building. Two rectangular wings spread out on either side. Native palmetto trees thirty feet in height surrounded the hotel and stood sentry on the short drive from Folly Beach Road to the parking area. An array of flowering bushes—camellias, bougainvilleas, magnolias and azaleas—added color around the lodge and cottages.

"You don't have to decide today," Connor continued, persuasively stating his case. "You can take some time to think about it."

"I don't have to think about it," Kristy stated. What was

it about these two guys that they didn't understand when a business offer was being refused?

Before Connor could reply to that, Kristy's obnoxious neighbor to the south, Bruce Fitts, suddenly rounded the side of the lodge. As always, the too-tanned, penguin-shaped man with the thin black mustache was dressed in swim trunks—trunks that were, in Kristy's estimation, way too brief. He also wore expensive Italian sandals and an open shirt accessorized with several thick gold chains.

"I told you and your partner she was unreasonable!" Fitts declared as he rushed across the wide front porch the locals liked to refer to as the piazza. Looking to Connor for help, Fitts ran a hand over his slick-backed ebony hair.

Kristy turned to Connor, barely able to believe that an aristocratic man like Connor would associate with the oily "entrepreneur" inhabiting the luxurious new beach house just south of her resort. Unlike the other hardworking inhabitants of Folly Beach, Bruce Fitts made his money from sleazy schemes. He was constantly threatening lawsuits, ripping off insurance companies and doing whatever he could to rake in easy money. And when he wasn't scheming and conniving, he was spying on other residents, including Kristy and her girls, through the telescope mounted on his deck. She had been trying to ignore him, and his near constant complaints, but with him in such close proximity, it wasn't easy.

"What are you doing here, Fitts?" Connor turned to glare warningly at Bruce.

"Yeah," Kristy said sarcastically to Connor, "I bet you've got a real deal on some prime marshland you want to sell me. For a friendly little discount, of course." How stupid did Connor and his partner think she was? Clearly, they would do anything to get her to throw in the towel, even, it seemed, employing her thoroughly disreputable neighbor. Not that the idea was without merit, Kristy had to admit. Being around Bruce Fitts for any length of time did make her want to split.

Bruce glared at Kristy resentfully as he declared, "You're just like your aunt."

Kristy smiled. Her poor aunt had had to put up with this, too. "Thank you," she said sweetly. "I'll consider that a compliment, since my aunt Ida was one of my all-time favorite people."

"Forcing the rest of us homeowners to look at this eyesore!" Bruce sputtered.

Kristy conceded that Paradise Resort was in need of a lot of tender loving care. But that was why she was here—to bring it back to life.

"Mr. Fitts, please leave us," Connor stated firmly.

Bruce stared at Connor. Obviously realizing that he was not a man to tangle with if you could help it, Bruce backed down reluctantly. "Fine." He snorted, then wagged a finger at Kristy. "But not before I tell you, missy, that I am not going to let you keep on devaluating my property with this dump for very much longer, even if I have to personally find a way to shut you down!"

There was no way he could do so legally, Kristy knew. She had complied with all state and local regulations as she worked to get the aging property looking good again.

Letting her neighbor know with a glance that she had no intention of falling victim to any of his shenanigans, she warned right back, "Try it. Give it your best shot!" She marched closer, fists knotted at her sides. "Now get off my property, Mr. Fitts, and stay off, before I call the police!"

Bruce Fitts glared at Kristy, unwilling to budge, until Connor clapped a hand on his shoulder and murmured something in Fitts's ear. Kristy had no idea what he said, but Fitts calmed down immediately, and with a last condescending glance at Kristy, headed off the porch and back down the beach toward his own home, a luxurious beach-front house overlooking the Atlantic.

"I would thank you for getting rid of that horse's behind," Kristy said, turning back to Connor. "Except I have the distinct feeling you're on Fitts's side in all this."

He focused on her face and loosely pinned up hair. "I'm not on anyone's side."

Kristy shot him another disgruntled look. In her thirty-three years, she had never met anyone quite this persistent. "A few minutes ago you were trying to convince me you were on *my* side." At least that's how his sales pitch—and the sum he was offering to buy the place—had sounded to her.

Connor folded his arms in front of him, leaned against the wooden post again and looked deep into her eyes. "I want everyone to be happy," he explained. "And I honestly think, if you were to listen to me and sell this property to people who could afford to build the kind of luxury condo project this area of Folly Beach needs, we would all be better off."

THIS WAS THE POINT in the conversation, Connor thought, when Kristy Neumeyer was supposed to relax and begin to seriously consider his and Skip Wakefield's very generous offer to purchase her property. Instead she was glaring at him as if he were a piece of gum stuck to the bottom of her shoe. Sighing, she shook her head, picked up her paint-brush and went back to the louvered shutter she had been painting. Her back to him, she said, "I think we've said everything there is to say."

Or in other words, Connor thought, it was time for him to be shoving off. The only problem being he didn't want to leave. And that was a little hard to fathom. At thirty-eight, Connor had long ago given up on spending time with people who did not enjoy his company, or vice versa. In his opinion, life was too short to force personal relationships, even the most useful or casual of ones.

But there was something about the delectable beauty next to him that completely captured his attention. And it had to do with more than her incredibly sexy looks. Although those were pretty remarkable, Connor had to admit. Even in the midst of what looked to be a very physically challenging workday, she was drop-dead gorgeous. Her hair was a glossy dark brown, and the straight, silky locks had been loosely twisted and caught at the back of her head in a tortoiseshell clip—a look that would have been very neat and businesslike had it not been for the wispy tendrils that had escaped along her cheekbones and neck. She didn't seem to be wearing any makeup, but then, Connor noted with a satisfied sigh, she didn't need it. Her skin was flawless and golden, her lips pink and luscious. Color bloomed in her cheeks, emphasizing the delicate bone structure of her face. Her nose was slender, her dark brown eyes sparkled—especially when she was sparring with him. And as for her stubborn chin…it was as pretty and feminine as the rest of her.

She looked to be several inches shorter than he was—which made her about five feet five inches tall, he guessed. The snug-fitting jeans and cap-sleeved, yellow T-shirt she was wearing made the most of what was a very nice figure—so nice that Connor was having trouble keeping his eyes off her slender, showgirl-sexy legs.

Determined to find some way for them to connect, as friends as well as future business allies, he walked over to stand beside her. What was that old saying? If you can't beat 'em, join 'em? "I could lend a hand here," he said, noting she still had several shutters to paint.

Kristy made a face at him. "In those clothes? I don't think so."

So okay, he wasn't dressed for hard manual labor. That

didn't mean he wasn't capable of it, however. Connor took off his sport coat, loosened his tie. Still searching for some way for the two of them to connect, he said easily, "Daisy says you're great, that you gave her a place to stay when her whole world was turned upside down." Connor knew his little sister was a great judge of character. Plus Daisy never said anything she didn't mean.

Kristy shrugged off the praise and continued painting. "It's Jack Granger you should be thanking," she said softly. "Jack's the one who helped her get her life back together."

Connor knew that, too. Jack and Daisy were not just married, they were crazy in love. The way he wanted to be someday. If he ever met the right woman, that was. One who wasn't the least bit interested in his blue blood or his wealth. Thus far, he had yet to meet a woman who loved him more than his pedigree or bank account. Connor looped his jacket over the railing that edged the piazza and removed his tie. "I understand you're a widow." Losing a spouse was something they had in common…

Kristy turned to give him a frosty look.

So she didn't want to talk about that, Connor noted.

Moving on. "You have twins." Who would likely be needing college funds. And many other things that money from the sale of Paradise Resort would provide. If he could get her to sell it, that was.

Kristy regarded him with exasperation. "Did you ever hear the expression about wearing out one's welcome? Well—" She broke off when she heard the sound of a car in the parking lot on the other side of the lodge.

"Expecting someone?" Connor said, aware that the place wasn't slated to reopen for another week or so.

"No," Kristy admitted as the car motor shut off. She set down her paintbrush and regarded Connor smugly. "But then I wasn't expecting you, either."

Touché.

Connor followed her around the building and down the walk that led to the parking lot. When she spotted the two people inside a late-model station wagon, she released her breath in a low hiss and muttered a most unladylike phrase.

"Problem?" Connor asked. He was surprised because up to now, Kristy had seemed so cool, calm and collected. Now she looked anything but.

"My mother and brother." More color swept into her cheeks.

"You don't look very happy to see them."

Kristy released an unsteady breath. Dread filled her dark brown eyes. "That's because I'm not."

Connor knew all about unpleasant family situations. He had grown up with them. He started to put on his jacket.

Kristy wrapped her fingers around his forearm and gave it an imploring squeeze. "Please stay. They'll be less likely to go on the attack if you're here."

Connor always had been a sucker for a damsel in distress. And to have Kristy Neumeyer looking at him so imploringly...

"Kristy! Hello, dear!" A woman emerged from the driver's side of the car, just as a big guy got out of the passenger side. Both resembled Kristy in looks and were also dressed casually in jeans, sneakers and shirts.

Kristy's smile looked frozen as she exchanged hugs with her mother and brother. "What brings you to this part of the world?" she asked cheerfully.

Her mother removed her sunglasses and placed them atop her soft gray curls. "A medical conference on the latest in ultrasound techniques at Hilton Head. We're on our way down." Unlike Kristy, though, her mother and brother looked genuinely happy to see her, Connor noted.

Her slender shoulders relaxing slightly, Kristy turned to Connor. Urging him forward, she made introductions.

"Mom, Doug, this is Connor Templeton. Connor, this is my mother, Maude Griffin, and my brother, Doug. They're both obstetricians. They practice in Raleigh, North Carolina."

"Nice to meet you." Connor shook hands with both. As the silence strung out awkwardly, he began to regret staying. Clearly, there was something that needed to be said here....

Kristy latched on to his arm in a way that seemed to indicate the two of them were very close. "I wish I'd known you were coming," she said. "I would have cleared my schedule."

"Or been out," Doug said dryly.

Kristy gave him a tolerant smile that didn't reach her eyes. "But the twins are still in school," she continued, as if her older brother had not spoken.

Maude beamed. "Darling, we're spending the night!"

Kristy blinked. Obviously, Connor thought, this was not in Kristy's game plan.

"Here?" she said.

"Well, yes. It's not as if you don't have plenty of room." Maude gestured expansively at the lodge and the dozen or so cottages fronting the beach. "There are...how many cottages here?"

"A dozen," Kristy admitted reluctantly.

"And how many rooms in the lodge itself?" Doug inquired.

"One hundred. But only one of the four wings is open, and those rooms are still undergoing renovation," Kristy warned. "None of those rooms are ready for guests."

"So, we don't mind roughing it as long as we get a chance to see you and the twins and have dinner together this evening. Do we, Doug?"

"Not in the slightest, Mother."

Kristy looked at Connor as if somehow expecting him

to bail her out. No way was he going to do that. If there was a family problem—and it looked like there was—then it wouldn't help any of them to sweep it under the rug. As his family had for so many years. No, they needed to deal with it, like it or not, and if the rest of Kristy's family was ready to do so… "I think it's great your mother and brother are here," he said kindly.

"Would you like to join us for dinner then?" Kristy replied, just as sweetly. "Good!" she exclaimed before Connor had a chance to reply. "We'll eat at seven, in the dining hall. And in the meantime…" she gestured for everyone to follow her around to the lobby entrance "…I'm going to have to send you and Mother to the market, Doug, because I wasn't planning on feeding quite so many people this evening."

CONNOR WATCHED as Kristy quickly wrote out a grocery list, produced some cash—which was summarily rejected by both her mother and brother—and then waved them off, with directions to the closest food store.

"A little rude, weren't you?" Connor said dryly, as the station wagon moved through the palmetto trees and disappeared down Folly Beach Road.

Kristy scowled and sat down in one of the green wooden rocking chairs on the piazza. She leaned forward, her paint-stained hands clasped between her knees. "You don't know them."

True, Connor thought, as he sat down in the chair beside her. He turned it so they were sitting knee to knee, then he leaned forward and looked into her eyes. "It sounds as if I'm going to get to know them, though."

"I'm sorry about that. I…" Kristy floundered, for the first time that afternoon looking regretful. "I was desperate."

Connor had seen that, and for that reason, his heart went

out to her. He knew what it was like to want to connect closely with family, and be unable to do so. For years he had not been as close as he wanted to be to anyone in his family. Since his parents' acknowledgment of their problems, that had changed. But he still regretted all the years when he and his mother and father and two sisters hadn't been able to talk. Or even spend any meaningful time together.

He took one of Kristy's hands in his. "Why are they here?" he asked.

A demoralized expression on her face, she pulled away. "The same reason you are. To talk me into giving up the ghost, so to speak, and sell the place to a high roller like you."

Connor sat back in his chair, began to rock. "But you're not about to take the money and run, are you?"

"Nope." Kristy pushed against the floor with the toe of her shoe. "I love this place. I know it's still a work in progress," she confessed as she rocked gently back and forth, "but I am determined to return it to its former glory and then some."

Connor was beginning to see that. Which, of course, made his own mission all the harder. "You have a history here?" he asked.

She nodded. "My siblings and I visited here every summer when we were kids," she told him, oblivious to the way she was sitting, giving him an unobstructed view of her fabulous body.

She turned to look at him, a mix of subdued temper and sentimentality glowing in her dark eyes. "When we got older, I worked here in the summers while my brother and sister were off at science camp, or volunteering at the hospitals in Raleigh, in hopes of getting into medical school."

"Which they did," Connor guessed.

"Oh, yes." Kristy squared her shoulders, took a deep,

regretful breath. "Both my brother and sister followed in our parents' footsteps."

Connor took a moment to consider what that must be like. "Everyone in your family is a doctor?"

Kristy nodded. "Except me. My father is a lung transplant surgeon and my sister is a pediatric oncologist. My late husband was a pediatric heart surgeon. I'm the only one who didn't choose medicine as a career."

"Wow."

"Yeah," Kristy said dryly, rolling her eyes at his reaction. "Wow."

Before Connor could comment further, they heard a large vehicle lumbering slowly up Folly Beach Road. Kristy glanced at her watch. "That's the school bus!" She jumped out of her chair and headed around the lodge again, just as a big yellow bus pulled up Folly Beach Road and stopped at the entrance of the resort. Two little girls got off the bus and began walking up the palmetto-lined driveway. One had shoulder-length corkscrew curls, the same rich hue as Kristy's, and was dressed in a pretty pink cotton smock and lacy white apron. The other's hair was caught in two messy braids. She was wearing shorts and a striped T-shirt and sneakers. Only as they neared could Connor see, by the sameness of their charming features, that they were indeed identical twins.

They were halfway to Kristy and Connor when the one in the smock said something to the one in shorts. The second little girl took offense, dropped her book bag onto the grass and shoved the one in the dress. She shoved back, even harder, and the next thing Connor knew, the two were down on the ground tussling and rolling.

Kristy gaped at them as if unable to believe what she was seeing, then rushed toward them. She separated the twins, who came up kicking and screeching. "Stop it!"

Kristy demanded as Connor caught up with her. "Both of you! Stop it right now!"

The cute little girls glared at each other and Kristy tearfully. "What in the world has gotten into you?" Kristy demanded as the twins wiped the tears from their long lashes with the backs of their hands. "I've never seen you fight like this before!"

"It's all her fault!" the one in the dress yelled abruptly, her frustration with her sister apparent. "She is just so dumb sometimes!"

"No, it's not! It's your fault, you big scaredy-cat!" the one in shorts shouted back.

"All right, you two, that's enough," Kristy said firmly. The girls faced each other, sniffling. "Go on inside. I'll be in directly to talk to you."

As the twins meandered off, still glaring at each other intermittently, Kristy turned back to Connor. "I'm sorry about that. I don't know what's going on." She paused, her expression conflicted. "About dinner... Forget the invitation, okay?"

"You're sure?" For some reason Connor didn't mind being used by her like that, although in any other situation, with any other person, he would have.

"Positive," Kristy said, smiling apologetically, as if trying to make it up to him.

He shoved his hands in the pockets of his slacks. Now he was the one feeling bereft. "What about your mother and brother?"

Kristy shrugged as if it were no big deal. With barely a backward glance in his direction, she strode resolutely after her girls. "I'll tell them you couldn't make it, after all," she said.

"SO SHE'S NOT GOING to sell," Skip Wakefield said, when Connor got back to the downtown Charleston office of Wakefield-Templeton Properties.

Connor draped his sport coat over the back of a stylish chrome-and-leather chair and dropped into the one next to it. He faced his old friend. "Not yet."

"Meaning what?" Skip asked, his probing green eyes alight with curiosity as he ran a hand through his close-cropped, reddish-brown hair. A risk taker with a practical streak, he was always focused on the bottom line. "You think you can change her mind?"

Connor reached for the necktie in his coat pocket and began to put it back on. "I think it's possible, given enough time."

His expression thoughtful, Skip watched as Connor buttoned the top button on his shirt and pushed the knot into place. "We don't have a lot of time," Skip warned as he tapped the end of a pen against his desk. "The investors we've rounded up to underwrite the costs of building the condo project aren't going to wait around indefinitely. Even though suitable beachfront property is so darn hard to come by these days, and this place is ideal. If this project doesn't come together soon, they may find another place to put their money."

Connor had to agree with his partner on that. It seemed everyone wanted to live at the beach, and no one wanted to sell what they had. Not a twenty-five acre parcel, the amount Skip and Connor needed, anyway.

"Kristy Neumeyer's property is worth waiting for."

"Only if she'll sell. If she won't—" Skip shrugged, looking unhappy again "—then she and her resort are of no use to us."

Speak for yourself, Connor thought. He had spent only thirty minutes or so with her, but she had definitely made an impression on him.

Skip tilted his head. "You're not getting sweet on her, are you?"

Guilt swept through Connor, even as he denied the possibility. "Why would you think that?" he demanded. He had never been one to mix business and pleasure. Not since Lorelai, anyway.

"I don't know." Skip studied Connor. "Maybe because I haven't seen you look that starry-eyed when talking about a woman since junior high."

Connor grinned. "Are you sure those aren't dollar signs you're seeing in my eyes?"

Skip clasped his hands behind his head and leaned back in his chair. "I wish your main desire was to make money because if it were, our partnership would be a lot more profitable. Instead, you want everyone to like you." He said that as if it were the worst quality on earth.

Connor knew differently. "It helps if people don't hate your guts when you're trying to broker a deal between two warring parties."

His partner's eyes gleamed with a cynical light. "It's more than that, and you know it," he scoffed. "You just can't stand making an enemy of anyone."

It was true, Connor admitted to himself. Probably because he had spent so much time as a kid feeling caught up in the animosity simmering between members of his family. For years he had suspected that his parents and his older sister had secretly resented the heck out of each other, but he hadn't understood why. Not that his younger sister, Daisy, who had been adopted as an infant, had escaped the family penchant for stifled emotions and supersecret angst. No, she had been as unhappy as all the rest, albeit more openly so. To the point that everything had finally exploded during the course of the previous summer. The truth had come out. And his parents had reluctantly ended the deception as well as their forty-eight-year marriage. Now, everyone seemed content to go on with their lives. Only

Connor, it seemed, was still reeling, still trying to take it all in. Still wondering where the hell it left him.

Aware that Skip was waiting for a response, Connor stood and moved lazily about the office. "So I don't like fighting."

"I know, you just want everyone, and I do mean everyone, to get along," Skip intoned dryly, shaking his head. "Speaking of which, that neighbor, Bruce Fitts, called here, said you weren't doing a good job with Kristy, not at all. He suggested I go back out there myself."

Connor objected fiercely to that. "It was you talking to Kristy in the first place that really set her off."

His partner spread his hands wide. "All I did was offer her a cool five million dollars for her land and buildings."

"Which wouldn't have been a problem had she been at all interested in selling." She wasn't.

Skip flashed him a sly smile. "She'll come around—if I know you. And I think I do."

"I hope so, too," Connor allowed. "But in the meantime, Skip, where Kristy's concerned, let me do the talking."

His partner agreed without argument. "When are you going to see her again?"

"Tonight."

Skip blinked. "You got her to agree to go to dinner?"

"Actually, she invited me to have dinner there." Then she had dis-invited him, but Connor figured that was beside the point.

"Way to go, buddy!" Skip came out of his chair to high-five Connor. Grinning, he predicted, "You'll have her seeing things our way in no time."

Connor hoped that was the case.

Chapter Two

"Kristy, dear, please come and look at this." Maude Griffin said, pointing to the television screen mounted near the ceiling of the hotel kitchen. "This is exactly what I was talking about."

Kristy left the crab cakes frying in the skillet and walked over to stand beside her mother. The TV was set to the Weather Channel. "...tropical storm Imogene, with winds of sixty-five miles an hour, is gathering strength five hundred miles southeast of Bermuda...."

"Mom," Kristy explained patiently, "it's October. It's hurricane season. And thus far a very mild one. So of course there are going to be tropical storms and, yes, even hurricanes headed our way till the end of hurricane season." Which Kristy knew was usually around November 1. "It's a fact of life on the Atlantic Coast."

Maude lifted a pot from the stove, carried it to the stainless steel sink and emptied its contents into a mesh strainer. Steam rose from the cooked redskin potatoes as the boiling water ran down the drain. "Suppose Imogene hits Paradise Resort?"

Trying not to let her mother's worry transfer to her, Kristy handed her milk and butter. "Suppose Imogene does?"

Maude put the potatoes in a bowl and sprinkled them

with salt and pepper, before switching on the mixer. "Kristy, you are sinking so much money and effort into this place without any reassurance at all that you are going to make it back."

They had been over this dozens of times since Aunt Ida died and left Kristy Paradise Resort, and Kristy had announced her decision to sell her house in Chapel Hill, and move the girls south in time to start the new school year.

She stabbed the green beans with a fork and found them tender. "I need a life, Mom."

Maude carefully added the milk and butter to the mashed potatoes. "You're only thirty-three. You're still young enough to go to medical school."

Kristy took the remoulade sauce out of the fridge and garnished it with a few sprigs of parsley. "That was your dream for me, not mine."

Maude scooped the mashed potatoes into the serving bowl, then paused to regard Kristy hopefully. "Only because you never gave it a chance."

Kristy layered the cooked crab cakes onto a large white serving platter. Doing her best to contain her exasperation, she asked, "Don't we have enough doctors in the family?"

Her mom ladled the steaming green beans into a dish. "We could always use one more. Think about it, honey," Maude persisted as they carried the food out to the table set up in the hotel dining room. "Your house in Chapel Hill hasn't sold yet, and University of North Carolina has a medical school. You could still move back there and get your medical education while the girls are in school. You had the grades and medical college admission test scores you needed to get in. And if not there, you could go to Duke or Wake Forest. Wherever you want."

If Kristy thought it would bring her happiness, she would have headed for medical school right out of college. But it wouldn't. Unfortunately, she couldn't seem to make her family understand that. Although Kristy supposed that, too, was her fault. She should never have let her parents pressure her into taking the premed courses and the medical school qualifying exam while simultaneously earning her college degree in hotel management. But she had....

Maude looked out the door toward where Doug was walking along the beach with his nieces. As usual, whenever they were home or just hanging out, Sally had Lance's old beach towel slung around her neck, and Susie had his beat up Frisbee clutched in her hand. Maude rang the dinner bell Kristy had mounted next to the door, and signaled them all in. Kristy smiled as they waved and headed toward the lodge.

"The twins would enjoy going back to North Carolina, too."

Kristy wasn't so sure about that, either. "The only thing that will make the twins happy is if they could have their father back," she answered soberly, as she brought out pitchers of sweet tea. "And that's not going to happen."

Maude paused. "You still miss Lance, too, don't you?"

Kristy didn't know how to answer that. She missed the man she thought Lance had been when she married him. She lamented all the dashed hopes and lost dreams, and she still felt tied to him in some way. Unable to go back, not quite willing to move on. At least in that sense. Her throat aching, she busied herself getting a plate for store-bought rolls and a bowl for coleslaw. "When do you and Doug have to leave for your medical conference?" she asked instead, as the twins and Doug walked in and went straight to the bathrooms off the lobby to wash up.

"Tomorrow. Early, about seven." Maude started to close the doors behind them, then began to smile.

"What is it?" Kristy asked.

Her mother turned back to her, surprise in her eyes. "I thought you said your friend wasn't coming."

HE WASN'T SUPPOSED to be here, but you would never know that by looking at Connor Templeton's face, Kristy thought, her heart racing as she went to the front door of the lodge to show him in.

Unlike the rest of the family, who were in shorts and T-shirts, Connor was still in the casual business clothes he'd had on earlier, including tie and sport coat. He had two bottles of wine—one white and one red—a bunch of flowers and a basket of gourmet cookies in his arms.

"My goodness!" Maude said cheerfully, rushing past Kristy to lend a hand. "You really went all out this evening!"

Connor looked past Kristy to the table in the middle of the hotel dining room, set with steaming food. "Looks like I'm just in time." He smiled, stepping closer.

Kristy bit her lip in embarrassment, knowing she was serving dinner a full half hour before she had told him she would, prior to privately uninviting him. Inhaling a whiff of his brisk masculine cologne, she replied, "Supper got ready quickly." Which was true.

Doug and the twins came out of the powder rooms in the lobby, smelling of hand soap and sea air. Susie and Sally looked at Connor curiously. Remembering she hadn't made formal introductions earlier, Kristy said, "Girls, this is Mr. Templeton. Connor, my daughters, Susie and Sally. Connor is going to be eating dinner with us this evening."

Susie and Sally eyed Connor curiously, but didn't seem to care one way or another whether he joined them. Kristy wished she could say the same. She, an accomplished hostess with years of experience entertaining guests, was suddenly all thumbs. Her mother, on the other hand, had already sprung into action and was quickly adding another place to the banquet table.

The six of them sat down and said grace.

"Everything looks delicious," Connor said, as they began passing the food.

"My husband and I taught all three of our children to be proficient in the kitchen," Maude stated proudly.

"What about you?" Doug asked, with an assessing look. "Can you cook?"

"Uh, no, actually, I can't," Connor admitted as he helped himself to a crab cake and passed the platter. "In my house all the cooking was done by the chef. We weren't even allowed in the kitchen. If we wanted something we had to request it and then wait in the dining room, or if we were sick, in our room."

Everyone was looking at him as if he were a Martian. "I'm guessing you're wealthy?" Maude said eventually.

"Very," Kristy said.

Undaunted, Connor shot her an assessing look. "I'm not sure I'd say very—"

Aware she was risking his ire, she persisted anyway. "I don't know what else you call old money and trust funds and multimillion-dollar business deals," she said with a shrug. "But to me—to us—that's wealthy, Connor."

Recognizing a shot across the bow when he saw one, Doug looked at Kristy curiously. "How do you know all this, sis?"

"For one thing, I read the Charleston newspaper—Connor's business deals are always being reported on the front page of the business section." He was a full-fledged tycoon and then some. An entrepreneur herself, Kristy had to respect him for that. "I'm also friends with his younger sister, Daisy. And she's talked about what it was like growing up in one of the wealthiest families of Charleston." It hadn't been all pleasant. Although, according to Daisy, these days Connor, his sisters and his mother were pretty close. His father, Richard Templeton—who had gone off to Europe to recover after a considerable scandal of his own making—was another story.

"Plus," Kristy continued, answering her brother's questions, "when Connor and his partner, Skip Wakefield, started sniffing around my property, I made it my business to find out everything I could about their commercial real estate and development dealings in the area." She had wanted to know what, and with whom, she was coming up against, in refusing to sell to them. Although to this point, it had been mostly Skip Wakefield, a pleasant if determined thirty-something bachelor, who had been darkening Kristy's door every other week or so and putting forth proposition after proposition. Until this afternoon, Connor had been conspicuously absent. A fact she hadn't really appreciated until now. Skip she could resist. Connor…well, he was not so easy to disregard. Both were handsome, successful, affable men. But there was something about Connor. Something in his eyes. A gentleness, an intuitive awareness of what she was thinking and feeling and considering, that left her on edge. She wasn't used to having anyone able to read her mind or predict her next move. Even Lance hadn't been able to do that. But Connor seemed at least a half step ahead of her. Like now, for instance. He seemed to realize she was planning to use not just his interest in her property, but his blue-blooded background to keep them from becoming friends. And seemed just as determined to prevent said action.

"Why would they be sniffing?" Sally interrupted, perplexed.

Connor grinned. "I think that is just a figure of speech," he said, looking the little girl in the eye. "Kind of like when you say you're really ticked off about something. You're not really ticking, right?"

"Our hearts are." Susie piped up as she touched the center of her chest. "My daddy was a heart doctor for kids and he used to let me listen to my heart with his stethoscope.''

"Mine, too," Sally added seriously.

"That's nice." Connor smiled at them gently, as if he were really enjoying their company.

"Not to change the subject," Doug interrupted soberly, "but how come you don't have any guests here, Kristy?"

Kristy swore inwardly. She had not wanted to get into this with her know-it-all older brother, who never hesitated to tell her what she was doing wrong with her life. "I'm not reopening until October 15."

"You have bookings then?" Maude asked hopefully.

Kristy cut into a crab cake that was golden brown on the outside and white and flaky inside. "Not exactly." She dabbed a bite of it into the river of yellow remoulade sauce on her plate.

"Partially booked then," Doug ascertained, a worried frown creasing his square face.

Kristy did not want to be discussing her business problems in front of Connor Templeton. But unless she wanted to lie, there was no helping it. She looked at her mother and brother resolutely. "I'm in the process of trying to hire a concierge slash assistant hotel manager, as well as a chef, handyman and several maids."

Maude nodded. "I saw your Help Wanted sign out front."

"But in the meantime, I am going through Aunt Ida's old booking records and sending out brochures to travel agents and groups that used to hold business conferences here," Kristy continued. She sipped her tea.

"But you still don't have any bookings?" Doug asked.

Kristy's throat felt parched. Wondering how much worse the familial inquisition was going to get, she said somewhat hoarsely, "I have to open first."

"Actually," Connor interjected, as he reached across the

table and gave her hand a brief reassuring squeeze, "I think my sister Daisy rented a cottage here, and so did her new husband, Jack Granger."

"When they were first getting to know each other," Kristy remembered, thankful for the gentle steering of the conversation away from what her brother considered her business mistakes.

"I still don't see how you're going to make any money here, never mind enough to live on and put the girls through college," Doug said worriedly. He looked at Connor, man-to-man, and asked, "What were you and your partner willing to pay for this place?"

"That is not dinner table conversation," Kristy interrupted, with a telling look at her daughters.

To Kristy's relief, Doug backed off, albeit reluctantly, and the rest of the meal was devoted to discussing the wonders of the South Carolina autumn.

"Wonderful dinner, Kristy," Connor said.

She smiled and rose, picking up plates in both hands. "My mother helped me cook it."

"And we're not finished yet," Maude said, getting up to help clear the table. "We still have dessert and coffee."

"Well, my hats off to both chefs," Connor said, just as a knock sounded on the door and a handsome blond man in his mid-forties walked in.

"I'M HARRY BOWLES," the stranger said in a charming British accent, as Kristy walked across the room to greet him. "And I've come to apply for the concierge job advertised in this morning's newspaper."

She turned her back to the lodge dining room, where the rest of the family sat, watching with an annoying amount of interest, and guided Harry back out into the lobby.

"I'd like an interview with the hotel management as soon as possible."

"I'm Kristy Neumeyer, the resort owner and manager." Kristy shook his hand, noting that Harry had a firm, businesslike grip. "And if you like, we could do it now," she said, aware that that would mean missing dessert with her family, but happy for anything that would cut short her brother's annoying questioning.

"Everything okay?" Connor Templeton walked up to them and nodded at Harry Bowles. "Nothing has happened to Winnifred, has it?"

"Winnifred...?" Kristy said. Obviously, the two men knew each other quite well.

"Deveraux-Smith." Connor supplied the rest of the name, before nodding again at Harry Bowles. "Harry here has been her butler for years."

"Twenty to be exact," the man replied as he straightened the lapels on his exquisitely cut dark business suit. "And, no, nothing is wrong. I am simply here to apply for the job. I resigned my other position this afternoon and find myself in need of work and a place to stay. And while I could check into a hotel or rent an apartment, I prefer to simply take another position right away."

He reached into his pocket and withdrew an envelope. "My résumé is inside." He waited expectantly while Kristy opened it. "As you can see, my talents are extensive and varied. I believe I would make an excellent addition to your staff."

No kidding, Kristy thought, running down the list of Harry's talents. "I'm not sure the salary I am offering is going to be enough for someone of your background," she said.

"Why don't you let me decide that?" he suggested.

"If you'll excuse us." Kristy looked at Connor, then took Harry by the elbow and guided him toward the front desk. "Why don't we step into my office?" she said. "We can talk privately there."

CONNOR HAD NO IDEA what Kristy and Harry said to each other behind closed doors. But it was clear when they emerged that Kristy had hired herself a concierge and assistant hotel manager. She gave him a key. "Cottage 1 is right next to the lodge. You can get settled in this evening and I'll show you around tomorrow morning."

"I'll look forward to it," Harry said. He tipped an imaginary hat to Kristy, nodded at Connor and left by the same doors he had come in.

"Your mother is serving ice cream in the dining room. She'd like to know if you want to join the rest of the family," Connor said.

"Sure," Kristy answered as the telephone rang. "Tell her I'll be right there."

As Connor headed off, he heard Kristy scrambling for a pen and paper and talking in the background.

"Friday, October 15? Yes, we do have availability for that. Twenty-five rooms. Hmm, let me see here. Yes. I think we can do it. Absolutely. No problem. I'll fax you the cost breakdown first thing tomorrow morning. Thank you!"

"Got a booking?" Connor said, when she slipped into her seat at the table.

Kristy grinned. "A group of twenty-five insurance agents from the Oak Park area of Chicago. They used to come here for their annual sales conference, and bring their spouses. For the past two years they went to another resort, but there was a mix-up in reservations and the place that was supposed to house them, on Kiawah Island, suddenly can't. So they're coming here instead."

"That's great," Connor said, looking surprisingly happy for her, considering that he was still trying to buy her out. Kristy noted that Maude and Doug, on the other hand, appeared ambivalent about her first success. As if they were glad she was getting some business, but not so happy that bookings would delay her going back to North Carólina to pursue what they felt was her true calling.

"The peach ice cream was yummy, Mommy," Susie said, as she and Sally yawned and pushed their empty ice cream dishes away.

Kristy smiled. "Thank Grandma—she made it for you."

The twins chorused, "Thank you." And yawned again.

"They look exhausted," Maude noted. She glanced at Kristy. "Would you like me to supervise their baths and get them ready for bed?"

"If you wouldn't mind," she said, noting that it was already seven-thirty, and the twins' school night bedtime was in another half hour.

"I have to call and check on a few patients back in Raleigh, but then I'll come help you with the dishes," Doug said, excusing himself, too.

"You don't have to do that," Connor said, already getting up. "I'll assist Kristy."

"Have you ever done dishes?" she asked, as she picked up several ice cream bowls and carried them across the lodge dining room to the big kitchen.

Connor grinned. "I know how to put things in a dishwasher."

That surprised Kristy. She wouldn't have expected a man like Connor to do even that. But she supposed life was different now that he had his own place, as opposed to the mansion where he, Iris and Daisy had grown up.

Connor stopped in front of the big commercial dishwasher in the kitchen and looked at it uncertainly. "Although I've got to say," he drawled, "the dishwasher in my loft does not look like this."

"THANKS FOR THE HELP," Kristy said, when they had finished cleaning up. She started the big machine and the two of them walked out of the kitchen, through the dining room, to the lobby.

"I really like what you've done here," Connor murmured appreciatively. The last time he had been here, shortly before Kristy's aunt had died, the once-popular lodge had been in decline. All he had seen of the interior were the common areas, but even those had been in a state of disrepair and neglect.

Today, Connor noted, things were different. Although the floor plan of the solidly built establishment remained just as he recalled, the ambience had undergone a stunning transformation. Once outdated and stodgy, the common areas were now fine examples of sunny, oceanfront chic.

One side of the lobby opened onto the main dining room. On the other side was a large club room, featuring a high cathedral ceiling with exposed beams and a large fieldstone fireplace that took up half of one wall. There were several intimate seating areas, with overstuffed sofas and club chairs. White plantation shutters on the windows were opened during the day, revealing a stunning ocean view. The lobby walls were a soothing pale green, the club room and ceiling white. Sisal rugs dotted the warm distressed-wood floors, and brightly colored Persian runners and unique artwork added color and interest to the lobby.

"Thanks," Kristy murmured proudly.

"You've turned it into a very peaceful place," he continued admiringly.

She nodded. Appearing distracted, she shot a glance at her brother, who was standing behind the reservation counter, talking with the hospital by phone, and making notations on a paper in front of him. "I'll walk you out," she said.

Doing his best to hide his disappointment—Connor had hoped to spend more time with Kristy that evening—he moved ahead to open the heavy wooden lobby door.

They stepped out onto the wide piazza that faced the beach. When Ida had been alive, and running Paradise, the porch had been filled with nylon folding chairs. Now wooden rocking chairs, and potted plants and flowers scattered here and there, created a homey look.

"I'm really happy about what I've managed to accomplish here, although I have a lot more to do before any guests arrive. And I appreciate your congratulating me on the booking…" she paused to search his eyes "…although I can't imagine that you really feel that way."

Connor knew he shouldn't have been happy for her. Any success she had on that score went counter to his business plans. But he was. Maybe because he knew how hard she had been working. And had seen how much revitalizing the old resort meant to her.

Nevertheless, he didn't like what her assumption implied. He slid a steadying hand beneath her elbow as they walked down the steps to the sidewalk. Loving the way her bare skin felt beneath his palm, so silky and warm, he guided her around the side of the building, toward the parking lot. "You think I'm insincere?"

Kristy slid her hands in her pockets as they strolled, side by side, past the flowering bushes that lined the northern edge of the building. Tensing, she slanted him a brief, assessing glance. "What I think is it's not in your best interests for me to make a success of this place on my own. Because then I'd have absolutely zero interest in selling out to you."

They paused as they reached the front grill of his black Mercedes sedan. Connor found himself more reluctant than ever to leave her company as he turned to face her. He let his glance rove over her expressive features. She had been beautiful earlier—in work clothes. Now, in a white, V-necked knit top, knee-length navy shorts and sandals, with her dark, silky hair loose around her shoulders, she looked even more amazing. Connor didn't know if it was the soft swell of her breasts, the indentation of her slender waist or her slim, sexy legs that put his hormones in overdrive whenever he was around her. All he knew for certain was that when he was with her, he was completely entranced by the feisty tilt of her chin and the intelligence and wit sparkling in her dark brown eyes. Without even trying, Kristy Neumeyer challenged him in a way no woman ever had. "You have zero interest in letting me buy you out now," he pointed out dryly.

"Correct." Kristy leaned against the grill of his car and lifted a skeptical brow. "So why are you here?"

"I was invited to dinner, if I recall."

"And then dis-invited," she reminded him archly.

Connor lounged against the front of the vehicle, as well. "My sister Daisy speaks so highly of you I figured I should get to know you, too."

Kristy folded her arms in front of her and glared at him somewhat contentiously. "Um-hmm."

Connor grinned as fire leaped in her pretty eyes. "Don't believe me?" he teased.

"Right now," Kristy sighed, whirling away from him, "I don't know what to believe."

Connor came up behind her. He put his hands on her shoulders and turned her around again. "Or whom to trust?"

She tilted her face up to his, admitting candidly, "Or whom to trust."

An awkward silence fell between them.

Deciding trust would not come until it was earned, and that that would take time, Connor moved on to other pressing matters that needed her attention. "I hate to bring it up—" he inclined his head toward the tall palmetto tree they were standing next to "—but I noticed on the way in this evening that those trees lining the driveway and pathways aren't looking too good.''

"I know.'' Kristy glanced upward with a frown. The fan-shaped leaves at the very top should have been a healthy green. Instead, they seemed to be losing both color and luster, and the edges were tobacco-brown and curling. "I've called an arborist," she said with a troubled sigh. "She's coming out tomorrow to have a look.''

"It'd be a shame to lose them," Connor stated gently. "It would cost a mint to have to replace them.''

When Kristy narrowed her eyes at him suspiciously, he lifted both hands in a gesture of surrender. "Hey, don't shoot the messenger!''

"As long as that's all you are," Kristy allowed.

"I would never sabotage your lodge," he declared.

She raked the toe of her sandal across the cement walk in front of her. "What about your partner?''

"Skip would never do anything like that, either," Connor stated firmly. They didn't have to. Not when they were ready, willing and able to pay top dollar for any property they were interested in acquiring and developing.

Another silence fell between them, even more potent and full of chemistry. Connor was just getting ready to say good-night and leave when he saw a flash of movement in the window behind Kristy. "Don't look now," he murmured.

"What?'' Kristy's chin angled up defiantly.

"We're being observed," he murmured. "By your brother.''

Kristy groaned and raked both hands through her hair. "I really wish he would mind his own business," she muttered beneath her breath, still not looking at the window.

"Well, I can think of one way to make him turn away," Connor said.

Aware that he had never wanted to possess a woman

more than he did Kristy at that very moment, he put one arm around her waist and slid his right hand beneath her chin. He had the advantage when her lips parted in surprise. Knowing it wouldn't last, he lowered his mouth to hers, and then did what he had wanted to do since the first moment he'd laid eyes on her.

Just as he'd expected, her lips were warm, enticingly feminine—and once again tightly closed. Aware of their audience, and his mission to rid them of it, he persisted anyway, letting her know he could be just as stubborn and reckless and impulsive as she was. He parted her lips with the pressure of his and his tongue swept inside, drawing in the taste of her, the softness. Kristy made a sound—half pleasure, half protest—low in her throat. Not one to be content doing anything halfway, he continued kissing her, long and hard and deep, stroking her tongue with his, tenderly coaxing a response from her even as he tasted the sweetness that was her, until she began to melt against him. The softness of her body giving new heat to his, he used the arm anchored about her waist to bring her closer yet, and show her what they could share, given half a chance. As their bodies fit together, softness to hardness, woman to man, Kristy trembled and uttered another breathy sigh. Her arms curled around his shoulders, and she began kissing him back every bit as passionately as he was kissing her. Satisfaction pouring through him, Connor swept a hand down her spine and continued caressing her, until their hearts were thudding rapidly and they were both completely caught up in the moment, yearning for more.

Which would have been fine, Connor noted, had they been anywhere else. But they weren't. So at least for now… With a sigh of regret, he halted the tempestuous kiss and lifted his head.

Taking a deep breath to steady herself, she looked into his eyes and demanded irritably, "What was that for?"

"Our audience," Connor replied matter-of-factly. Keeping his arms around her, he glanced at the windows. "Yep. Just as I figured. Your brother's gone."

"Good." Trembling all the harder, Kristy splayed both her hands across Connor's chest. "Then you can stop kissing me," she said.

She didn't look or act as if she wanted him to stop kissing her, Connor noted. "I don't think so," he replied dryly.

Kristy blinked. "What?"

"The first kiss was to get rid of your pesky brother. This one," he said, "is for me."

Chapter Three

Kristy hadn't been kissed in a long time, and she didn't think she had ever been kissed quite like this. As if she was someone precious and rare, someone he couldn't quite resist. And the truth was, as she surrendered to the strength and warmth of him, loving his taste and feel and scent, so dark and male and sexy, she was feeling just that. She wasn't sure what it was about Connor Templeton. Whether his kiss was so searing and sensual it took her breath away and sent emotions swirling through her at breakneck speed. Or that he had persisted when others would have walked away, and that he seemed to see so much more in her than everyone else. All she knew for certain was that he had identified a need within her that even she hadn't been aware of—the deep yearning need to be close to someone again, to feel wanted and respected and understood. She wanted to forget, just for a second, all the demands upon her. To ignore the unprecedented risks she was taking, and her worry over the future, and just live in the here and now. Not as someone's mother or sister or daughter, but as a woman. A flesh-and-blood woman with passionate needs and desires.

But like it or not, Kristy thought, as Connor deepened the kiss even more and stroked his tongue intimately against hers, she was all those things. And as such was required to keep her wits about her even when that was the last thing she wanted to do. Because she had responsibilities that were not going to go away.

She laid a hand on his chest and broke off the wonderfully evocative kiss, as slowly as it had begun. "Well," she said, reluctantly stepping back, and doing her best to behave as if he hadn't just turned her whole world upside down—with just one kiss! She drew in a deep, stabilizing breath. "I guess you've proved your point."

His brows knit together. "And what would that be?" he murmured just as softly.

Kristy's pulse pounded when she realized he looked as if he still wanted to kiss her. Aware it was all she could do not to give in to impulse and let him take her in his arms again, she countered equably, "That I'm just as human as everyone else." She turned her back to him and pretended to study the resort's ailing palmetto trees.

Connor rested both hands on her shoulders. He ducked his head so his mouth was close to her ear. "Ah, but you're not like everyone else, Kristy. If you were, I would have been able to say good-night without mixing business and pleasure."

She turned to face him. "I take it that's forbidden," she said lightly.

He dropped his hands abruptly. "Oh, yeah. I don't want the lines blurring between work and play."

Then you'd better not kiss me again, Kristy thought.

"And acquiring my resort is still on your agenda."

He shrugged his broad shoulders. "I've found there's usually a way to make everyone happy in the end, if the lines of communication—and negotiation—are kept open."

Which meant what? Kristy wondered, upset. Had his praise of her efforts to revitalize been disingenuous, after all? Or did he now have some other business scheme in mind? Something he thought she might actually cotton to?

Deciding she didn't need—or want—to know, since she had no plans to sell Paradise Resort anyway, Kristy merely smiled. "I'll keep that in mind," she said dryly, walking away.

"I'll see you tomorrow," he promised.

Kristy didn't reply, wave, or in any way acknowledge what he'd said. She just kept walking and let her actions speak volumes.

"WE'LL TRY AND STOP IN briefly on the way home to Raleigh," Maude said as she and Kristy's brother carried their suitcases out to the car the next morning.

"Sounds good," Kristy said. Doug hadn't mentioned seeing her kissing Connor the evening before, but she knew from the way he and her mother were looking at her that they were both aware she had made a misstep in judgment. And both were taking that as yet another sign that she was slowly but surely going off her rocker, in the wake of Lance's death.

Kristy loved her family and didn't want them worrying about her, but she didn't want to be put in the position of defending her every action to them, either. Darn it all, she was an adult, with the freedom to venture out of her self-imposed little world whenever she wanted to, for whatever reason. Even if it was, as it had been last night when she was wrapped in Connor's arms, an exceedingly foolish and impetuous one.

"Maybe then we can talk more about Connor Templeton's offer to you," Doug said soberly, appearing to believe that the sooner they got her out of South Carolina and back home to Chapel Hill, the better.

"I've made up my mind about that," Kristy said firmly but pleasantly, as her brother opened the back of the station wagon. "I'm turning him down."

Doug made a soft harrumph.

"I think you might want to talk to your father and his accountant about it before you make a definite decision," Maude said.

No, Kristy thought, just as resolutely, she did not. Because they would look at the sum Connor and Skip Wakefield were offering her and realize that after she had paid off both the first and second mortgage on the resort, she would still have a good two million dollars to bank. Managed properly, she and the girls could live off the interest on that for years. And while it was a tempting thought, to know she would never have to worry about money again, Kristy knew it was also the easy way out. Plus she'd be guaranteeing the demise of the resort her aunt Ida had spent her life taking care of.

"Aunt Ida bequeathed Paradise Resort to me because she trusted me to take care of it and bring it back to its former glory."

"Ida would also understand that you are waging a losing battle here," Maude said gently.

Doug nodded. "You have to face it, Kristy. You can't compete with the fancy places that have sprung up along the coast."

"I don't want to compete with the golf and tennis resorts," Kristy retorted, beginning to be irked again at the lack of understanding and support she received from her family in this regard. "I want to offer a different kind of place for a different kind of vacation." And if they didn't understand that...

Maude and Doug sighed.

Deciding there was no use in rehashing the same old argument, or continuing to make her case that there was a place for many kinds of resorts along the South Carolina coast, Kristy glanced at her watch. "You'd better be hitting the road if you don't want to get caught up in rush hour traffic."

To her relief, Doug and Maude took the hint. They said their goodbyes, thanked her for the hospitality and drove off.

The twins, having "forgotten" about the math work sheets that were due that morning, were sitting at a table in the dining room, busily working the multiplication problems that had been assigned to them.

They finished about five minutes before the bus was due. Kristy made sure they went to the bathroom and had their lunches, then walked out to the end of the driveway to wait for their bus with them.

About the same time, Connor pulled into the drive. Kristy's heart gave a little leap at the sight of him, even as she reminded herself sternly not to get caught in the unexpected chemistry between them. Or spend any time at all remembering the warmth of his arms or the heart-stopping nature of his kiss, or the fact that he had made her feel like a woman for the first time in a very long time. Bottom line, he was here for one reason and one reason only—to buy her out. And, she reminded herself sternly, even when her body began to tingle as he got out of his Mercedes and strolled confidently toward her, holding her eyes all the while, she had to remember that. Because another kiss, another few hours of letting down her guard with him, was not something she could afford.

Not that Connor Templeton seemed to accept that fact, Kristy noted. As he deliberately closed the distance between them, he looked as if he was ready to pick up exactly where they had left off. With her wrapped in his strong arms, his lips fastened securely on hers...

Eyes twinkling, he leaned over to brush a light, careless kiss—a Southern-style greeting—against her cheek. "Morning."

Only because the twins were there to witness her behavior did Kristy resist the urge to glower at him. As she sought to get a handle on her soaring emotions, she could feel the blood rushing to her face. Passing up the chance to lightly kiss his cheek, too, she forced a cheerful smile and stepped back a pace. "Good morning, Mr. Templeton." She spoke as if he were a casual acquaintance she'd happened to see on the street.

And he wasn't buying it for a second, Kristy noted.

He knew she was thinking about the way they had kissed last night, just as he was....

Unlike yesterday, however, this morning he was dressed in jeans that made the most of his tall, muscular frame, and a T-shirt that did similar things for his broad shoulders and flat abs. He had recently showered and shaved, and Kristy tried hard not to notice how good he looked and smelled so early in the morning.

"You gals off to school?" Connor asked the twins cheerfully.

Susie and Sally both nodded.

In the distance, they could hear the rumble of the school bus stopping and starting as it picked up children at various stops along Folly Beach Road. Abruptly, Susie elbowed Sally. Sally elbowed her back.

"What's going on?" Kristy interjected. The twins had stubbornly insisted they hadn't been fighting about anything in particular the previous afternoon when they got off the bus. Kristy had suspected the reverse was true, but unable to prompt them to confide in her any further, she had let it ride, figuring they could talk about the unprecedented catfight this afternoon.

Sally unzipped the pocket of her backpack and pulled out a crumpled envelope with the Folly Beach Elementary School insignia on it. "We forgot to give you this," she said, as the school bus lumbered up to the end of the lane. Both twins heaved sighs of relief and started to bolt. Another bad sign. "Hold on just one minute there," Kristy ordered, latching on to both her daughters before they could take off. She quickly opened the letter, saw the words *parent-counselor conference.* Lifting a hand, she signaled the bus driver to go on. "I'm taking you two to school this morning," she said firmly.

"But Mom…!" Susie protested unhappily, even as Sally leaned against Kristy in defeat.

The bus driver waved in acknowledgment and drove on down the road.

"Is this what you two were fighting about yesterday afternoon?" Kristy demanded.

Susie looked at Connor hesitantly before turning back to her mom and saying, "I wanted to give you the letter last night, but Sally wouldn't let me. She said we ought to wait until this morning. 'Cause otherwise you would just worry about it all night long. And we didn't want you to worry, Mommy."

They had been doing enough of that already, Kristy noted, not sure whether to be unhappy with her daughters for keeping something from her, or proud that they had tried—in their own convoluted, eight-year-old way—to protect her from suffering any more grief. The only thing she knew for sure was that this had to be dealt with—now.

"Did you two get in trouble?"

They exchanged worried glances and shrugged in tandem. "We didn't do anything," Sally said, rubbing the toe of one patent leather dress shoe across the path. "Which is why it is so unfair that you have to go in and have a conference about us."

"Well, something must have happened to prompt this," Kristy said, frowning and glancing back at the letter. Otherwise the school counselor wouldn't have requested that Kristy make arrangements to meet with her privately as soon as possible.

The girls shrugged again, looking as mystified and out of sorts as Kristy felt.

"This looks like a bad time," Connor said.

Kristy glanced up at him. She had been so wrapped up in what was going on with the girls she had almost forgotten he was there. "Actually, yes, it is," she said, deciding she had enough on her hands trying to deal with her twins' current calamity without wrestling with her feelings about him, too. Glad that Connor seemed to understand and be okay with that, she rushed back inside, where she spotted Harry Bowles in the lobby. "I'm ready to get to work," he announced.

Kristy wasn't surprised to see the British butler looking as handsome and tidy as ever. What did shock her was that he was dressed in a formal-looking suit and tie. Which was not what she needed from him this morning.

Belatedly, Kristy realized she should have gone over that with Harry when she hired him. But it, too, would have to wait until later. "Harry, do you have some old clothes?" she asked.

Harry peered at her peculiarly. "Old clothes?"

"Like what I'm wearing," Kristy said, pointing to her clean but paint-stained blue chambray work shirt and loose-fitting shorts.

"Uh, no, actually, I don't have anything like that," Harry said. And he didn't look particularly eager to get some, either.

"Well, can you find something to wear that won't be a great loss if it gets ruined?" Kristy asked. Able to see the myriad questions in Harry's keen eyes, she promised, "I'll explain later. I've got to run the girls to school. They've missed their bus."

"Very well, madam. I'll do my best," Harry agreed cooperatively.

He strode cheerfully out to his luxury sports car parked

in the employee lot at the end of the driveway. Connor was still standing there, talking to the twins about flying kites on the beach. "Okay, girls, let's go!" Kristy said, opening up her minivan. She slung her purse into the front seat and opened the back for the twins.

The girls climbed in, Sally being careful not to muss up her pretty dress and matching crinoline, while Susie hopped in like the complete tomboy she had gradually morphed into since her father's death.

Harry turned to Connor. "Do you know where I might find some 'old clothes' similar to what Ms. Neumeyer is wearing?" she heard him ask.

Connor directed him down the beach to a discount store, and Harry got in his sport coupe and drove away as Kristy put on her sunglasses and seat belt. "We're going to be late," Susie said.

"No, we're not," Kristy stated. Confident she had plenty of time to get the girls to school before the bell, she slid her key into the ignition, turned it and got...absolutely nothing. Kristy stared at the steering column and the driver panel, and tried again.

Nothing. No groan from the motor, no spark as the ignition tried to catch. Just silence.

"Oh, no!" Susie moaned from the back seat.

"The van won't start!" Sally sounded panicked, too.

"Problem?" Connor appeared at Kristy's window.

Kristy scowled, already calculating how long it would take to get a cab out here. The answer: way too long. "My van won't start."

"Want me to have a look under the hood?" Connor asked.

The girls grew even more agitated.

"There's no time for that," Kristy said, getting out. She had so much to do today. She really didn't need this. "I've got to get the girls to school." And she had very few options, unless she wanted them to miss half an hour or more of their school day. She looked at him, hating the position she was in, but—for her kids' sake—not too proud to ask. "Can you take us?"

"Sure. You'll have to direct me."

"No problem."

They piled into Connor's Mercedes, and Kristy directed Connor to the elementary school. Unfortunately, there was a traffic snarl at two of the intersections, and by the time they reached the school, the bell had already rung and the grounds were deserted.

"Now I don't want to go at all," Sally grumbled from the back seat.

"It'll be fine. I'll go in with you and explain what happened at the office," Kristy said.

"Do you want me to go inside with you or wait in the car?" Connor asked, willing to do whatever was best.

"You can just wait here if you don't mind. It should take me only a minute to sign them in," Kristy promised.

"EVERYTHING OKAY?" Connor asked Kristy when she finally emerged from the school some twenty minutes later and climbed into the car beside him. It didn't look as if things were okay, he thought. In fact, she looked pretty upset.

"No." Kristy lowered her glance and pressed her fingertips to her forehead.

Connor turned to her, no longer sure if this was merely a business encounter or a love affair about to happen. He only knew for certain that kissing her last night had stirred something deep inside him that he thought had been exhausted long ago. And though he wasn't sure if passion like that was good for anything except messing up the best laid plans, he still wanted to experience it again.

"You want to talk about it?" he asked, as he started his

car and guided it back onto the road. Right now she seemed to need a friend, and even if it interfered with what he was trying to accomplish workwise, he wanted to be there for her.

Kristy sighed and, with the flat of one hand, pushed her silky, dark brown hair away from her face. "I ran into the school counselor as I was checking the girls in at the office."

"And...?" Connor asked as he turned onto Folly Beach Road.

"She asked me to step into her office, since I was there." Kristy drew a deep breath and turned to face him. "She told me the girls have been talking about their dad a lot to their classmates and teachers. Susie acts as if Lance is there with her every day after school and commented to that end to her music, art and physical ed teachers. And Sally's been telling the other kids that her dad is away, but he'll be coming back real soon."

Not good, given the fact that—according to the information Skip and Connor had gleaned, anyway—Kristy's husband had died nearly two years before. "Do the other kids know Lance died?"

"Well, the twins' teachers hadn't mentioned it. But that all happened long before the twins moved here or started in this school six weeks ago. Now the third grade teaching team is wondering what to do, which is why they turned it over to the guidance counselor."

That seemed like a good move, Connor thought. "What did the twins have to say?"

Kristy lowered her window and let the warm ocean breeze blow across her face. "I haven't talked to them yet. They weren't there when I spoke to the counselor."

Connor switched off the air-conditioning and opened his window, too. "What is the counselor recommending?"

"Ms. Meyes is going to meet with them frequently at

school to talk about things. Both together and separately. She's a clinical psychologist and has experience handling stuff like this. She said it could just be a coping mechanism they're employing due to the move here over the summer. That they feel they need their dad to help them through the transition or something, and it's just a temporary thing."

"Do you think that's it?"

"I don't know, Connor." Kristy sighed. Her teeth worried her lower lip as she shot him a troubled glance, confiding, "The thing is, they've never talked too much about their dad's passing. Young kids can't really comprehend the concept of death, the finality of it. So that was no surprise. I mean, they know he is in heaven, and that he hasn't come back and isn't going to. And they *seemed* to be soldiering on."

"But…?" Connor prodded, his heart going out to her and her girls, and all they had obviously been through. It couldn't have been easy, losing a husband when you still had two children who were depending on you to take care of them, he thought. It was hard enough to get over losing a spouse, period.

"But there's no doubt they've changed since Lance died," Kristy continued in a low, troubled voice. "Susie used to be a princess, and now she's a tomboy. And Sally is so particular about things. Susie carries around a Frisbee, and Sally carries around that old beach towel that was Lance's. You probably saw them with those things yesterday."

"Yeah, I did," Connor said compassionately. He hadn't known what the significance of the items were at the time. He had just noticed that the girls had brought them in to dinner and then carefully recouped them as soon as dinner was over.

"But Susie won't play Frisbee anymore, and neither will

Sally, because that's something they used to do with their dad.''

"They're still grieving the loss of their daddy."

Kristy nodded, a look of unbearable sadness coming over her face.

"What about you?" Connor asked, not sure why this should be so important to him, just knowing it was. "Are you?"

GOOD QUESTION, Kristy thought as they arrived back at Paradise. Noting Harry Bowles's car was not in the drive, she released the catch on her safety belt and got out of Connor's Mercedes. "I think I've moved on."

"And yet," he pointed out quietly, as he circled around the end of the car and fell into step beside her, "you're still wearing your wedding and engagement rings on your left hand."

Kristy looked self-consciously down at her hand, embarrassed that Connor had noticed that about her. She knew she should have taken her rings off when Lance died, and put them away. But she hadn't been able to. Feeling herself growing defensive, she shoved her hands in the pockets of her shorts and turned to face him. "What's your point?"

Not about to pull any punches with her, he said quietly, "If you want your girls to be able to accept the finality of their father's passing, maybe you have to start accepting it, too."

Kristy glared at him. "I don't believe I asked for any armchair psychology, Mr. Templeton!"

He shrugged his broad shoulders indolently. "Just making an observation."

"Well, don't!" Kristy advised with every ounce of dignity she possessed. Not sure when she had been so furious with anyone in her life, she stalked away without a backward glance.

CONNOR STARTED TO GO after Kristy, to find some way to make amends, then changed his mind. Whether she wanted to or not, she had to think about what he had just said. And in the meantime, there was still the matter of her nonfunctioning minivan....

In the distance, the lodge door slammed behind Kristy.

Connor sighed and started toward his car.

Without the keys to Kristy's minivan or her permission to take a look under the hood, there wasn't a lot he could do except call his favorite mechanic and ask him to make a house call. Connor reached into his pocket and pulled out his cell phone. He had just started to dial when a maliciously grinning Bruce Fitts rounded the corner.

"What are you doing here?" Connor demanded, irked to have to deal with Kristy's obnoxious neighbor to the south.

"Helping 'our cause,' of course."

Connor didn't want to be lumped in with the likes of someone like the lawsuit-loving Bruce Fitts. "By...?" Connor prodded.

"Loosening the distributor cap and a few wires on her minivan, of course. Fool woman, she didn't even think to check."

"You deliberately sabotaged her car?" Connor asked in amazement.

"The lady needs to realize she is not welcome here."

"Listen..." Connor took a threatening step toward Bruce. Then, reminding himself it wouldn't do any good to make enemies here, he reined in his temper. "Antics like this could sour the deal," he pointed out coolly.

That stopped Fitts, but only for a second. "Has she agreed to sell yet?" he asked.

"No, but—"

"Then I plan to continue my campaign to help her toward that decision," he announced with a sneer.

Connor's temper inched higher. Much more of this and he would lose it.

"What are you still doing here?" Kristy's voice rang out behind Connor. "And what are you—" she pointed at Bruce "—doing on *my* property?"

"I was saying hello to my friend Connor," Bruce said.

Kristy's eyebrows climbed higher. "Well, I'd like you both to leave," she said firmly.

Connor wanted to tell her this jerk was not his friend. Not anywhere near it. But knowing that wouldn't help Kristy, he merely clapped a hand on Bruce Fitts's shoulder and propelled him toward his beach house. He would deal with Kristy. Make her see he hadn't meant to offend her with his observation about her wedding and engagement rings. But it would be later, after they had both had the time and opportunity to cool off.

"So HOW IS IT GOING with the widow woman?" Skip asked Connor over a late breakfast at a local café.

"We've got a problem with her neighbor." Connor explained the harassment Kristy was receiving from Bruce Fitts.

"Well, I hate to say it, but as loathsome as I find Fitts and his actions, what he's doing only seems to help our cause," Skip said practically.

Exactly the words Fitts had used, Connor thought uncomfortably. "Bruce Fitts is a jackass and a half," he said.

"I know," Skip answered bluntly. "But look at it this way. He doesn't want Kristy Neumeyer resurrecting Paradise Resort. He does want something built in its place."

"At this moment he does," Connor corrected. "But that could change. And Fitts could be just as much a pain in the butt to the new condominium owners as he is to Kristy Neumeyer right now."

"Then that will be their problem, not ours," Skip replied

unsympathetically. "Besides, the consortium we put together can always buy him out, and they can turn his luxurious beach house into a restaurant or something."

Connor had already had thoughts along the same lines himself. Not that Fitts's property would come cheap. Or even reasonably priced.

"Meanwhile, how are you doing at convincing the delectable Ms. Neumeyer to change her mind and work with us on this?" Skip asked.

Connor frowned and took a sip of his coffee. "Don't call her that."

"Why?" Skip paused and narrowed his eyes. "She's a beauty and you know it. Unless…" He studied Connor all the more. "You're not really getting sweet on her, are you?"

Was he?

Connor knew better than to mix business and pleasure.

Knew better than to let anything cloud his judgment.

Yet there he had been last night, having dinner with her family and kissing her, and this morning, driving her and her children to school. Listening to her most intimate problems. Offering unsolicited advice!

"And what's with the clothes, anyway?" Skip demanded as his glance swept Connor's T-shirt and jeans. "You heading out on someone's boat or something?"

He shrugged and said casually, "I was planning to see if I could help Kristy." Which was another anomaly, as Connor knew nothing about the kinds of tasks she was doing. If he needed something fixed, he simply hired someone to do it for him. Kristy was a lot more hands-on.

"Good plan." Skip nodded approvingly. He leaned forward and whispered conspiratorially, "Infiltrating the enemy camp."

Connor and Skip had been friends for years, and business partners for the last fifteen. They'd enjoyed many a success together, Skip doing the business analysis and Connor working with all the parties to soothe the rough edges and get the deals implemented. Until now, Connor had appreciated Skip's ability to keep his emotions out of any work situation. This time it was different. Maybe because for the first time someone stood to get hurt by what they were proposing. And Skip seemed either not to comprehend that or not to care. "She's not our enemy," Connor said flatly. He drained the last of his coffee and found it as cold and flat as his mood.

"She is if she won't sell to the group we've put together," Skip warned.

Connor was silent.

Beginning to look as upset with the situation as Connor was, Skip leaned forward and warned, "You're not for one minute forgetting we've spent the past five months putting this project together or that we each stand to make a fortune from the deal, are you?"

No, Connor wasn't forgetting that.

The problem was, he realized with a weary sigh, he couldn't seem to forget Kristy Neumeyer, either. And that made it awfully darn hard to push on with a business proposition he knew she not only loathed, but was also resisting with every fiber of her being.

Chapter Four

When Harry Bowles returned from his shopping expedition, he was wearing a pair of loose-fitting trousers, a short-sleeved shirt and sneakers. He'd added a souvenir cap that said Folly Beach across the front, and he looked a lot more relaxed as he and Kristy sat down in her office to go over the work she had slated. Kristy took two bottles of water from her office fridge and handed him one. "I hate to tell you this, Harry," she said as she sat down behind her desk, "but we've really got our work cut out for us if we want to be ready for that insurance agents convention next week."

Harry smiled, unperturbed. "I'm used to hard work."

Kristy was glad to hear it. "If you don't mind my asking, what exactly did your duties as Winnifred Deveraux-Smith's butler include?"

Harry unscrewed the lid to his water and drank sparingly. "A little bit of everything, as it happens," he said rather formally. "I arranged parties, oversaw the household help that came in to cook and clean, dealt with the decorators and handymen that were hired for various tasks. I even managed Winnifred's social calendar until her aunt Eleanor came in and took over those duties."

It sounded as if he was a flexible guy, willing to take on whatever needed to be accomplished.

Kristy frowned. Here came the hard part. "Well, we don't have maids yet and probably won't for another week or two, so for the moment all those duties are going to fall to the two of us." She paused, not sure how this was going to go, and regarded him seriously. "Are you up to that?" Because if not, he was not the man for the job, after all.

"Absolutely." Looking ready for action, Harry put the cap back on his water bottle. "What do you need me to do today?"

Kristy rose and escorted him out, past the reservation desk to the center of the lodge. "Well, as you can see the lobby, club room, kitchen and dining room are in fine shape. So is the exterior of the hotel now, and all the cottages, and the apartment on the second floor of the south side of the building where my daughters and I reside. But all four wings of guest rooms are in need of a lot of TLC," she warned, knowing he was in for a shock there. "We only need one wing for the conference next week, but all twenty-five rooms have got to be stripped and cleaned and put back together again, before next Wednesday. Actually, Tuesday, since the guests will be arriving Wednesday before noon, and we don't want to still be doing any of that when they get here."

"Sounds doable," Harry said. "Where would you like me to begin?"

"I'd like you to take down all the draperies in the rooms. They're going to need to be laundered. And the same goes for all the bed linens, including blankets and bedspreads." Still not entirely sure that Harry wasn't going to change his mind and bolt when he grasped the gargantuan task ahead, Kristy led him down a short hall to the big laundry room, where a half-dozen large commercial washers and dryers lined the walls. Kristy made her way over to a canvas cart. "You can put the linens in this and then bring them back here, and begin washing them."

"Which rooms will I be stripping?" Harry asked, as he pushed the cart out into the hall.

"One hundred to one twenty-five. I'll be working in the same wing. I'm going to start on the bathrooms." Kristy handed him the maid's set of room keys.

"Right-o, madam."

Kristy stopped in her tracks, figuring they might as well get this cleared up right now. "And, Harry?"

He paused. "Yes, madam?"

"You've got to start calling me by my first name," she insisted.

"Oh. Right. Kristy." He smiled at her. She smiled back. He began pushing the linen cart again as the front door of the lobby swung open and Connor Templeton walked in. He was dressed as he had been earlier that morning, in a T-shirt and jeans. Kristy's shoulders tensed, even as her heart took a little leap. She should not be so glad to see him. Particularly after the way they had parted a few hours ago....

Harry looked at her, the polite, formal butler again. "Would you like me to see what the gentleman wants, mad—er, Kristy?"

She shook her head. "I'll handle Mr. Templeton." She pointed in the direction of the north wing. "You go ahead and get started."

Kristy crossed the lobby. Unsure whether it was excitement or annoyance speeding up her pulse, she noted dryly, "Like a bad penny, you keep turning up."

"Ha, ha." Smoky-gray eyes twinkling, he strode over to her. Before she could do anything to stop him, he curved a possessive hand about her elbow and leaned over to kiss her cheek in that casual Southern style of greeting he favored. Kristy knew it didn't mean anything—Connor probably kissed dozens of female cheeks in the course of a single day as he said hello to women he knew—but she couldn't keep her face from tingling at the soft-as-a-butterfly touch of his lips. Or keep from thinking how those same lips had felt—so sure and so right—over hers the night before, as they had ended the evening in a way that had felt anything but casual.

"So? What's going on around here today?" Connor asked, as he stepped back.

"We're working." *Or about to start,* Kristy amended silently. "What did you need?"

Connor looked deep into her eyes. "I thought maybe we could go for coffee," he suggested softly.

And darned if she didn't want to forget everything and just go. "I don't have time for that." She had a business to run, even if it was a fledgling operation at the moment.

Some emotion she couldn't quite identify flickered in Connor's face. Kristy didn't know why, but suddenly she felt as if she were in the midst of some sort of test. A test she was destined to fail.

"Why not?" he asked, still holding her gaze.

"Because," Kristy continued, attempting to insert some levity into the conversation, "I'm getting ready for a group of insurance agents and their spouses."

Connor shrugged his shoulders. "That's not until next week." For him, that was light years away.

It didn't matter, Kristy thought, beginning to feel completely overwhelmed again. She turned and headed for the reservations desk. To her chagrin, Connor was right behind her.

"I have a lot to do between now and then," she told him bluntly.

"Such as…?"

His sympathetic attitude invited confession. And right now Kristy needed someone to unburden herself to. "Clean rooms, do something about the ratty-looking carpet in the one-hundred wing, see if I can't get a crew in to paint the hallway. Polish everything until it gleams. Wash windows. Scrub down bathrooms that haven't been touched in over six months. Need I go on?'' Feeling as if she was wasting time standing there gabbing—or flirting—with him, she yanked open the drawer where all the room keys were kept. Grabbing the old-fashioned master key ring for the north wing, with all twenty-five keys on it, she brought it out and clipped it to the belt loop of her shorts.

As if he had all the time in the world, Connor lounged against the polished wooden counter. ''Sounds like you have your hands full.''

Kristy shot him a wry look. ''Gee. You think?''

He straightened. ''What would you like me to do?''

Stop standing there as if you were my white knight, riding in to the rescue, she thought. But not about to say that, she brushed past him purposefully and headed for the end of the reservations desk. ''Besides leave me alone and stop badgering me about selling the resort?''

He followed her through the swinging wooden door that separated guests from the check-in clerk. ''I won't say another word,'' he promised as he caught up and fell into step beside her.

Kristy narrowed her eyes at him. If she didn't know better, she would think she wasn't hearing right.

''I'm serious, Kristy,'' Connor insisted softly. He reached out and gently clasped her upper arm, stopping her headlong flight. ''I'd like to help you.''

She folded her arms and regarded him skeptically. ''Why?''

Once again the agenda he wasn't quite willing to reveal to her—in its entirety, anyway—became part of their conversation. Connor rubbed his chin and sent her a playful grin. ''Because I'm trying to get on your good side?''

Telling herself she was not going to get involved with a man who deliberately kept things from her—hadn't she already done that once, with disastrous results?—Kristy responded, "Not possible."

He merely smiled, looking every bit as determined to have his way in this as she was to have hers.

Which brought them to another subject Kristy knew they had to discuss. "Also, while we are on the subject of you helping me out…"

"Yes?" Connor said, giving her his full attention.

Kristy regarded him grimly. "I appreciate you sending out your personal mechanic to look at my minivan, Connor, but it really wasn't necessary for you to go to all that trouble."

He paused, his demeanor abruptly serious. "Was he able to get it running?" he asked protectively.

Telling herself all the while that she most definitely did not need Connor watching over and taking care of her and the girls like some guardian angel, Kristy nodded, and didn't bother to mask her relief about that. "It turned out to be a loose wire," she explained. "And something about the distributor cap not being on quite as tight as it should have been. That doesn't usually happen." She paused, eyeing Connor carefully. "You wouldn't happen to know anything about that, would you?"

Connor looked even more uncomfortable.

"I mean, I'd hate to think you would sabotage my vehicle just so you could come charging to the rescue this morning."

His forehead creased. "I did not show up this morning just to rescue you," he stated indignantly.

Put that way, Kristy could almost—almost—believe him. Just as she also believed he had very much enjoyed aiding her, nevertheless. "Then why did you?" she demanded, still feeling a little piqued about his timing and his call to his mechanic, and a lot attracted to him. Too much so for comfort, she noted inwardly, as she took another step back, away from him.

"I came for the same reason I'm here now," Connor explained patiently, his gray eyes taking on a new, ardent gleam. "I wanted to ask you out on a date."

CONNOR COULD SEE his invitation was going over like a lead balloon. But that didn't mean he would give up. And if she thought she could irritate him into leaving, she was wrong. For one thing, he had a job to do here, and Connor hadn't gotten to be a commercial real estate tycoon by leaving tasks undone. Hence he had to make good on his promise to Skip and get close enough to Kristy Neumeyer to find out just what it was they could offer her so that she *would* sell them her property. And then everyone else in the consortium he and Skip had put together would get what they wanted, also. Connor had to protect her from her obnoxious neighbor, Bruce Fitts. And there were other things he wanted to do, too, such as be a friend and soundingboard to her as she dealt with the problems she was having with her twins. And last but not least, he wanted to take her out on a date. For purely personal—not business— reasons.

He wanted to take her in his arms and kiss her again. Heck, he wanted to do more than that—he wanted to make love to her. But he couldn't contemplate either option until they knew each other a little better. And to know each other, they had to spend time together. Something Kristy was doing her best to avoid.

She angled her chin at him icily. "I don't date."

Connor stepped closer until they were standing toe to toe. "Why not?" he demanded.

The soft edges of Kristy's lips turned up in a complacent smile. "No time."

Silence fell between them as Connor thought about that.

As he continued to study her—and the various paths he could take to make her wrong about that, after all—she smirked up at him. "You don't believe me, do you?"

He didn't think he liked the look in Kristy's eyes. It guaranteed trouble. At his expense. Feeling as if he was in the midst of a romantic comedy about to happen, he said, "I believe you could do anything you set your mind to." And it was true. He did. Including save this aging resort, if he and Skip couldn't convince her to do otherwise.

"Well—" Kristy smiled at him merrily "—right now, I'm off to clean twenty-five toilets, so unless you care to join me..."

Obviously, she expected him to turn tail and run.

Had it been anyone else throwing down that gauntlet, he probably would have.

But it wasn't.

With that sassy look of hers and that sassy tone, she had dared him not to leave, and no way was Connor letting her have the upper hand in this blossoming romance of theirs. If that was indeed what it was. Right now he wasn't sure. It felt more like a rivalry.

The only difference being he'd never had the hots for a rival the way he had the hots for Kristy Neumeyer.

Keeping his own game plan to himself, he lifted an arm and gestured broadly. "Not the most scintillating invitation I've ever had, but lead the way."

For a second Kristy looked taken aback, as if she couldn't believe he was actually going to agree. Then her cheeks pinkened, her chin lifted defiantly and she gave him a challenging smile. Pivoting sharply on her heel, she marched away. Connor fell into step behind her, appreciating the determined sway of her hips beneath the rumpled cotton shorts. And her pert knees and lightly suntanned legs peeking out from beneath the hem were pretty fine, too. And then there were her breasts, Connor thought, as Kristy stopped at the supply room and walked in. She might think the oversize man's work shirt she was wearing overtop of her clinging white T-shirt disguised them, but Connor could see the softly rounded curves, as easily as he could see her slender feminine hands and graceful neck, her trim waist and provocative hips. She might not realize it, but she had a body made for loving. And a heart, too...

Kristy picked up a pair of heavy-duty rubber gloves, a scrubber sponge and a big can of powdered disinfectant cleanser. She looked at him smugly. "I think this is your cue to exit," she said dryly.

"When the work begins?" Connor countered, in the same know-it-all tone. "No way."

She began to look frustrated. And annoyed that her plan wasn't working. "You can't just be a passive participant here and stand around and watch me work my tail off, Connor," she pointed out irritably. "If you're going to hang around, you're going to have to help."

"I get the picture," he stated matter-of-factly, beginning to realize how much fun it was going to be to get under her skin.

"Going or staying, Mr. Templeton?" She pushed the words through tightly gritted teeth.

Connor's smile broadened all the more. "Staying," he said.

Looking peeved rather than pleased by his valor, she slapped the gloves, sponge and cleanser into his hands. "Okay. It's your adventure. Just remember, you signed up for this," she said, as she led the way back out of the storeroom and down the hall to the north wing of the lodge.

Connor caught a glimpse of Harry Bowles in room 100, stripping linens off a bed, as they swept by. "We'll go down to the other end of the hall," Kristy said.

She led the way to room 125 and unlocked the door. Connor's eyes widened as he got a good look at the interior.

It needed a lot of TLC. The walls needed painting, the carpet was worn and scuzzy and the bathroom… Connor swore silently to himself. He'd never seen anything as disgusting in his entire life. "What," he asked, physically recoiling as he pointed to the orange-and-black streaks inside the commode and around the tub, "is that?"

"Rust and mold," Kristy replied sweetly. Her eyebrows climbed higher. "Don't tell me you've never seen either."

What could he say? He hadn't. But then he'd had servants to clean when he was growing up, and his mother had advised him to hire a housekeeper as soon as he moved out on his own. Which Connor, who had no earthly desire to clean toilets himself—never mind toilets other people had used!—had promptly done.

Kristy was still looking at him, a lot more victoriously now that she'd made her point. "Well, put your rubber gloves on," she said with a let's-get-on-with-this tone, "and I'll walk you through it."

She wasn't the only one who could be stubborn and irascible, Connor thought. He looked down at her earnestly. "I thought you'd show me." He paused to flash her a crocodile grin. "Me being a novice and all."

"No need for that," she replied airily. "I'll talk you through it. Unless—" she batted her eyelashes at him coquettishly "—you'd like to get out while the going's good and run along home or wherever it is you spend your days?"

Connor knew when he was being challenged. He also knew what Kristy didn't—that he never backed down from one. Or let anyone intimate, through word or deed, that he was a gutless wonder. His eyes holding hers, he inched on one rubber glove, then the other. He drew in a deep, determined breath. "Let's go, then," he commanded, with the same inflection he would have used to say "Saddle up!"

Pretty color swept Kristy's face. Her wicked grin widened, and Connor had the sharp sensation she was close to bursting into laughter. "The first thing you do is lift the lid."

Ugh. She really was going to go through with this. Keeping his face expressionless, Connor picked up the lid with two fingers and pulled it away from the ceramic bowl. Unfortunately, in his eagerness to be done with that nasty bit of business, he let it go a little too quickly and it slammed against the back of the toilet.

Kristy sighed, shook her head and watched mutely as he did it again, this time not letting go too soon.

"Okay, now. Sprinkle cleanser all around the inside of the bowl." She edged closer, watching approvingly as he followed her directions to the letter. "Good. Now take the sponge and work that cleanser in, being careful to get up around the inside of the rim."

Very glad he had industrial-strength gloves on, Connor dabbed a little here and there. Kristy leaned in closer still, until the enticing softness of her breast brushed his extended arm. Connor began to have a different problem, starting near the front of his jeans. Fortunately, she was still focused on the task at hand.

"Don't be afraid to give it a good scrubbing." She straightened and winked. "It won't bite."

Tired of bending over, Connor got down on his knees. "Har de har har."

Kristy braced her hands on her hips. "I thought you would see the adventure in this, eventually."

Kristy Neumeyer was an adventure. Definitely. He didn't know about the rest of this, though....

"Keep going," she directed enthusiastically. "We're going to scrub and rinse the whole commode, inside and out, until it's clean enough to eat off of."

Connor shook his head at that image as he put a lot more

power into his scrub arm. He shot her a glance. "I don't know about you, but I will not be taking any meals here."

Connor thought, but couldn't be sure, that he saw a hint of respect in her lovely brown eyes. She chuckled. "A sense of humor. Nice."

As Connor continued working, the porcelain bowl began to sparkle the way the commodes in his own home always did.

"Be sure you get around the base of the toilet, too," Kristy directed, backing away. "It can get pretty icky around the floor."

Connor looked down. And promptly wished he hadn't. No wonder women were always complaining about aim. "No kidding."

Kristy leaned against the wall as Connor finished cleaning and rinsing around the commode. "That's good enough," she murmured at long last. "In fact," she stated respectfully, "it's excellent."

It ought to be, Connor thought. He was sweating. He never perspired, except on the tennis court. He stood up again.

"Okay!" Kristy said enthusiastically, clapping her hands together. "One down, twenty-four to go!"

Connor had words for that particular goal. But none, he knew, that should be muttered in front of a lady. And despite her goading, Kristy Neumeyer was a lady. And a fine-looking one at that.

"I'm kidding," she said humorously after a moment, attempting to take the cleanser can from him, despite his resistance to giving up or giving in. "You've proved your point. You can do this. Just as I've proved mine."

Connor paused as their hands fought over the cleanser. He didn't like the sound of this. "And your point was what, exactly?"

Kristy's eyes gentled compassionately, letting him know

it was okay, she forgave him. "That I'm not the kind of woman a tycoon-about-town like you wants to date."

Connor stiffened. He had encountered attitudes like this before. He just hadn't expected one from someone as down-to-earth and inherently compassionate as Kristy Neumeyer. "Next thing I know you'll be calling me a blue blood."

Kristy blinked, surprised by his pique. "Aren't you?"

Connor grimaced. "That's beside the point."

She eyed him up and down, her glance scanning him slowly before returning to his face. "I don't think so," she said, stepping intimately closer as she angled her head up to his. "You see, Connor, I'm as common as they come. College educated, yes. In hotel management, no less. But there isn't a drop of blue blood in my entire body."

So? What did that have to do with anything? "That hasn't stopped you from being friends with my sister Daisy," Connor pointed out.

With a sigh of exasperation, Kristy waved off the comparison. "Daisy is her own woman. Besides, she rejected her aristocratic roots from the get-go." She pointed a finger at him. "You don't seem to have done that."

Connor was not going to apologize either for being okay with who and what he was, or for being financially successful. He edged closer. "Now who's the snob?" he demanded, irked.

"What?" Kristy blinked.

"I didn't mention your background. I didn't know what it was." He pulled off the gloves, first one and then the other. He tossed them onto the sink, then continued in the same taut tone. "Nor did I care."

"How reassuring." Kristy made a face at him and tossed down her gloves, too. They landed next to his, in the sink.

"I'm attracted to you," Connor explained, not embarrassed or ashamed about that, either. "It is as simple and complicated as that."

Kristy looked him up and down as if to say, *Yeah, right.* "And the resort located on prime beach property that I recently inherited has nothing to do with said attraction," she repeated disbelievingly.

Ignoring her gasp of dismay, Connor took her into his arms and brought her close. Knowing there was only one way to make his point, he looked deep into her eyes and said, "You tell me."

Chapter Five

Kristy saw the kiss coming and reminded herself she had sworn to resist him, if he tried to possess her lips again. But as his mouth took hers, a thrill swept through her and she felt herself wanting and needing Connor Templeton the way she had never wanted and needed anyone. She moaned softly as he bent her backward and deepened the kiss until it was so hot and sensual it stole her breath away. He kissed her as if he meant to make her his, and yearning surged through her, overwhelming her heart and her mind. Surrendering helplessly despite the reservations still swirling inside her, Kristy wreathed her arms about his neck, curving her body into his, and kissed Connor passionately. She loved the dark, male scent of him, and the feel of him pressed up against her, so strong and warm and sexy. She loved the reckless, womanly way he made her feel. As if she still had her whole life—and plenty of passion and tenderness—ahead of her. Her lips parted all the more and she drew his tongue deeper into her mouth, continuing to stroke it with hers, and somehow the parity of their love play made the culmination of their desire all the sweeter. And more erotic. And still he kissed her as if he didn't care how many roadblocks she threw in their way, or how difficult she made it for them to be together.

His hand slipped beneath her blouse and cupped her

breast through the lace of her bra. Trembling with helpless pleasure, Kristy arched her back and luxuriated in the warm ribbons of sensation sweeping through her. She wanted so much more. She wanted them to make love. But they couldn't, not here and not now, not when she still had so much work to do, and so little time to do it in. She couldn't afford to mess around here, wearing her heart on her sleeve. Especially knowing that she would likely end up getting her heart broken when Connor inevitably approached her for what he had wanted from her from the first—her resort. So, telling herself it was for the best—for both of them— Kristy splayed her hands across his chest, tore her lips from his, and breathlessly, resolutely, pushed him away.

THE ABRUPT END to their hot embrace caught Connor by surprise. He had wanted to forget the business deal that had brought him here and just let their feelings—instead of logic and reason—take over today. He had wanted to let the complications of their circumstances be damned, and take Kristy somewhere quiet and private and make wild, passionate love to her, so thoroughly and completely that neither one of them would ever forget a single instant of it. And then, only then, deal with the unresolved specifics of their situation. Which, he admitted, were considerable. Not that they had stopped Kristy from responding to the chemistry flowing between them. He could tell by the look in her eyes that she had been as affected as he had by the spontaneous kiss, but was predictably—just as she had the evening before when he had kissed her good-night—determined not to admit her desire for him.

Kristy regarded him feistily. Stepping past him, she muttered, "Okay, Connor. You've proved your point. You are off the hook."

He closed the distance between them and kept her from exiting the bathroom. Putting a hand to her shoulder, he turned her to face him. "What are you talking about?" Obviously, she deemed him guilty of something nefarious. He wanted to know what, precisely.

Kristy pressed her lips together resentfully.

"You didn't have to take me in your arms and kiss me like that to get tossed out of here. Or get out of a chore you are obviously not cut out to do."

"You don't honestly think I kissed you to get out of cleaning another commode, do you?" Connor asked incredulously. Did she really think he was that shallow?

Kristy lifted her slender shoulders in an elegant little shrug. "I wouldn't blame you if you did," she told him with exaggerated civility as she danced away from him yet again. Sympathy lit her dark brown eyes as she regarded him kindly. "It's the worst chore around here."

Connor couldn't disagree with her on that as she picked up her discarded rubber gloves. He took them from her and tossed them down again, saying flatly, "And one you as owner of the resort, and an executive in your own right, should not have to do yourself."

The flush of temper filled Kristy's cheeks as she swung around to square off with him. "I'm not above any of the work around here, Connor," she stated archly, as if her upper-middle-class background was somehow more noble or laudable than his aristocratic one. She jabbed a finger at the middle of his chest. "If I can assign an employee to do it, I have to be able to do it myself. Besides—" Kristy let out a quavering breath as she backed up against the bathroom wall "—there's nothing undignified about doing an honest day's labor."

Another dig at his profession, Connor thought, his own seldom used temper beginning to heat up.

She flicked her fingers toward the door. "So you can run along now."

His lips thinned. "And stop hounding you?"

"Yes," Kristy snapped, looking even more irked.

Hands braced on his waist, Connor swaggered closer. No way was he going to let her slur on his character go unanswered. "That would be fine, if we were finished here," he stated calmly, deliberately holding her glance. "We're not. As you pointed out earlier, we still have twenty-four commodes left. I said I would help you do that. I will."

She glared at him from beneath thick, dark lashes. Obviously, he thought with satisfaction, she resented his can-and-will-do attitude, his determination to earn her respect and her trust, no matter what it took, or how arduous she made the getting-to-know-each-other process.

"Thanks, but I can take it from here." She started to move past him. He put out an arm to prevent her from leaving. She heaved a beleaguered sigh and he studied her upturned face.

"You don't think I have it in me to finish cleaning twenty-four more commodes, do you?"

"No. Frankly, I don't."

Connor smirked. This was going to be easy! "Well, I bet you that I do," he said audaciously. "In fact," he added, when she continued to stare at him with a combination of amazement and pique, "I bet I could handle working here for an entire week without complaining or being tempted to give up once." He wouldn't mind being near her, either.

She rolled her eyes in frank disbelief. "Sure. Whatever, Connor." Looking as disinterested as it was possible to look, she started to step past him.

Once again he blocked her path. "You don't believe me?"

"No." She lounged against the bathroom wall and folded her arms in front of her. "I don't. In fact, if you want the absolute truth…"

"I do." He egged her on with a provoking grin.

Kristy lifted an imperious brow. "I don't think you could last for even a day here doing the kind of work that Harry and I will be doing for the next week, to get ready for the conference coming in."

"Well, I can. And furthermore, I'll prove it to you."

"You're nuts," Kristy exclaimed, looking at Connor in a way that made him want to haul her into his arms again and kiss her until she melted against him.

"Ah. So you are afraid to make this wager with me," Connor taunted playfully, edging closer.

Color flooded her cheeks. Her soft lips formed a kissable pout. "I most certainly am not!" she declared indignantly, her stubborn gaze still trained on his.

"Then prove it to me," he challenged mildly.

"Fine." She regarded him with the steely resolve of a Carolina belle, born and bred. "You want to make this stupid bet? We'll do it."

Connor grinned in satisfaction at once again getting the upper hand in this battle of wills, whether she knew it yet or not, before going on to stipulate audaciously, "If I win, I get that date I wanted. One night. With you. On the town." He would use it to good advantage. To romance her and hopefully—finally—get her right where she belonged, in his arms—and in his bed!

Kristy stomped closer. "And if I win," she stated, eyes sparkling, "and you do cry uncle before the week is out, you—Mr. Let's Make a Deal—have to promise to never ever mention the sale of my property again. Furthermore, you have to get your partner, Skip Wakefield, to back off, too."

Connor felt that was a fair price to pay, should he lose the bet. Not that he was going to. "Done," he said, holding out his palm.

They shook hands. Kristy laughed then, the sound soft

and musical. "This is going to be like taking candy from a baby," she declared happily.

Connor grinned right back, feeling even more confident than she did as he taunted her mischievously, "You just take your prettiest dress out and get it ready to wear. Because come one week from today, sweetheart, you and I are going to paint the town red."

KRISTY WORKED ONE SIDE of the hall, Connor worked the rooms on the other. To her surprise, he didn't seem to mind the hard physical labor of the task they had undertaken. Two hours later, they were headed out to the lodge kitchen for a much needed respite and cold drink, when a beautiful woman in her early fifties walked in. Her dark hair was cut in stylish layers that nicely framed her patrician features, and she was wearing a beautiful ultrasuede suit the same color blue as her eyes. Kristy had never met Winnifred Deveraux-Smith, but she recognized the social doyenne of Charleston from pictures on the society page of the *Herald,* as Winnifred was always presiding over one charity function or another.

Curious as to why she would be there, Kristy strode forward to say hello and introduce herself. "I'm Kristy Neumeyer."

Winnifred smiled like the gracious lady she was. "I'm Winnifred Deveraux-Smith. Pleased to meet you, dear. Connor..." Winnifred released her clasp on Kristy's hand and shook Connor's, too, leaning forward while he kissed her cheek. "Nice to see you, dear. Give your regards to your mother and sisters when you see them."

"Thanks," Connor said, regarding Winnifred affectionately. "I will."

Kristy wasn't sure why someone of Winnifred's ilk would be at her place. Unless she wanted to see Harry Bowles. "I'm afraid we're not open yet," Kristy said.

Winnifred smiled. "I'm here to see my butler."

Just then Harry appeared, rolling a cart overflowing with dusty draperies toward the laundry room. He gave the older woman a look simmering with resentment. "I'm not your butler anymore."

Winnifred propped her hands on her hips and stared at Harry with equal pique. "You have made your point, Harry," she murmured, clearly upset. "Now get your suit and tie back on and come home."

Harry paused, straightened and glared right back at Winnifred. "Has anything changed?" he demanded.

Winnifred became flustered. She touched a hand to her hair, making sure it was in place. "You know why it can't," she stated miserably, still holding her ex-butler's eyes.

Harry shrugged, looking as comfortable in his chinos and loose-fitting, tropical-weight work shirt as he had in his impeccably tailored suit and tie the previous day. "Then I'm staying."

"Harry, for heaven's sake! This is beneath you. Sorry, Ms. Neumeyer, but it is! Harry's trained for so much more than…than laundry work or whatever it is he's doing here!"

Harry let go of the laundry cart and stomped closer. "Don't you mean that I am beneath you, madam?" he asked coldly. "Socially speaking, of course."

Fearing things would be said that would later be regretted, Kristy cut in and told Winnifred cheerfully, "Harry is simply helping me out here. As soon as we get the resort up and running next week, he will be managing it for me."

Winnifred looked even more upset. She stared at Harry in stunned amazement. "That means you've accepted a permanent position here?" She was obviously aghast.

Looking every bit the handsome blond Brit he was,

Harry folded his arms in front of him. "Yes, madam, I have."

"Then I want one, too," Winnifred commanded, not to be outdone. She turned to Kristy and asked, "What positions are currently open?"

This was getting really strange, Kristy thought. She shrugged her slender shoulders. "Well, for starters, head chef and dining room manager."

"I'll take that one," Winnifred said, setting down her stylish Kate Spade handbag.

Kristy frowned, aware that this demonstration of one-upmanship had gone on long enough. "This isn't a game, Mrs. Deveraux-Smith."

"Call me Winnifred, please."

"We have fifty guests checking in next Wednesday for a five-day stay. Menus have to be planned. Supplies ordered. The cuisine has to be first-rate." Otherwise, Kristy would consider the sales conference a failure no matter how much badly needed revenue it brought in.

Winnifred looked both hurt and incensed. "You don't think I can cook, is that it?"

Beside Kristy, Connor coughed, as if hinting that she should tread carefully here. What was it about Charleston society people and their egos? "I'm not trying to insult you," Kristy said gently. "But preparing food for fifty people plus the staff three times a day is a real challenge."

"One I assure you I am up to," Winnifred said starchily, slipping off her exquisitely tailored jacket, to reveal a silk shell underneath. "And to prove it, I'll prepare dinner this evening for as many as you like."

Kristy hesitated.

Winnifred looked at her, almost daring Kristy not to give her a chance. What did she have to lose? Kristy wondered. Perhaps it would give Harry Bowles and Winnifred a chance to work out whatever problem they had, in any case.

Because it was clear that something pretty important was going on between them. "Fine. You'll have to make do with what is currently in the refrigerator and pantry, though." She didn't have the time or inclination to go out and look for any gourmet delicacies required in whatever haute cuisine Winnifred might want to whip up.

"How many will be here?" the woman asked, all-business now.

Kristy did some rapid calculating. "Six. But if you wanted to make more, we could eat leftovers tomorrow."

"Nonsense." Winnifred tossed Harry a challenging look, then turned back to Kristy, promising resolutely, "I'll prepare every meal fresh. That is my job, after all. Should you decide to forgo any prejudice my blue-blooded background might engender, and award it to me." She glanced at the set of swinging double doors at the other end of the dining hall. "I presume the hotel kitchen is this way?"

Kristy nodded.

Winnifred took off.

Scowling as if he had just been trumped in an important bridge match, Harry stomped back to the cart of draperies and pushed it on into the laundry room.

"Now what?" Connor asked, when he and Kristy were alone again.

Deciding it might be wise to stay out of the kitchen until Winnifred cooled down, and at the same time give Harry a clear path to apologize to her, or vice versa, Kristy said, "Let's go outside and get some sodas out of the drink machines next to the building."

They had just popped the tabs on their drinks when the arborist Kristy had been expecting pulled into the resort driveway and circled around to the portico in front of the lobby. The woman, Shirley Lane, jumped out of her pickup truck. She had short, red-gray hair and a friendly freckled face, and was clad in a pine-green landscaping-company uniform, with a badge pinned to the lapel of her cotton work vest.

"I see what you mean about those palmetto trees," she said, indicating them with a wave of her hand. "They aren't looking good at all."

"I'm afraid they might all be dying," Kristy said worriedly.

"I hate to say it, but I think you might be right." Shirley got a couple of plastic bags and a sharp instrument that looked like a surgical tool out of the tackle box on her front seat. "I'm going to have to take some samples, but off the cuff, I'd say something has attacked the roots."

Connor was watching the procedure with interest. "Insects?" he guessed.

Shirley pursed her lips. "Generally speaking, palmettos are pretty resistant to pests and disease," she said. "That's why they're so popular down here. Because they are such a strong tree, with such deep root systems. But never say never."

"How long will it take you to find out what is happening to them?" Kristy asked anxiously. It seemed to her that every day now the trees looked worse. And with them comprising the bulk of the landscaping and providing both shade and a tropical aura, it could be a problem. Especially if she ended up eventually having to take the trees out.

Shirley shook her head thoughtfully. "It could be as short as a couple of weeks or as long as a month, depending on how hard it is to isolate and identify the problem."

"That long?" Kristy gasped. At the rate the leaves were curling up, her trees could be dead by then!

The arborist shrugged her shoulders helplessly. "I'll put a rush on it. But you have to understand, it takes a few weeks to grow the cultures in the lab. And a while after that to get the disease identified, especially if it's something unusual. And right now, it looks to me as if it might be."

Great, Kristy thought. "In the meantime, is there anything I can do to help them get better or at least not any worse?" The edges of the leaves were brown and curling, a definitely unhealthy sign.

Shirley shook her head. "Until we know what we are dealing with, it's best not to do anything. But just to be on the safe side, in case this is a disease of some sort that's attacking the root systems, I wouldn't plant any new shrubbery or flowers around them. Whatever is affecting your trees could be in the soil."

Kristy thanked the arborist, then stood with Connor, watching her drive away.

"Well, that could hardly have been worse news," he noted.

"At least she didn't say they were definitely dying and there was no hope," Kristy answered. It would cost thousands of dollars to replace the trees, and would take years for new ones to reach the same towering heights. Without trees, the resort would lose a lot of its charm, resembling one of those hotels that sprang up along barren stretches of the freeway, instead of a carefully cultivated haven in nature.

"Well, let's hope Shirley Lane comes back with good news," Connor said.

"No kidding." Kristy took a sip of her soda.

"What next?" Connor said, as he finished his.

Kristy glanced at the school bus coming down the drive. Reminded of her talk with the counselor that very morning, she sighed. These days it was always something. She shot Connor a concerned look. "I talk to my twins."

"ARE WE IN TROUBLE, Mommy?" Susie asked, as Kristy carried beach chairs down to the dunes for the three of them. The girls walked beside her, Susie carrying a small cooler of canned lemonade and Sally three individual bags of pretzels for their snack.

"No, sweetheart, you're not." Kristy selected the place in the dunes where they had the most privacy and the best view of the ocean at Paradise Resort. It was the spot where she and Lance had always taken the girls to enjoy the sunset, whenever they vacationed and visited here, and she was hoping it would make them feel closer to their father, being here.

"Then how come the guidance counselor gave us that note so she could talk to you?" Sally asked, her lower lip trembling.

Kristy gave both girls a reassuring look as she explained matter-of-factly, "She was concerned. She said the two of you have been talking about Daddy a lot lately. At school."

Susie blinked, her confusion evident. "And that's why we're in trouble?" she asked.

This was so hard. Suddenly Kristy wished she didn't have to do it alone. She wished Connor were here with her. But she had asked him to stay back at the lodge and do whatever he could to assist Harry or Winnifred.

Kristy finished setting up the chairs, close together and facing the ocean. "Your teachers said you've been sort of acting like Daddy didn't die," Kristy murmured, seating her daughters on either side of her.

The girls scowled at her in confusion. "But he did die and go to heaven," Sally protested heatedly.

"I know that, honey." Kristy wrapped an arm around each girl and cuddled them close. "Which is why everyone is a little confused." *And I am worried out of my mind about what might be going on here.* "Because your teacher said you told the other kids your daddy was helping you learn your multiplication tables."

Sally nodded soberly, admitting this was true.

Kristy turned to Susie. "And she said you were telling

the kids your daddy was away on a long trip and you couldn't wait to spend time with him again.''

"That's right." Susie nodded vigorously. "Daddy did go on a long journey—to heaven. You and Grandma and Grandpa told me so. And I'll get to see him again when I go to heaven."

"But that won't be for a long time."

"I know," Susie said with perfect eight-year-old logic. "But I still can't wait," she finished eagerly.

Okay, that made sense. To an eight-year-old, anyway. Kristy turned to Sally. "What you said about Daddy helping you with your homework..." She paused, not sure how to word this. "Do you see Daddy when he helps you?"

"No, silly." Sally made a face, as if that was the stupidest question on earth. "He's in heaven!"

Beginning to feel a little better now, Kristy asked curiously, "Then how does he help you?"

Sally clasped her hands over her chest. "He helps me in here. Don't you 'member, Mommy? You told us that Daddy was always going to be with us—in our hearts. Whenever I needed him, all I had to do was close my eyes and think about how much I loved him, and he would be with me again. And I needed him to help me with my math."

Kristy felt tears gathering behind her eyes. She loved her little girls so much and felt so bad they'd had to suffer through this loss. "I see now," she said thickly. She couldn't wait to explain it to their schoolteachers and counselor.

"So are we still in trouble?" Susie asked. Both girls looked at Kristy urgently.

"No."

The twins smiled at each other, relieved.

Not sure this was as simple as it appeared on the surface, however—her experience as a mother told her there were always layers to things, whenever any sort of trouble occurred—Kristy dug a little deeper. She wanted to make sure the girls weren't feeling as if she was letting them down, too, by not being there for them when they needed her. "How are things otherwise?" she asked kindly.

Both girls' eyes widened. They exchanged glances. Then Sally demanded, "What do you mean?"

"Are you happy at your new school?"

Both of them shrugged. Sally worked on opening her snack bag of pretzels. Susie did the same.

"Are you sad when you're there?" Kristy persisted.

Neither twin said anything. Nor did they look at her.

Certain she was on to something, Kristy said, "Lonely, maybe?"

The twins looked at each other intently. Finally, Susie spoke for both of them, "Sometimes we miss our friends in North Carolina." She attempted to smile at her mom reassuringly.

"But most of the time it's okay," Sally added quickly, her own melancholy evident. "The kids here are nice, too."

So they had been having some trouble adjusting, Kristy thought. And because they knew she was so overwhelmed with trying to get the resort up and running again, they'd decided to keep their worries to themselves. "You know, I've been working so hard trying to get the lodge ready to reopen, that I haven't had much time to play with you two kiddos. I'm really sorry about that," Kristy said, ruffling their dark hair affectionately.

"It's okay, Mommy." Susie leaned against Kristy's shoulder. Sally did the same.

No, Kristy thought, as she continued to cuddle both her daughters, it wasn't okay. The girls needed more from her, and she hadn't been as accessible to them as she should be. But that was going to change, starting today. She looked down at Sally, knowing her "princess" hadn't chosen the most comfortable shoes to wear to school that day. "Would you like to change your clothes and take a long walk on the beach?"

"I can't." Sally plucked at the frilly apron covering her gingham school dress.

Kristy studied her, recalling how much Sally had once liked wearing shorts and T-shirts. That had been before Lance died. Was this somehow connected to her husband's death, too? Instead of just a "phase," as she'd been assuming it was? "Why not?"

Sally seemed to withdraw into herself as she studied the toe of her leather shoe. "Because."

"Because why not?"

Sally plucked at the buckle on her shoe and admitted in a very small voice, "Daddy wouldn't like it."

Suddenly, they were talking as if Lance was still here, impacting their daily lives with his definite and not always so supportive or encouraging opinions. Recalling how tough to please her perfectionist husband had been at times, Kristy pointed out kindly, "You used to wear shorts and T-shirts every day and it didn't bother you." Now only the ultratomboy, Susie, did that.

Sally looked even more guilty and unhappy. "But Daddy always wanted me to wear dresses and tights and stuff, and I wouldn't 'cause I didn't want to, and that made him sad."

"I think Daddy was perplexed, honey, at the way you wanted to wear only play clothes back then." It had been an ordeal to get her into a dress for a special occasion, Kristy recalled, and Lance had never been one to appreciate a little drama on the family front. "But he wasn't sad."

"What's purr-plexed?" Susie interjected.

"Puzzled. Confused. Like he really didn't understand little girls as much as he wanted to understand them."

"Oh." Sally ate another pretzel while she thought about that.

Kristy studied her daughter. "Is that why you want to wear dresses all the time now? And carry Daddy's old beach towel around with you, so you can sit on it, and not get your clothes dirty?"

Sally's face contorted as she struggled with her most secret emotions. "I thought maybe Daddy would come back and see us if I got dressed up like he wanted me to, back when he was still 'live. You know?"

Kristy knew. She had wanted to please Lance, too, and realized in the end, after all was said and done, that she had always come up short in his view. And that had hurt. She just hadn't realized until now that the twins had also felt the harshness of his unspoken criticism.

"And you girls figured this out all by yourself," Kristy said out loud, doing her best to keep her own sense of failure to herself.

They nodded.

Sally rubbed the toe of her shoe in the sand. "Are you mad at us now that you know about that, too?" she asked warily.

"No, honey," Kristy said tenderly. *Just a little embarrassed at how long it took me to catch on.* "You know, it's okay for you both to wear what you want." *And be who you are.*

"That's okay, Mommy," Sally and Susie said in unison.

"We think we'll just leave things the way they are," Susie added.

They might know intellectually it was impossible for their daddy to come back, but in their hearts, they still wanted him in their lives so they could have a complete family once again.

Kristy understood that and empathized with their feelings, even as she felt increasingly anxious to put the marriage that had never once given her what she really needed or wanted behind her, so she could get on with her life, too. She'd thought, prior to those kisses from Connor, that she would be moving on without a mate. And that she'd be happy about her romantically unattached life. Now she wasn't so sure. Because Connor's kisses…well, they had stirred up a lot of things within her she thought were over. They had made her yearn to want—and be wanted—again.

Kristy sighed inwardly as she turned her attention to the sun glistening off the blue-gray waters of the Atlantic. She didn't know what she was going to do about that, either. Especially with their ongoing bet and Connor underfoot constantly for the next week, trying to simultaneously prove her wrong about him and win a date with her as his prize.

"WELL? WHAT DO YOU THINK?" Winnifred asked, when the six of them had finished the meal she had prepared. Cooking all afternoon had left her hair disheveled, a warm blush of color in her cheeks, excitement in her Deveraux-blue eyes.

Kristy couldn't believe the social doyenne of Charleston had made such a kid-friendly meal. And so cheerfully and efficiently. Who would have known a woman who had never had children of her own would be so accomplished a chef? Or even want to do something like this, even if just to prove a point to her former butler, Harry Bowles?

"The chicken fingers were yummy," Susie said.

Sally grinned. "I liked the mashed potatoes."

Connor patted his tummy. "You won me over with the crumb-topped pie."

Kristy grinned, too, and complimented Winnifred warmly. "It was all excellent."

"But you were surprised by the menu I chose, weren't you?" Winnifred said with a sly smile.

Kristy didn't want to fib or to hurt the prominent socialite's feelings. "Well, yes, actually, I was. It was the perfect choice for a low-key family dinner. But I can't imagine you serving it often at the parties you give.''

"You're right. Those menus tend toward oysters in champagne cream sauce, and spinach torte. But neither would have been appropriate here, and the key to successful entertaining is pleasing your guests, rather than just the host.''

"Ah. I'll remember that," Kristy said. She regarded Winnifred admiringly. "Perhaps while you're here you could give me some tips on putting on memorable parties for conferences and so on?''

"I'd be delighted to help you with that," Winnifred said.

Harry Bowles remained silent.

Connor looked at him, and in an effort to ease the tension, queried pleasantly, "What did you think of the meal, Harry?''

Harry rose with dignity and began to clear the dishes. He gave Winnifred a pleasant but aloof look. "Superb as always, madam.''

Ooh, chilly, Kristy thought.

Two spots of color appeared in Winnifred's cheeks. She turned to Kristy and squared her slender shoulders purposefully. "Do I have a job?''

Although Kristy doubted a sophisticated woman like Winnifred would last long as head chef at a small beach resort, she didn't see how she could not hire her after such a wonderful culinary audition. "If you're sure you want to cook three meals a day starting now," she stipulated bluntly, more than willing to give her a chance if that was what Winnifred wanted. Kristy couldn't, however, afford for her to take the job, then quit abruptly and leave her without a chef during the conference next week.

"Contrary to some people's opinion of me—" Winnifred shot a telling look at Harry "—I am not now nor have I ever been averse to a day's work.''

Sensing fireworks, Kristy decided to leave it at that.

Connor looked at the twins. "What about you two ladies?" he asked genially. "Do you have any homework?"

They both nodded and looked reluctant to get started on it.

"We have a math work sheet to do," Sally said.

"Yeah, and I don't think our daddy can help us anymore," Sally confessed with a tentative glance at Kristy. "I think our mommy wants us to learn it all by ourselves."

Connor looked at Kristy.

She nodded, doing her best to hide her mounting feelings of inadequacy as a mother. Obviously, her talk with the twins hadn't accomplished all that she had wanted. If it had, her girls wouldn't be staring at her as if she hadn't just ripped them from their home and all their friends and moved them to another state, plus taken away their daddy, too.

Unfortunately, she couldn't explain to them all the reasons why she had needed such a change. That was definitely too much for them to handle.

Sally looked at Kristy. "May we be excused so we can show Connor what we got to do?"

"Yeah, maybe he can help us." Susie's face shone with enthusiasm.

Well, that was better than calling on a dear departed father, and pretending he was still here to do those kinds of things, she guessed. If Connor was willing, anyway.

He smiled, obviously ready for any challenge that came his way. "I would be delighted to assist two beautiful and extremely intelligent young ladies," he said, indulging in a courtly bow from the waist that made both Susie and Sally giggle. He held out a hand to each of them. "Just lead the way...."

"THANKS FOR HELPING THEM with their math," Kristy said two hours later, after the twins had been tucked into bed. This was the first moment she'd had alone with Connor since dinner. And now that the twins were asleep—and Harry and Winnifred nowhere to be seen—Kristy wanted a chance to bring Connor up to speed, so he'd understand where her girls were in this recovery process, such as it was.

"I was glad to be of service," Connor said cheerfully.

"You like kids, don't you?"

"That apparent, is it?"

When Kristy nodded appreciatively, he continued, "I thought by now I'd have several of my own."

"But it hasn't happened."

"No. Although..." he met and held her eyes, a gentle smile curving his sensual lips "...I'm still hopeful it will."

It was easy to imagine him tenderly caring for his own kids. Kristy knew he was not the kind of man who would ever be too busy to see to their needs. His children, she was certain, would always feel very loved and accepted for who and what they were. She looked deep into his eyes. "I think you'll make a good father."

"Thank you."

Silence fell between them. Kristy didn't know how to broach the subject she wanted to talk about. But as if he was reading her mind, Connor turned to her, a concerned light in his eyes. "About what the girls said earlier, at dinner, about their father," he began.

Obviously, Kristy thought, studying the compassion on his face as he sought to understand, Connor had been able to tell the twins' reference to their late father had upset her, too. "I suppose I should explain," she said awkwardly as she stepped out onto the covered porch that ran the length of the lodge, and gestured for him to follow.

After charging to her rescue both this morning and this

evening, and helping her out all day, he had earned the right to know the full story. And she needed a sympathetic ear and a shoulder to lean on tonight. Because he was acting as if he wanted to be the man in her life, the man her girls turned to also, Kristy found herself ready and willing to confide in him.

In a low voice, she filled him in on what her daughters had told her out on the dunes that afternoon, while Connor had been helping Harry strip beds inside the lodge. He listened to her attentively. Once again, Kristy was amazed by the compassion and tenderness in his eyes.

"Sounds like they really miss their dad," he finally observed, leaning a shoulder against a post.

Kristy perched on the railing that rimmed the piazza and turned to face him. "I'm sure they do," she said sadly, swallowing around the growing knot of emotion in her throat. Bitterness she had worked long and hard to erase welled up inside her. "Unfortunately, that's nothing new."

Hands thrust in the pockets of his jeans, Connor remarked, "How so?"

Kristy glanced over at him, aware that the impossible was happening. She and Connor were well on their way to becoming not just business adversaries, but friends. Aware that she had never really talked about the problems within her marriage to anyone, never wanted to until now, Kristy continued in a low, halting voice. "Like all surgeons, Lance worked extremely long hours, and was usually gone well before the girls got up in the morning, and not home until several hours after they were asleep. He was with the girls at most two or three hours every week. Sometimes a lot less than that."

"Sounds hard for you," Connor said, respect glimmering in his gray eyes.

It had been, Kristy recalled stoically. For her and the girls. Kristy had had to be both mother and father to them, most of the time. And worse than that had been the loneliness, the fact that Lance had never had time for her, for their marriage, either.

Warming to the quiet acceptance in Connor's low voice, Kristy continued hoarsely, "I tried to make Lance see that although the girls were very little, they still needed a lot more than that. And so, for that matter, did he, because this was the only childhood they were ever going to have."

Connor reached across the space separating them and covered Kristy's hand with his. "Did it change things?"

"No," she admitted, even as she absorbed the comforting warmth. "Lance never did slow down, never did spend much time with them. Not even at the end, when his life was in danger," she recollected.

Connor's brow furrowed and his eyes searched hers. "What do you mean?"

She shrugged as her thoughts turned to one of the memories she had been running from when she left North Carolina. She extricated her hand from his. "Lance had a very stressful lifestyle. Too little sleep, no exercise, too many meals grabbed on the run. He also had a family history of heart disease."

Connor scowled. "And that didn't prompt him to take better care of himself? If for no other reason than to be around for you and the girls?"

Kristy compressed her lips ruefully. If only Lance had thought like Connor did! "Like most doctors, Lance felt that because he was in medicine, he was invulnerable, immune to all that. But he wasn't." Restless, she stood up, began to pace the length of the piazza. "A couple of weeks before he died, he began having chest pains."

Connor followed her to the end of the porch, well away from the lobby doors. He stood in the pale yellow glow of the porch light, concern sharpening the handsome planes of his face. "You must've been frantic."

Kristy folded her arms in front of her and did her best to keep a lid on her lingering anger and resentment. She glanced at Connor, admitting unhappily, "I didn't know about it." When he quirked a brow in disbelief, she continued relating her sad tale matter-of-factly. "He didn't want to tell me. Probably because he knew I would've insisted he have right away the double bypass surgery his cardiologist was recommending. Instead, Lance decided to do things his way and wait until he had performed another month of surgeries he had scheduled. Only problem was, he wasn't strong enough. And after a particularly grueling round of back-to-back emergency surgeries he had a massive heart attack and died, leaving me a widow and my two daughters without a father."

Connor tucked a hand beneath her chin and lifted her face to his. "You're angry," he observed softly.

"Yes, and I probably always will be." Kristy paused, leaning into his warm, compelling touch. "Do you blame me?"

Chapter Six

Connor had had his own share of life's disappointments. But becoming bitter or resentful had never been an option for him, maybe because he had seen firsthand, in his own family, how destructive such emotions could be. So instead, he had worked hard on finding a way to reconcile everyone, because only in harmony, he had found, were people ever truly happy.

"That explains why the girls are holding on to Lance's memory so hard," he said. "They still want and need a father's presence in their lives."

"Except he can't come back," Kristy stated, turning her eyes to the ocean waves rolling into shore. Moonlight glistened on the water and a warm breeze was blowing. If not for the subject matter, it would have been a romantic setting, indeed, Connor thought. But Kristy's mind was on heartbreak from her past, not the future, with him or anyone else.

"Even so," he said gently, "your girls have something not every child has. The knowledge that their father loved them and wanted the best for them."

Connor hadn't had that. His father had regarded him and his sisters as pawns on a chessboard, to be moved around at his advantage, and forgotten and discarded when he had no use for them. Richard Templeton had treated his wife the same way. Unfortunately, it had taken Connor's mother, Charlotte, most of her adult years to realize that, and then take action to free herself for a life of love, respect and hope again. Connor admired the courage his mother had shown recently. Even as he still wished there had been some way to repair or reverse the damage his father had done with his selfish actions. Because the Templeton family unit would never be whole again. Connor, his mother and sisters lived on one side of the Atlantic, his father on the other, with any contact between them cursory at best. And sadly, that was the way his dad wanted it.

Kristy, however, wasn't in that kind of situation, Connor knew. Yes, her husband had passed away, but she still had family who loved and supported her. She still had a chance to work things out with them, get along better, just as she had a chance to give her girls the kind of childhood they needed. She was still holding herself accountable for so very much, at least where her children's happiness was concerned. Her marriage appeared to be another matter. She seemed to realize that she and her husband had not been as well-suited as they'd needed to be to have a happy marriage.

"In any case," Kristy sighed, raking both her hands through the silky length of her hair, "I'm hoping the school counselor is right. That this is just a phase the twins are going through, brought on by the stress of moving here. And the counseling she is going to give them, plus the attention I plan to heap on them at home, should help them move on and embrace their life here as much as their past."

Connor nodded encouragingly. He had always thought it was better to seize the day and immerse yourself in the present, rather than worry too much about the past, which was over, anyway. Or the future, which would likely take care of itself.

Aware that she could easily get used to having Connor

around all the time, to talk to and be with, Kristy perched on the porch railing and asked, "Where are Harry and Winnifred, by the way?"

Connor sat down beside her and stretched his long legs out in front of him. He wished he could take Kristy to bed and make love to her until all the sadness and uncertainty in her eyes went away. Until she forgot the hurts and disappointments of the past and concentrated only on the future. "Winnifred went back to Charleston to pack a few bags and tell her great-aunt Eleanor she'd be staying here. Harry didn't want her trying to lift her bags alone, so he went with her."

Kristy bit her lower lip. "So they'll both be residing on the premises. Not just Harry."

"Looks like it." She and Connor both fell silent, thinking about the ramifications—and romantic fireworks—that arrangement and the resultant proximity might bring. His mood tense but hopeful, Connor dared ask, "What about me? Given the fact I'm now working here, too—at least for the next week, according to the terms of our wager—do I get the same courtesy?"

"You can't really want to—" Kristy broke off, self-conscious color illuminating the delicate bone structure of her face.

Connor grinned. Lazily, he anchored an arm about her waist and pulled her over so she was ensconced in the open V of his legs. "Suppose I do?" he remarked playfully as her rounded bottom settled against him.

Kristy pivoted to face him, her thighs rubbing against the inner sides of his. "Connor?"

He looked down to where her shorts had ridden up her bare legs, and struggled to contain both a groan and the rising heat in his groin. "Hmm?"

Kristy twisted some more and splayed her hands on his

shoulders. "There's not going to be a romance between us," she warned.

Connor knew she wanted that to be the case. He, however, was more of a realist. And he knew if they were around each other even half as much as they had been today and last night, other kisses and intimate confidences, and further emotional involvement, were not only inevitable, they were desirable. The task would be to convince her of that, make her see that the two of them were undeniably, irrevocably drawn to each other, and that an attraction as electric as theirs came along once in a lifetime.

"Kiss me again, like you *don't* mean it, and then I'll believe that's the case."

She had time to evade him if she wanted, but she didn't. She merely stared up at him with a look of cautious yearning and soul-deep wariness that made Connor feel all the more protective of her as he clamped an arm about her waist and ever so deliberately brought her against him. Threading a hand through the silky hair at the nape of her neck, he tilted her head back and lowered his mouth to hers. Her body was soft and warm as it molded to his length. His lips caressed hers—gently, seductively this time, with slow, gentle passion—until they parted helplessly under the onslaught, and she was meeting him stroke for stroke. Until she was moaning softly and clinging to him helplessly.

He knew she didn't mean to kiss him back, any more than he could keep himself from kissing her, and somehow that made their desire all the sweeter. Luxuriating in the clean, fragrant scent of her, he kissed her deeply, lingeringly, as his hands swept down her body, charting her dips and curves. She made a soft, helpless sound of pleasure low in her throat, and unable to help himself, he gripped her hips with both hands and pulled her closer still, fitting her snugly against his arousal, until the need to have her and make her his was a hot, incessant ache.

Knowing this had to either move to a bedroom—now—or end, and that she wasn't ready for the first, not nearly, he reluctantly pulled away. They regarded each other breathlessly, both trembling, and Kristy shook her head. "I knew from the moment I met you that you were bad news."

Connor grinned, knowing that although her reaction wasn't exactly the one he wanted, it wasn't all bad, either. "So do I get a cottage, too?" he asked.

KRISTY KNEW SHE SHOULDN'T give him one. Having Connor close by would mean nothing but trouble and nearly constant temptation, two things she could ill afford right now. On the other hand, if she refused to give him a cottage, she knew everyone there would think it indicative of her unusually spirited reaction to him. When the truth was she had no feelings for him except friendship. Okay, she amended hastily, friendship and desire. But that still didn't amount to any kind of romantic future. Because Kristy was not looking to get married again. At least not for a very long time. Even if she had taken off her rings before she got in the shower that morning and declined to put them back on. Nor was she looking to have a steady man in her life, a lover or a companion. And it seemed, unless she was mistaken, that Connor was determined to be all three.

Sensing he was waiting for a response, Kristy said, "I enjoy talking to you." *And confiding in you. And having one person in my life who truly seems to understand and accept what I am feeling.* But Connor had that effect on everyone, she reminded herself. Kristy only had to watch him with the twins and Winnifred and Harry to know that. He got along with everyone, even her nosy, intrusive neighbor, Bruce Fitts.

Connor leaned toward her earnestly, his entire attention

focused on her. "Now that sounds like a kiss-off," he teased, giving her a very knowing, very male grin.

Obviously, he didn't buy it for a single minute. Which was the problem in dealing with a tycoon, Kristy thought. They were way too confident and self-possessed for their own good. She folded her arms at her waist. "All you will find out by moving in here for one week is that I intend to be your friend, and nothing more."

He grinned, all scoundrel again. "So? I can always use more friends."

Her body still tingling with the memory of his passionate kisses, Kristy kept her eyes on his and adapted a devil-may-care tone as she asked, "Which cottage do you want?"

Connor sent her a probing gaze. "Which ones are Harry and Winnifred bunking in?"

"One and two," Kristy reported, as her pulse kicked up another notch. Honestly, she didn't know why Connor had this effect on her, he just did. "They took cottages closest to the lodge," she continued matter-of-factly.

"Then put me way at the other end," Connor decided, as considerate of others as ever. "I want to give them maximum privacy."

She thought about the simmering romance between the two, the way Winnifred had followed Harry all the way out here—an unusual occurrence, to say the least. Kristy studied Connor's face. "You really think they are going to make up, and that Harry will go back to work as her butler?"

"I don't know about that," Connor allowed, his brow furrowing, "but I do think they are going to make up eventually. And the more time they spend together, the quicker it will happen."

Kristy paused, troubled by this revelation. It was what she had been thinking, too. "I wonder if I should be looking for backup kitchen help for next week,'' she worried out loud. Heaven knew she wanted—needed—this business conference to go well. She wanted to be able to use the group for reference, as a foundation for building up the resort's, and her own, reputation. Especially among business folk.

Connor shook his head. ''I've known Winnifred for a long time. She's a woman of her word. If she said she'd be here to cook for the conference next week, she will be. After that, if she can't talk Harry into returning to her employ, well, I don't know what will happen. I would expect that she would go back to her own life, but I could be wrong about that, too,'' he cautioned. ''Because I never in a million years would have expected Winnifred to follow Harry all the way out here and take a job at the resort just to be near him.''

''Me, neither.'' Kristy had certainly lucked out. Winnifred was an excellent chef and superb hostess, and Kristy expected to learn a lot from the social doyenne, however long Winnifred Deveraux-Smith was at the resort.

''And speaking of them,'' Kristy continued as a car turned into the parking lot. ''It sounds like they're back.''

''I'll go and see if they need some help bringing in Winnifred's things,'' Connor offered.

For a self-made tycoon who had been reared in a luxurious environment, he sure was a hands-on kind of guy. Kristy nodded. ''I'll come, too.''

They walked around to the front of the lodge. Winnifred had been driving her Bentley. Harry looked disgruntled as he got out of the passenger side and went around to the trunk. He lifted half a dozen suitcases and two large hanging garment bags out of the rear of the car and set them on the pavement. Connor slipped inside the lodge and returned with one of the wheeled baggage carts that were stored to the left of the reception desk. He took it to Harry.

Winnifred walked over to Kristy. Although smiling purposefully, she seemed just as distressed as Harry, which made Kristy wonder how well this arrangement was going to work out. Nevertheless, she handed her the key to cottage 2. "You are supplying the linens, aren't you?" Winnifred asked.

"Yes." Kristy hesitated. "Although I doubt they are of the quality to which you're accustomed."

"Don't you worry about that," Winnifred said with an airy wave as she followed Kristy into the linen closet to collect a complete set of bed linens, towels and pillows as well as a cache of complementary toiletries. "I can rough it as well as the next person."

Behind her, Harry scoffed.

Winnifred whirled to face him. She gave the man a goading look that dared him to try and prove her wrong about that. "I can handle the cart and unload my belongings myself," she announced stiffly.

"Don't be silly," Connor and Harry said in unison. There was no way they were letting a woman do that task when two able-bodied men were standing right there.

Harry looked at Connor, man-to-man. "I'll take it. I'm headed that direction, anyway."

They charged off, leaving Kristy and Connor in the lobby. "I think this is where we say good-night also," Kristy said dryly.

Connor knew the evening was still young, as it was only nine o'clock. Most evenings he didn't return home until midnight, and he rarely left his loft before nine in the morning, unless he had a business appointment or mission to complete, as he had that day. But because Kristy was on a different schedule, with her work and her kids, he nodded agreeably. She went around the reservations desk and came back with the key to Cabin 12. "You're sure you want to do this?" she said skeptically.

The accommodations weren't what he was accustomed to living in, but Connor couldn't have cared less. He had learned a long time ago that it wasn't the quality of the bed linens or furniture that made him feel at home. It was the people who lived in a place. The warmth they exhibited toward one another. The finest accommodations in the world couldn't counter an emotionally chilly or aloof atmosphere. But Kristy obviously had yet to learn that. Probably, Connor noted inwardly, because she hadn't ever lived in the stone-cold, stiffly formal atmosphere he had endured in his youth around his father. Had it not been for his mother, her inherent warmth and loving nature, well, who knew what kind of jerk Connor might have grown up to be?

Admiring how fresh and lovely Kristy looked, despite the very long day she'd had, Connor said, "We had a bet, lest you forget."

She regarded him with equal parts amusement and challenge. "I haven't forgotten."

Connor didn't imagine she had, since if she lost, she owed him a night on the town. "I'm supposed to be available to do hard labor twenty hours a day for seven days if I want that dinner date with you, and I do. So I have to live up to my commitment," he told her seriously.

HE LOOKED, Kristy thought as she led the way back to the linen room, prepared to live up to much more than that. The only problem with that, she mused as she opened the door to the twenty-by-twenty-foot room filled with floor-to-ceiling shelves, was it had been so long since she had had a date, she wasn't sure she remembered how to go on one.

"Seriously," Connor added, as Kristy led the way to the back of the room, where the boxes of new pillows were kept.

"I'll give you eight hours off if you want, with no problem," she offered seriously as she pulled a box from the bottom shelf.

Connor lounged against the shelving unit as Kristy opened the box and removed two plastic-wrapped pillows. "Those weren't the terms of our bet."

Trying not to think how cozy it was, being back here with him, she shrugged her shoulders amiably. "So I'm flexible," she retorted.

Connor grinned as yet another meaning of her words sank in.

"About some things," Kristy amended hastily. *Not about going to bed with you.* There, she was determined to be as aloof and practical-minded as they both needed her to be.

Connor smiled again, in a way that let her know he had thought of several other sexy ways her offhand comment could be interpreted. "Besides," he continued casually, "I'd like to stay here."

Kristy laid the pillows in his waiting arms. "Why?" She moved over to the shelf where quilted mattress pads were kept.

Connor followed amiably. "I want to understand what has you so tied to Paradise Resort that you'd give up millions to stay here."

"How about I simply love it?" Kristy said dryly. She added a mattress pad to the two pillows in his arms.

Connor quirked a brow, and they studied each other in silence, until Kristy leaned against the opposite storage shelf and murmured, "You've never been attached to any one place, have you?"

Connor shook his head as his eyes roved her face. "I love Charleston," he confided softly. "But I suspect I'd be just as happy in any other charming antebellum Southern city, if my family and friends were there. But they're not. So Charleston is where I've put down my roots, too."

Kristy led the way over to where pillow covers and pillow cases were kept. She selected two of each and, deciding he had enough in his arms for the moment, carried those herself. "How is your family, by the way?"

Connor waited as she plucked a white, thermal cotton blanket and bedspread printed with a beach scene from the shelves, and added them to the cache in her arms. "You heard about my parents' divorce?"

Kristy nodded. It would have been impossible not to read about the scandal of the year. It had been in the society page of the *Herald,* in Bucky Jerome's highly touted "Around the City" column. And although Kristy didn't spend much time reading that, or keeping up with the activities of Charleston's society set, everyone who was anyone in the area had been talking about it. It was news when two members of one of the most prestigious families in the entire Charleston area split up.

Kristy gave him a sympathetic look. "Daisy mentioned it. She said your father had gone off to Europe." And although Connor's sister had been pleased and relieved when her mother had left her father after finally discovering his blatant philandering, there was no telling how Connor felt about what had happened.

"It was for the best," he said grimly, a look of abject disapproval coming into his smoky-gray eyes. "Given the flagrant nature of my father's affair and his complete lack of remorse. Even now," he sighed wearily, "my father thinks he had every right to run around that way."

Kristy could see that Connor did not agree. Relieved that he didn't share his father's morals, or more accurately, lack thereof, Kristy picked up two freshly laundered sheets. "Is he still seeing the other woman?"

"No." Connor followed Kristy over to the cabinet where the complimentary toiletries were kept. "She washed her hands of him, too. Although I've no doubt Father has taken up with someone else in Europe. I don't think he understands even now what a betrayal his actions were to Mother and the entire family.''

"But you do," Kristy noted softly, as she filled a plastic laundry bag with all the small items the room needed, like tissues, soap, shampoo and plastic beverage cups.

He trained his glance on her. "When a man pledges himself to a woman, he's honor bound to keep that promise."

Kristy could tell Connor believed that with all his heart and soul. "I gather that means you have never been unfaithful to a woman?" she queried lightly, realizing she was as deeply curious about him as he was about her.

"No."

Aware that this pleased her, though she had no reason to feel that way, she said, "Have you ever been married?"

Evidently in no hurry to leave the intimacy of the linen room, Connor set the pillows and linens down on the waist-high table next to him. "Yes."

This was news, Kristy thought.

Sadness crept into his eyes. "She died."

Kristy felt her heart go out to him. She knew firsthand how that felt. Losing your mate was devastating no matter the situation. She'd been numb for at least a year. Connor looked as if a part of him were still recovering from the enormity of his loss. "When?" she asked quietly. Putting down her things, too, she reached over and touched his hand compassionately.

Connor twined his fingers with hers as he muttered, "Eleven years ago." And judging from the closed look on his face, that was all he planned to say.

Kristy had not known Connor's sister back then. They had become friends recently, at a women-in-business group that encouraged young women to take charge of their own destinies and begin their own businesses.

Before Kristy could change the subject, Winnifred and

Harry came back into the lobby. Seeing Kristy and Connor standing near the doorway of the storage room, Winnifred headed straight for them and asked purposefully, "Kristy, do you have any paper I could use? I want to start planning menus for the conference next week."

"Sure." Letting Connor take charge of the linens, pillows and bag of toiletries, Kristy went behind the front desk for some stationery and a pen.

"What kind of meals do you want?" Winnifred asked, her expression all-business. Kristy noted she was as busy ignoring Harry as Harry was her.

"It's up to you," she answered. "You're the expert at entertaining. The group is from Chicago, but they will be expecting regional fare. I'd like to stay in the fifty-dollar-per-person range, per day, however. Think you can do that and still have them raving about the cuisine they had here?"

"Leave it to me," Winnifred said.

His expression grim, Harry headed for the laundry room. "I'm going to keep working on those linens," he told Kristy.

"You know you don't have to work this late," she said. "I'm aware you've both already put in a very full day."

"Believe me, I couldn't sleep a wink if I tried right now," Winnifred said stiffly. "I'll be much happier working."

"Same here," Harry said.

Harry and Winnifred headed off in different directions as Connor stood there, his arms laden with the things meant for his cottage. "Now I'm beginning to feel lazy," he murmured, obviously displeased.

Kristy chuckled as she ducked behind the reservation desk and opened a drawer. "Don't. I'm going to work your buns off tomorrow."

He grinned, as if anticipating just that.

"I presume you can find cottage 12 and make up your bed yourself?" Kristy said, handing over the key.

Connor hesitated just long enough for her to realize her handy-guy-to-have-around wasn't as skilled as he wanted to pretend, even when it came to something that rudimentary. "Sure," he said, the confidence in his voice at odds with the look in his eyes.

Kristy studied him cheerfully. "You've never made a bed in your life, have you?"

"Well, uh…"

She tamped down the smile that tugged at her lips, along with the amused warmth that went with it. "Who does it for you at home?"

He made a comical face, admitting, "Actually, I usually don't make it at all during the week. But the sheets get changed every Friday when my housekeeper comes in."

"So I suppose putting hospital corners on a bed is probably beyond you, too," she guessed, telling herself it was no big deal if she lent him a helping hand.

Connor blinked in confusion. "Hosp—what?"

"Never mind. I'll show you." It would only take a moment. And given all the commodes he had cleaned, it was the least she could do, Kristy figured. She walked briskly through the dining room and stuck her head into the kitchen. Winnifred was seated at one of the long, stainless steel counters, writing busily. "I'm going to run down and show Connor how to make up a bed. Can you keep an ear out for the girls? They're asleep. But if they should wander down from the owner's suite upstairs, looking for me—"

"I'll tell 'em where you are, and then come and get you," Winnifred said.

"Thanks." Kristy smiled. She strode back to where Connor was patiently waiting for her, and walked out the door with him, heading for the paved walkway that led from the lodge to the cottages. It was a beautiful October night, breezy and warm. Moonlight shimmered on the water, and the sound of the ocean rolling in to shore made a peaceful backdrop. The leaves of the palmetto trees rustled quietly in the wind.

"Now I see why you like this," Connor murmured, as they walked side by side. He slanted her a glance overtop the linens and pillows in his arms. "But all you would need to have is a home on the beach."

"Is this a sales pitch, Connor?" Kristy asked as they walked up to the front door of cottage twelve. So he wouldn't have to put his things down, or hand them over to her, she took the key from him and unlocked the cozy little unit. "Because if it is…"

"You're not interested in hearing it," Connor guessed as he sidled past her.

"Nope," she said firmly. "I've made up my mind. And once I have done that it stays made up. Just ask anyone who knows me."

Connor set the stack on the dresser. As he turned back to her, he drawled, "Ah, a stubborn woman."

"Yes. I am." Kristy looked around and tried to see the unit through Connor's eyes. Unlike the hotel, the cottages had all been cleaned to perfection. And though the queen-size brass bed wasn't made up, the dresser, desk and windows were all sparkling clean. The cotton drapes and matching upholstered armchairs were fresh and spotless, the adjacent bathroom gleaming. Kristy moved across the distressed hardwood floor to stand on the brightly colored rag rug near his feet. "I suppose you don't have a stubborn bone in your body."

"Probably not," Connor conceded, as he looked around approvingly. Then he turned his probing glance to her. "I'm usually too busy trying to help everyone get along to take a stand and stick with it just for the heck of it."

"Instead, you're the consummate middleman," Kristy

noted, not sure when that had started sounding like a good thing to her.

Connor shrugged his broad shoulders unapologetically. "Pretty much."

Upon further reflection, Kristy wasn't sure how she felt about that. Oh, she could see how his ability to view all sides of a problem had its advantages, but she wanted him to take sides, too. Specifically, her side. Although she had no right to expect or even ask for that, Kristy knew. Deciding her thoughts about him were becoming far too intimate and personal for comfort, she gave him a bracing smile. "Okay." She rubbed her hands together. "Ready to learn how to make up a bed, hotel style?"

Connor watched as she retrieved the mattress pad. "Sure."

Kristy opened it up and spread it over the bed, pulling the contoured elastic edges over the two corners on one side, and then, more awkwardly, on the other.

Trying not to think about what it would be like to be in a bed with Connor, instead of just making one up together, Kristy went back to the dresser to retrieve the sheets. The sooner she got out of here, she decided, the better. Feeling a self-conscious heat move from her body to her face, she kept her eyes away from his and explained, "The first thing we do is unfold the sheet and center it on the bed."

Connor looked at the flat, hemmed edges of one sheet, then checked out the other. "Shouldn't one of these sheets be different from the other?" he asked, frowning.

So he knew a lot more than he thought, Kristy noted, feeling oddly pleased that he wasn't a complete novice on the domestic front. "At home, yeah, you can buy contoured sheets with elastic around the edges, but in a hotel or a hospital you usually just use two flat sheets. Which is why we need hospital corners."

He listened intently, his expression so deadly serious and

perplexed that it was all Kristy could do not to laugh. "This really isn't hard, Connor," she soothed, reaching over to touch his arm reassuringly. "Guys in the military do it all the time."

"Oh." He began to relax.

Kristy opened up the sheet and spread it across the bed. With a quick flick of her wrists, she centered it on the mattress, then tucked the excess linen between the mattress and box springs at both the head and foot of the bed on her side. Connor did the same on his.

"Now tuck it in along the edges on your side, just like I'm doing. Yeah. Like that. Good. Now miter the ends—"

"Miter?" Connor paused, confused.

"Angle the corner of the fold." Kristy demonstrated what she meant, so the sheet was wrapped snugly and neatly on all sides. "The way you do the ends of the wrapping paper on a Christmas present."

Connor's hands stilled on the sheets as he made a perplexed face. "I don't wrap presents, either."

Kristy burst out laughing. "Oh, Connor." She shook her head. "You have so much to learn."

IT TOOK ANOTHER ten minutes, but Kristy finally talked him through the process, including putting cases on the pillows. Connor had never figured that domestic chores could be fun. The household help his mother had employed had never particularly looked like they were enjoying themselves, so he had always assumed it was serious drudgery. But Kristy made it fun. In fact, she made everything fun. So he hated for her to leave him and head back to the lodge.

"Well, if you're all settled," she said, "I've got to be getting back." She stepped outside onto the small private porch of his cottage, which was just wide enough to hold a couple of beach chairs and a table.

Connor followed her out onto the porch, stood in the

glow of the lamplight that lit the exterior of the resort. He wanted so much to take her in his arms and kiss her. But this wasn't the end of a date, he reminded himself sternly, even as he noted that Kristy was looking as if she wouldn't mind being kissed. Until she glanced down the beach. Then she scowled. "Darn it all," she muttered as she turned away immediately. "That man is at it again."

Connor surreptitiously followed her glance and saw Bruce Fitts on the deck of his luxurious new beach house, his eye pressed to the end of a telescope that was pointed their way.

Kristy folded her arms in front of her. "He's spying on us."

"Looks like it." Connor had never wanted to punch someone out. But he was beginning to understand why guys did things like that in defense of their women. With intrusive idiots like Fitts it was the only way to get the message across.

Frowning, Connor looked back at Kristy. "Want me to go and have a word with him?"

"And say what?" she demanded, pushing her hands through her hair as she blew out a frustrated breath. "Don't look at the resort? Whether I like it or not, Mr. Fitts is well within his rights to sit on his own deck and use his telescope to look at whatever he wants to view."

Connor couldn't argue with that. Nevertheless... "It's still an invasion of privacy," he said.

Kristy's expression grew even more troubled. "And one our guests are not going to like."

Connor was silent. "Maybe you can plant a hedge or something," he suggested finally.

"Only to the inland edge of the dunes." Kristy recited current restrictions enforced by both the state and the county. "Plus, a hedge would take years to grow to a height that would block his view."

She smiled tightly at Connor, the mood between them spoiled by Fitts's intrusive behavior. Not wanting to discuss it further, she simply said, "I'll see you tomorrow."

Connor watched her walk down the path to the main building. She disappeared into the lodge without a backward look.

Aware that he hadn't had a chance to drive back to the city to pick up any clothes, he locked the cottage and headed around the main lodge, out to the well-lit parking lot to his car.

Connor knew Kristy didn't really want him acting as a buffer between her and her nosy neighbor, but he also knew someone had to do something, so he stopped off at Bruce Fitts's home en route to the city. By then, Bruce was no longer on the deck, but in his garage, polishing his car. He smiled evilly as Connor got out of the car and walked toward him.

"Saw you working on Ms. Neumeyer. How's it coming? Convinced her to sell yet?"

"No." And, Connor thought, he was fast losing the will to do so, even though he knew it would be a lot better for Kristy and her girls financially if he could do that. Because then she wouldn't have to work so hard. Connor stepped farther into the garage, so the two could talk quietly, and saw twenty gallon-size jugs of weed killer concentrate lined up along the edges. Connor didn't know anything about yard work, either, but he knew that was way more than anyone needed.

Bruce Fitts studied him with a mixture of unhappiness and contempt. "The little lady's got you by the short hairs, hmm? Well, don't you worry," he promised with a nasty leer. "I'll drive her out one way or another. And sooner than you might think."

"So you think Ms. Neumeyer is in danger?" Harlan Decker said, when he met with Connor in the shadows behind cottage 12 an hour later. The burly ex-cop turned private detective was dressed in a loud shirt and rumpled khaki slacks, an outfit suited to the warm autumn weather. He had a straw boater on his head, a cigar clamped in his mouth.

Connor folded his arms in front of him and kept his voice low. "Her resort is definitely in danger. The only problem is I can't prove Bruce Fitts is behind any sabotage. Yet, anyway. Which is why I need you, Harlan. I think Bruce Fitts has been poisoning all of Kristy's palmetto trees around the resort with those jugs of weed killer concentrate I saw in his garage."

"But you need to catch him in the act," Harlan guessed, as he jotted a few notes on the pad in his hand.

Connor nodded, his blood boiling at the thought of anyone putting Kristy's and her daughters' health at risk by putting out so much poison on the grounds where the girls played. "So can you put up some surveillance cameras around the property that will catch him tampering with cars, and pouring poison on tree roots?"

"Sure," Harlan agreed, sliding the notepad and pen back in his shirt pocket. "I'll be out first thing in the morning."

"That's the problem," Connor cautioned. "I don't want Kristy to know."

Harlan arched a curious brow.

"She's got so much on her plate now," Connor continued worriedly. "I don't want to go off half-cocked, making wild accusations. If I'm going to say anything to anyone about this, I've got to have proof first. Only then will I be able to do something about it." And Connor wanted to get rid of Fitts and his incessant troublemaking in the worst way.

Harlan rubbed the flat of his hand across his jaw. "I don't have a problem setting up some cameras. I can do that in the middle of the night tonight, with no one being the wiser, especially your neighbor Mr. Fitts. I'll just wait until his lights go out and I'm sure he's asleep. But I really think you should tell Kristy, Connor.''

Connor shook his head, his decision firm. ''I don't want to go to her with information like that unless I'm able to do something about it then and there. I want to protect her, Harlan.'' He wanted to help her feel as if her world was the way it should be once again. He paused to study the P.I.'s face. ''So will you help me or not?''

''I'll help you, all right,'' Harlan said. He looked Connor in the eye, despite his continuing reservations. ''I just hope for both your sakes you know what you're doing.''

Chapter Seven

Although the day promised to hold more of the same tedious physical labor he had indulged in the day before, Connor had no trouble getting up and over to the main lodge at an early hour. "So what are we doing here today?" he asked, as soon as breakfast was over and the twins had left on the school bus.

"What are we doing," Kristy clarified with a flirtatious look as she breezed into the janitorial closet to get a fully loaded maid's cart, complete with vacuum cleaner, "or what do we wish we had time to do?"

Feeling game for anything she might want to tackle, Connor focused on the flushed contours of her pretty face. She was wearing a snug-fitting red T-shirt and gray overalls made out of a lightweight but sturdy canvas cloth. The combination of loose- and snug-fitting clothes only seemed to emphasize her slender body and sizzling curves, and Connor felt the wave of attraction all the way to his toes. "The latter."

"Well," Kristy sighed, as she clamped her hands over the handle. "First on my list would be to pull up the ratty old carpeting and get the hardwood floors beneath them looking good again. Second would be to paint the entire interior."

It was looking a little dingy, Connor noted, as he settled

his hands next to hers and pushed the wheeled cart down the carpeted hall.

"Unfortunately," Kristy sighed as she plucked a coated elastic band from her pocket, "there's no time."

Connor watched as she gathered her hair into a ponytail at the back of her head and secured it with the band. "It could all be done in a day if you hired a crew," he said.

"I don't have the money for that." Kristy sighed again as she picked up a red-and-gray Carolina Storm hockey team cap from the end of the cart and put that over her hair, so the brim was facing backward. "So we'll just have to get things as sparkling clean as we can and worry about painting and pulling up the carpet later, I guess."

Noting how cute—and young—she looked in the hat, Connor grinned. "I could at least paint the hallway for you," he said.

Kristy wrinkled her nose at him as she opened the first door and pushed the cleaning cart into the room. "It's got to be a professional job."

Connor slanted her a teasing glance. "Don't trust me to accomplish that, hmm?"

Kristy pulled on a pair of heavy-duty rubber gloves. "Not to insult you, Connor, but you've never done any manual labor."

Connor regarded her confidently. "Just tell me the color you want it and leave the rest to me."

As she studied him, she raked her teeth across her soft, kissable lower lip. "You're serious."

Basking in his ability to assist her—even though it went counter to his own agenda—Connor nodded. "I promised to help you, and painting this hallway will go a long way toward making this wing a lot more presentable."

Kristy stepped back out into the hall and looked at the faded, dirty paint. "I can't argue with you there," she said slowly.

"So what color?"

Kristy backtracked to the laundry room. She brought out a fresh laundered drapery with the old-fashioned beach print. "I'd like it to be this color green." She looked up at him earnestly. "Do you think you could take this to the paint store and have them match it?"

Touched by the trust she was putting in him, Connor nodded. "Sure." Telling himself that now was not the time to be thinking of kissing her again, he stepped back casually and asked, "What about the rest of the rooms? What color are you eventually going to paint those when you have the time and money?"

"The other colors in the drapes. I'd have one room ocean-blue, the next sand, the next grass-green, the next the deep rose of the beach umbrella."

"Ah. I see." Connor grinned approvingly. "All the room colors would correspond to one of the hues in the drapes. Nice."

"Thanks. Listen…" Kristy glanced at her watch. "If you really are going to paint the hallway for me, you better get a move on."

Connor would have liked her to come with him. "What are you going to do while I'm gone?" he asked, wondering if he could convince her to make this another joint project.

"I'm going to continue cleaning bathrooms this morning, meet with Winnifred at noon to go over the menus and the lists of supplies we're going to need, and then probably go with her to the warehouse club to pick up the nonperishable items. Obviously, it's too soon to buy fresh produce, meat and dairy products, but we can put orders in and have them delivered by the wholesalers on Tuesday of next week." Kristy paused. "You'll have to pick up paint rollers and tape and other supplies, too."

"I'll take care of it," Connor promised as he bent and kissed her cheek. It was a casual gesture, given often in the

South as goodbyes were said. But kissing Kristy's cheek didn't feel casual to Connor, any more than being there did. Instead it felt as if he were getting involved with her. Head over heels, irrevocably involved.

BECAUSE THEY WERE BOTH working in the area, Maggie Callaway Deveraux and Amy Deveraux Everton were able to meet with Connor at the coffee shop across from the paint store.

"So let me get this straight," Maggie said as she eased her slender but pregnant frame into a chair. "You want a top-notch paint crew at the Paradise Resort to do twenty-five guest rooms, bathrooms and a hall. Plus a flooring crew to remove some old carpet and spiff up some hardwood floors. And you want them all in and out of there today."

"Right," Connor said, looking at Amy, who was recently married, and also pregnant. "Although I understand the flooring crew might have to come back again tomorrow to finish their work."

"Why?" Amy asked, point-blank.

Good question, Connor thought, and one his business partner, Skip Wakefield, would soon be asking, too.

"Because I have no intention of cutting any corners," he said. He wanted Kristy and her girls to have only the best. Which was why he had called Amy, who had her own decorating business, and Maggie, who was a kitchen designer with her own contracting and remodeling business. He'd been friends with both women from way back, having gone to school with Amy and her brothers, and having hired Maggie to redo the kitchen in his loft several years before. Both were members of the Deveraux clan and extremely well connected in the business community. They would not only know who to call, they had the clout to see that a project got done when he wanted and how he wanted.

"Probably the ceilings and all the trim, too," Connor added.

Maggie, a very independent woman in her own right, rubbed her chin. "And you haven't run this by Kristy," she surmised.

A minor problem, as far as Connor was concerned, given all that was at stake. He leaned back in his chair and sipped his coffee. It was black, hot and delicious. "She'd just say she couldn't afford it."

Amy shook her head as if to clear it. "Then why are we even talking about this?" she demanded, looking even more confused.

Connor angled a thumb at his chest. "Because I'm paying." And he knew money talked. For the right sum, literally anything could get done.

"We're talking thousands of dollars here," Maggie cautioned, her light green eyes serious.

Amy nodded, backing her up. Her Deveraux-blue eyes were just as serious. "Maybe even double time if you want it done right away," she warned.

Connor shrugged. What were a few bucks if the outcome made Kristy happy and eased her worry, even a little bit? "That's fine."

Maggie let out a low whistle that spoke volumes. "You must really want to impress her," she said.

Amy, ever the romantic, agreed. She elbowed her friend and offered a conspiratorial wink. "I think it's more than that, Mags. I think he's really got a thing for her."

So it showed, Connor thought, and promptly wished it didn't. At least as far as the rest of the world was concerned. He took another sip of his coffee and pretended to glare at them. "Are you two going to sit there haranguing me or help me get something done?"

Abruptly serious, Amy came through for him, just as he

knew she would. "We'll help you," she promised, all sorts of romantic notions causing a glint in her eyes.

The more practical Maggie regarded Connor sternly. "You just better hope this is a happy surprise, fella. Or you're going to be in such deep quicksand you may never get out."

Connor scoffed.

There was no way Kristy was going to be irritated with him for giving her such a generous, heartfelt gift. Absolutely no way.

EVEN WITH WINNIFRED'S help, it took a lot longer to go to the warehouse for supplies and place the orders for meat, produce and dairy than Kristy had expected. Hence it was nearly four o'clock by the time she and Winnifred were driving down Folly Beach Road to the resort.

As they turned into the drive, Kristy noticed three things. First, the palmetto trees looked even worse than they had the day before. Second, there were large piles of the ratty old carpeting she had wanted torn up heaped in the parking lot. And third, the parking lot looked like a contractor's convention. There were several different paint company trucks. A flooring company van. And a half dozen more pickups, some with ladders mounted on the top.

"Looks like Connor did a little more than just go and get a few cans of paint," Winnifred observed as Kristy parked as close to the service entrance as she could get.

"You're right about that," she muttered, stunned at the sheer audacity of the man, even as she wondered what it would all mean to her business and her already troubled finances. Or was that what the sly Connor was planning? "And now I'm going to kill him," she declared heatedly.

"Don't be too hard on him, dear," Winnifred murmured as she got out of Kristy's minivan. "I'm sure his heart was in the right place."

Too angry to formulate a civil reply, since all the brouhaha currently going on meant Connor had deliberately ignored her plainly stated wishes, Kristy snorted and marched toward the entrance. The smell of new paint assaulted her as soon as she opened the door to the lobby.

Kristy expected Connor to be lounging about. Instead, he was in the north wing hallway, patiently getting painting lessons from a pro. He had paint in his hair, on his face and hands and especially his clothes. But, Kristy had to admit, she had never seen him looking happier than he did at that moment.

Her senses clamoring, she beckoned to him. Connor put down his paintbrush, wiped his hands on the rag he had tucked into his belt, and strode toward her. As he reached her, he was grinning from ear to ear. "Surprised, hmm?"

"Doesn't begin to cover it," Kristy replied sweetly.

Having no intention of making her disagreement with him public, she grabbed Connor's arm and guided him through the lobby and into her private office. She shut the door behind them, then turned toward him and let her fury show. "I can't believe you," she fumed, throwing down her shoulder bag so hard that the clasp opened up and everything, including things she would much rather not be seen, spilled out.

"I thought you'd be happy," Connor said, looking truly baffled.

"Well," Kristy said as she threw her wallet, cell phone and lipstick back into her purse, "I'm not!"

He watched as, red-faced, she crammed the transparent pouch containing her feminine products in, too. Advancing on her, he explained calmly, "Haven't you ever heard the expression 'to make money you have to spend money'?"

"Spoken like a true tycoon." Who, unlike her, had oodles and oodles of money!

"Or a successful businessman."

A tense silence fell between them.

"I was doing you a favor here," Connor continued.

"Well…" Kristy picked up a small can of hair spray and receipts from the warehouse club and wholesalers. She put the hair spray in her desk and the receipts in her purse, then had to stop and reverse them. "These kinds of favors I can do without!"

Connor rubbed the heel of his hand over his chin, turning two dots of fresh green paint into a lake-shaped smear. Exasperation tightened the handsome planes of his face. "What do you want me to do?" His gray eyes turned the color of the Atlantic on a stormy day. He flattened his hands on her desk and leaned toward her, looking more aggravated than guilty. "You want me to go out there and tell them to stop?"

Finished putting her purse to rights, Kristy turned away from him, muttering glumly, "It's too late for that. Now they have to finish."

Connor checked his jeans for paint and then sat down on the edge of her sturdy wooden desk. He folded his arms in front of him. "Look, they'll be out of here by nine tonight," he soothed.

"Great," Kristy stated sourly, irritated that she hadn't seen this coming, that she had trusted him and his willingness to help her—even if it was just to win a bet and get a date—so completely. She looked him square in the eye. "I hope you've got your checkbook ready," she said in a low, tortured voice. "Because as I stated before, there is absolutely no way I can pay for this." No way in Hades.

Connor shrugged negligently. "No problem. I've got it covered."

Kristy shook her head, her spirits sinking as fast as an anchor in the sea. "I don't think you understand, Connor," she explained with a great deal more forbearance than she actually felt. Shame made her face flame. "It could be years before I can pay you back. Unless…'' Abruptly, the heat and color drained from her face. She studied him, aghast. "You're not planning to put a lien on this place, to force me to sell out to you and your partner when I can't pay up, are you?"

It was his turn to look upset and insulted. Connor shot to his feet, cupped her shoulders in both hands. "Of course not!" he said. "I would never do that to you or anyone else! I'm here to find solutions! To make your life easier, not harder."

Silence fell between them. In the face of such righteous indignation, Kristy found it hard to stay angry. Sighing with a weariness she felt all the way to her soul, she sank down in her desk chair and buried her face in both hands. "You just don't get it," she murmured, distraught.

"Then explain it to me," he insisted, sitting down on the edge of her desk, facing her.

She studied his paint-stained hands. They were large and capable, and yet, she knew, also capable of being so very gentle and tender. She swallowed hard, forcing herself not to think about the way it had felt when those same hands had cupped and caressed her breast. "I've already done this, Connor."

Without warning, Connor latched on to her wrist and hauled her onto his lap. "Done what?"

Kristy shrugged as she settled against his warm, strong frame. "Given my opinion, only to have it ignored."

Connor curved a hand against the side of her face, forcing her to look at him. "Well, I've *done that,* too," he said curtly. "And I'll be damned if I'm going to make the same mistake again."

Kristy slid off his lap. She did not like that look in his eyes. As if he had just been wronged and was preparing to right the situation, no matter what. She hitched in a breath as she began to pace the small confines of her office. "Which was…?"

Connor sighed, then stood up, too. "Being wrongly convicted by a woman who constantly doubts my intentions and assumes the worst about me, no matter what the evidence to the contrary."

Kristy knew what it was like to have someone you cared about lack faith in you. It hurt. It surprised her to realize that Connor had suffered an injustice like this, too. She was silent a moment, taking it all in. "This happened to you before?"

Their gazes meshed and Kristy saw the pain and regret in his eyes.

"With my wife," Connor admitted in a low, tortured voice. "It didn't matter what I did or said. She constantly distrusted me."

Kristy found her anger over what he had done fading. Connor had listened to her problems. Maybe it was time she listened to his. She edged closer, wanting to understand him. "Tell me about her," she encouraged softly.

He studied her, as if he was trying to decide if he could trust her with his private demons. "It's not a pretty story," he warned gruffly, as his fingers tightened over hers.

"Neither is mine," Kristy commiserated quietly. But their marriages were part of their lives. It wouldn't help to pretend none of it had happened. Otherwise they would have learned nothing from their mistakes.

Connor's mouth compressed into a brooding line. "We met the year after I graduated college. I was in Atlanta, putting together a consortium there. It was one of the first big business deals I ever did and I was pretty pumped up about it. Lorelai's father was one of the investors. Anyway, she and I met through him and started dating, and got married later that same year."

Connor paused, shook his head. A faraway look came

into his eyes. "We should have been happy. We had everything going for us. We both came from old money and had our trust funds, plus successful careers that were just starting to take off. We didn't lack for anything."

Kristy perched next to him on the edge of her desk. "But you weren't happy."

Connor grimaced, admitting it with a shrug of his powerful shoulders. "Lorelai never really believed I loved her. I knew what a highly emotional and dramatic woman she was—she was the epitome of the spoiled, pampered Southern belle. But I thought that would change after we married. Instead, it only got worse. Whatever I did or said or didn't do or say was misinterpreted. Looking back, I see that Lorelai was addicted to the drama, the fights, but back then all I knew was that indulging her penchant for big emotional scenes only seemed to make things worse. Anyway, one night we were at an anniversary party for a couple of our friends and in the middle of it she accused me of not loving her, and stomped out. That was probably the fiftieth time she'd pulled something like that since we had been married, and I was in no mood to indulge her that night. So I stayed at the restaurant to placate our friends, thinking some time to cool off and calm down would help." Sorrow and guilt combined in his eyes as he continued in a low, choked voice, "Meanwhile, at home, Lorelai was busy creating her biggest, boldest drama yet. Unbeknownst to me, she had slipped into a beautiful negligee, put on some tragic opera music, penned a note and swallowed a handful of pills along with a glass of champagne." Connor swallowed, eyes glistening as he finished relating the story in a dull monotone. "I found her when I came in. The paramedics couldn't revive her and she was pronounced dead at the scene."

Kristy gasped, imagining the horror of that. "Oh, Connor," she whispered, her heart going out to him.

His mouth twisted ruefully. "No one who knew her thought Lorelai really meant to kill herself. She just meant for me to find her. And be really sorry. Which, believe me, I was."

Kristy squeezed his hand all the tighter, offering what comfort she could. Although she had the feeling Connor would always carry with him a certain amount of guilt.

He looked down at their entwined fingers. "Hindsight tells me the marriage never would've worked. That there was no way I ever could've convinced Lorelai I loved her. But, on the other hand—" Connor drew a deep breath, straightened "—if I had just figured out what she was up to, or gotten home an hour sooner, I probably could have saved her life and forced her to get some therapy. But I didn't and I have to live with that, Kristy."

He disengaged their hands and stood, squaring off with her yet again. "What I don't have to live with are accusations of underhandedness or impure motives or insincere behavior." He looked her straight in the eye and continued unapologetically, "I am who I am. I don't like fighting. I don't like to see people suffer unnecessarily. I'll do whatever I have to do to help people on different sides of an issue get along. But there's nothing underhanded about me or my motives."

Kristy saw that now. And although she still didn't like what he had done, she knew she owed him an apology. "I'm sorry I accused you otherwise," she said softly, meaning it.

"And I'm sorry, too," Connor said, just as steadfastly. "Because you're right. I shouldn't have presumed it would be all right to give you such a lavish gift. And that's what the fresh coat of paint and the touched-up floors are, Kristy. A lavish gift from me to you. I don't want or expect to be repaid."

Kristy could see that he meant it. "What you have done

is very generous,'' she said sincerely. She plucked the Carolina Storm cap she had been wearing earlier that day off the top of her file cabinet and handed it to him. ''So generous, in fact, that I'm going to give you this cap to wear as you proceed. Because you definitely need something to keep the paint off your hair.''

''Thanks.'' Connor's posture relaxed slightly as he widened the band so it would fit him. ''I'm glad you see it that way.''

''But there is no way, Connor. No way—'' Kristy emphasized bluntly, as Connor put the cap on his head and adjusted the brim so it sat squarely on his forehead ''—that I can accept it.''

He quirked a brow warily. ''Meaning?''

''Someway, somehow, I'm paying you back. In the meantime, before you go back to your painting, perhaps you could help Winnifred in the kitchen?''

''YOU GOT YOURSELF in one heck of a mess today, didn't you?'' Winnifred murmured as Connor hefted the fifty pound bags of rice, beans, flour and sugar onto the stainless steel kitchen counter. Thinking he might have a sympathetic ear in the older woman, he complained, ''Kristy is determined to read me the wrong way.''

Winnifred snipped the top off the flour bag. ''For someone of our background, the gift is no more than a necklace. But for someone of Kristy's, it's way too much. You can see that, can't you?''

''Of course.'' Connor helped pour the contents of the bag into several big stainless steel canisters. ''But I'm the one who gave the gift,'' he protested mildly.

''And she's the one who received it,'' Winnifred countered.

Connor watched as Winnifred moved on to the sugar. Maybe what he needed here was a woman's viewpoint.

"What should I do?" He wanted to make up with Kristy. Right now she still resented what he had done, if not him, specifically.

"First," Winnifred advised with a wise smile, "give her time to cool off and come to her senses."

That hadn't worked with Lorelai, Connor thought.

"Second, continue to prove you are not above demanding physical work."

Connor helped transfer the sugar from bag to canister. "Is that what you're doing, Winnifred? With Harry?"

Finished, Winnifred straightened and wiped her hands on her white chef's apron. "Harry thinks we're too far apart."

For what? Connor wondered. "But you two have been friends for years," he noted. Everyone in Charleston knew how close Winnifred and her butler were.

"That's what makes this so frustrating," Winnifred admitted with a sad sigh. "I know Harry and I can be a lot more than simply employer and employee."

Connor waited until it was clear nothing else was forthcoming. "But?"

Twin spots of color appeared in Winnifred's cheeks. "Harry wants more. He wants to date! At our age! Can you imagine?"

Connor snipped off the top of the brown sugar bag while Winnifred went to get another commercial-size canister. "You're hardly old." Plenty young enough, in his opinion.

Winnifred grimaced. "I'm fifty!"

So? Knowing there had to be something more here keeping them apart, Connor asked gently, "Is it the class thing?"

Winnifred huffed. "I am not a snob."

"Still," Connor pointed out as Winnifred put bags of pecans and walnuts onto the pantry shelves, "you come from old money and Harry's been your butler for years."

That would be enough to halt some blue bloods, but it didn't seem to be the fracturing factor for Winnifred.

"I know he loves me. I love him."

"Just not in that way?" Connor guessed.

Winnifred released a troubled sigh. "I promised my late husband, Ewan, I would never love anyone but him," she said earnestly. "When I married him, it was with my whole heart. I can't be another man's wife. I can't make that kind of lifelong commitment again. And I fear that is what Harry wants."

"Which is why he quit your employ," Connor said.

Winnifred sat down at the prep table. Hunching forward dispiritedly, she admitted, "He said it's too painful to be around me, knowing we can never be anything more."

Connor touched the woman's shoulder gently. "So why not let Harry go on and make a new life for himself, if that's the way you feel?" he asked quietly.

"Because Harry and I are also best friends," Winnifred said stubbornly. "And wonderful companions. And I have no intention of giving that up, no matter how unreasonable he's being at the moment!"

"Well," Connor said, as always trying to find some common ground upon which two battling parties could meet, "if that's the way you really feel—"

"It is!" Winnifred replied passionately.

"Then there's one thing you could do," Connor suggested helpfully.

Winnifred waited.

"You could ask Harry to be your friend. But also admit that you understand why, at age forty—"

"Forty-one," she corrected, making sure Connor knew there was only a nine years' difference in their ages, not a decade.

"Harry needs more to be happy," Connor continued. "And then advise him to find another woman to court. And give him your heartfelt blessing."

Chapter Eight

Connor finished assisting Winnifred in the kitchen, then went back to the north wing of the lodge, where he stayed to help until the painters had completely finished and cleared all their stuff out. At 10:00 p.m. he went in search of Kristy. She was in her office, sitting behind her computer. Connor only had to glance at it to see she was working on some sort of accounting spreadsheet.

"What are you doing?" he asked, afraid to interrupt, more afraid not to, as he didn't want the rift between them to continue.

Kristy kept her eyes fixed steadfastly on the screen in front of her as she replied in a low, noncommittal tone, "I'm working on a ten-year repayment plan for the painting that was done today. I'm not sure what would be fair—a variable interest rate or prime plus three, but I'll go by whatever you think is workable."

Connor sauntered forward, his thumbs anchored in the belt loops on either side of his fly. "I wish you wouldn't worry about that," he said.

A becoming blush stained her cheeks. "I'm aware this is penny ante stuff for you."

Connor stepped around behind her and checked out the figures on the computer screen. "That's not what I meant and you know it." He felt the first stirrings of panic. He was irritated with Kristy for continuing to act as if he had greatly overstepped his bounds here, despite the fact that his decisive actions were contrary to his own business agenda. All he had wanted was to help her feel better during however long it took for them to work out a deal that would financially benefit them all. He was trying to make Kristy see that even if the place was in optimum condition, and she had all the bookings she wanted, that the hard work would not be worth it on a daily basis. Not if she could just cash out and be a mom and never have to worry about money again.

"Obviously, I made a mistake today," Connor continued. "But my heart was in the right place."

Her luscious mouth pursed. "That, Connor Templeton, is debatable."

Connor wished he didn't recall quite so accurately how sweet that bare mouth of hers tasted, or just how well she could kiss. Wished he could stop imagining how wonderful it would be when they finally did make love. "All I'm trying to do is help you here," he said, doing his best to contain his exasperation.

"You don't understand." Kristy rested her elbows on either side of her keyboard. "I've got to do this on my own, prove that I am worth something, too."

Connor marveled at her stubborn need to be her own woman, even though a part of him couldn't really understand why she didn't just take the easy way out that he and Skip were offering her. Most people worked and dreamed and struggled their whole lives to have the kind of wealth Kristy had within easy reach. But to his surprise, she seemed to have no such ambition. Money per se meant no more to her than a blade of grass or a bucketful of sand. He studied her, sensing there was a lot more behind her feelings than she wanted to let on. "How could you ever think you're not worth something?" he asked, confused.

"Easy." Kristy pushed her chair back with a screech. "I'm thirty-three years old. I grew up as the underachieving misfit in a family of doctors. And thus far, unlike everyone else in my clan, and practically everyone else I know who's my age, I haven't a single professional accomplishment to my name."

Connor thought the job she was doing with her girls was a fine one, but sensing that she didn't want to talk about motherhood at the moment, he pointed out calmly, "What you do here, trying to create a cozy place for people to vacation, and to provide financially for your two daughters, is very valuable."

Kristy scoffed. She picked up a half-finished glass of lemonade from her desk. "You would never know that from my family's reaction to my chosen career," she muttered, taking a long, thirsty drink. "You should have seen the looks on their faces when I added hotel and restaurant management classes to my college course load, in addition to my premed classes. Both my siblings and my parents thought I was wasting my time."

Too late, Connor realized she thought he had underestimated her, too, by rushing to her aid the way he had. "Obviously you're not wasting your time if this is what you want to do with your life."

Kristy finished her lemonade and then stalked past him out the door, leaving him to follow at will. They walked across the lobby together, through the dining room toward the lodge kitchen, Kristy talking all the while. "They insisted I take the MCAT."

"That's the test you take to get into med school, right?"

She nodded.

Connor knew it was supposed to be a grueling exam that separated those with an aptitude for medicine from those without.

"Anyway—" Kristy walked across the kitchen to the big

refrigerator and brought out a pitcher of lemonade to refill her glass "—I was going to do really bad on it, on purpose, just so they would get off my back. But when I went in to the take the test, I couldn't fail on purpose. It was against my nature to even try." She scowled, as if resenting her natural inclination to be a good student. "So I did my best and ended up scoring phenomenally high on it."

Connor wasn't surprised about that. She was a very bright woman. "Which probably made them want you to become a physician all the more," he guessed.

"You got it." Kristy poured him a glass of lemonade, too, and added a few ice cubes. "But I talked them into letting me take a year off after I graduated, to work at a hotel and save money."

That sounded more like her, Connor thought. "What did your parents think about that?"

Kristy sighed and looked all the more miserable. "They supported my plan only because they thought working in a hotel would cure me of ever wanting to own one."

Which in turn sounded somewhat like his current plan to induce her to sell out, Connor realized guiltily.

Oblivious to his thoughts, Kristy continued her narrative. "Nevertheless, they kept introducing me to other young med students, hoping some of their ambition would rub off on me, and to their delight, I actually clicked with one of them."

"Lance."

"Right. I married him before the year was out and got pregnant with the twins right away."

Connor felt that should have made her family happy, but he could tell by her disgruntled expression it hadn't done anything of the sort. He regarded her curiously. "That didn't stop the campaign to get you into med school?"

"Nope." Kristy looked into his eyes as if searching for the understanding she had not gotten anywhere else. "Not that I really ever thought it would," she admitted with a candid shrug. "My mother had always worked. She only took six weeks off with each of her three pregnancies. But I wanted to stay home with my babies," Kristy said passionately. She paused, shook her head, before going on in a low voice tinged with frustration. "My mother and father didn't understand my desire to be a homemaker when I could be out saving the world. But I knew I had to be home with them, just as I know now that I have to strike out on my own. Don't you see, this is my chance to prove to myself and everyone else that I have what it takes to run a top-notch beachfront resort."

More important, Connor thought, this was a part of her long-held dream she had never had a chance to pursue. "So when your aunt died last spring and left you this place, it was a perfect opportunity, right?" he asked, letting her know he did understand now. Maybe more than he, or his conscience, would have wanted…

Kristy beamed with pleasure and enthusiasm. "I knew I had to run it. Get it back to its former glory, the friendly, fun family place it was when I was a kid."

And she was doing just that. With or without his help, Connor noted. For the first time since stepping foot on her property, he saw that this association of theirs might not have the ending either one of them had expected. But maybe that wasn't so bad, either, he mused, as long as when this situation finally got resolved, once and for all, they both were better for having crossed paths.

In the meantime, though, a lot had been done today that she hadn't even viewed. And it was time that much, at least, was remedied, Connor decided. He reached over and took her arm. "Speaking of restoration…how about coming down to see the paint job now that it's finished?"

KRISTY HELD ON TO HER lingering feelings of self-righteousness as they walked across the lobby, down the hall and into the north wing. But the moment they entered and she got her first glimpse of the transformation the crews had worked in just one day, her resentment faded. "Oh, Connor," Kristy breathed.

It was beautiful. Better yet, it looked brand-new, and yet had so much old-fashioned charm. Their guests were going to love it.

"The new paint smell is pretty heavy," Connor warned. He searched her eyes for approval. "We're going to have to leave the windows open all night for ventilation."

Kristy waved off his concern. "That's all right."

Connor directed her gaze downward. "What do you think about the floors?"

The hardwood glowed with the warm patina that comes with aged oak. There were pockmarks here and there, but they only added to the charm of the floors, Kristy decided with a grin. "They look stylishly distressed, don't they?" She had seen someone on the home-and-garden channel on TV make floors look like this with three days intensive labor.

Connor nodded. "One of the flooring people who helped tear up the carpet suggested they just wash and wax them, for now. I was skeptical, but now that it's done, I have to say I think what they did does look really good."

"I agree. With the colors of the walls and the white woodwork, the weathered look of the floors is perfect."

Being careful to stay away from the still-damp walls, Connor continued helpfully, "The flooring guy also suggested you think about some colorful rag or braided rugs."

Kristy considered that. "I may just do that when I can afford it. For now, though, I think we'll have to go with just washing all the windows and putting the drapes back up. We'll see how it looks then."

Connor nodded in approval as they continued to inspect all the work that, thanks to him, had been done that day.

"I hate to say it," Kristy said as she walked from room to room, inspecting the incredibly beautiful paint job, admiring how fresh and pretty it made the formerly drab and dingy guest rooms. She turned back to Connor reluctantly, knowing she owed him more than money; she owed him an apology. "You were right to insist we do this. It's going to make all the difference in the world to the conference guests coming in next week."

Which in turn would lead to even more bookings.

"As soon as we get the rooms put back together, I'm going to take some pictures for the brochures I'm sending out," she confided.

"Daisy could probably do that for you," Connor suggested.

Kristy had been planning to call her, since Daisy was not only her friend, but a very talented photographer in her own right who specialized in working with small-business owners. "I just wish I could get a business loan and pay you back and finish the rest of the hotel now."

"Why can't you—if that's what you really want?"

Kristy had the feeling Connor wasn't just playing devil's advocate with her, and that he already knew the answer to that. There were really no secrets in a business community the size of Charleston's. "Because," she said quietly, feeling herself begin to grow anxious again as talk turned to the mountain of problems she faced, "as I'm sure you and your partner, Skip, already know, this place has been going downhill for years and is currently mortgaged to the hilt."

Connor frowned. "If you had a business plan—"

Kristy held up a silencing hand. "I tried that. Let's just say in the current economic climate, the banks want to make sure they will get their money back before they fork over money for renovation on the scale we're talking. Plus, they also know you and Skip and that group of investors you've lined up are standing in the wings, waiting for me to fail so you can purchase this property, tear down the Paradise Resort and put up a luxury, hurricane-proof condominium community in its place.''

To Kristy's disappointment, Connor looked a little guilty at that. ''Maybe if you brought them out, showed them what you've managed to do over the summer and fall—''

''The banks are still going to want some sort of collateral for that and I just don't have it.''

''Surely your husband left you—''

''A lot of debt and not nearly enough insurance. I've already used a great deal of what I had left getting the outside of the cottages and the lodge professionally painted. I did as much of the interior work as I could myself, of course, but there were things, like the leaks in the roof, that required immediate attention, and I had to pay cash for those.''

Connor studied her, concern sharpening the planes of his handsome face. ''So how close to the edge are you?'' he asked.

Kristy's lips curved into a cynical smile as she related, ''I need to turn a profit by the end of this year or I really will be forced to sell. So you see, Connor,'' she said softly, feeling hopelessly discouraged once again, ''all you really ever had to do was play the waiting game. It might be yours to tear down, anyway.''

KRISTY WAS TELLING HIM what he wanted to hear. What he had been aiming for all along. But strangely, Connor was no longer enthused about the development project he and Skip had put together. He, like Kristy, was more interested in restoring the grand old lodge to its former glory. And then some. And that was a surprise. Connor had never put much stock in things that were old versus things that were new. For him, it had always been about getting down to the bottom line to serve all involved. "How did it get so run-down, anyway?" he asked compassionately as they left the wing.

Kristy shrugged and, as if on a whim, escorted him into the other wings, which were in even worse shape than the one they had been working on so hard. "For one thing, my aunt was getting older," she said, as they walked down one dingy hall after another. "She didn't have the energy to compete with some of the big outfits that have come in and built modern resorts and golf courses."

Connor could understand that. Most of the new places were pretty luxurious. "You had no idea of the condition of the rooms?"

"She told me the last time I was here—two summers ago, with Lance and the girls—that she was going to begin closing a wing down every winter during the off-season, in January and February, to redecorate. I assumed she had done so, but I didn't come back that first summer after Lance died. It was just too painful, so the girls and I went to Washington, D.C., to vacation instead. You know, just trying to do something different. Educational. Then my aunt fell ill, but she didn't want to worry anyone, so she didn't mention it, and the place fell apart even more. I had planned to come back again last summer, but before I could, my aunt died. And left the place to me."

Connor looped a hand around Kristy's waist as they walked along. "Were you her favorite?"

She moved in companionably close. Her glossy, clean hair brushed his chin as she turned her face up to his. "She said I was the only one in the family who had ever understood what this place meant or could come to mean to generations of families. She knew it was in bad shape, but she thought—hoped—I had the talent to put it together again, the way she had after her husband died, years ago. She entrusted Paradise Resort to me, Connor. And I am not—I repeat, not—going to let her down,'' she said determinedly. ''Not if I can help it.''

Chapter Nine

"Mommy, can you braid my hair today?" Sally asked as she sauntered into the cozy sitting room of their apartment, carrying her father's old beach towel. She was dressed in her usual dress and ruffled pinafore.

Susie came in right behind her, wearing a pair of coveralls suitable for roughhousing, and a T-shirt, her daddy's old Frisbee clutched in one hand.

"You sure you don't want curls?" Kristy asked Sally curiously. As per their usual routine, she already had the electric rollers heating, so she could make the spiral curls Sally loved.

"No. I think I want to wear my hair in a French braid today," Sally announced as she sat down in front of her mom.

"Well, I want pigtails," Susie said, as she waited her turn. "Only I want ribbons on 'em. Is that okay, Mommy?" She pulled hair adornments that only Sally usually wore from her pocket.

"Sure." Kristy smiled, pleased to see her ultradressy little princess, Sally, going a little more casual, while her determined little tomboy, Susie, was becoming a tad more feminine. That meant her talk with them on the beach the other day had cleared up at least some of their misconceptions about what their father—and she—had wanted and expected from them. Kristy wanted her girls to embrace all aspects of themselves and their personalities, but she wanted them to do it on their own terms and time schedule. She wanted them to be free to become whoever, whatever they wanted to be, and not be pushed in a single direction the way she had been while growing up.

As she reached for a hairbrush, Kristy switched on the TV. Bypassing the usual Saturday morning kid shows, she turned to the Weather Channel to get the latest on Imogene. She frowned as she saw it had been upgraded to a hurricane overnight, with winds strengthening to seventy-five miles per hour as it pushed past Jamaica, toward the Cayman Islands. The Weather Channel showed the several dozen houses it had damaged as it swept past the far western edges of the island before continuing on out to sea, where it was still slowly but surely gathering strength. "Is Imogene going to come here?" Susie asked.

Kristy patted her shoulder reassuringly, while Sally cuddled closer to her. "I don't know, honey. You know how it is with these storms—"

"One minute they're a hurricane—" Sally grinned.

"Then the next they're a tropical storm again," Susie stated.

"One minute they're headed toward us—" Kristy continued.

"The next they're headed away from us," Susie and Sally said in unison.

Kristy shrugged. "So we'll just have to wait and see. But most of these storms don't amount to much more than a few days of rain for us. You girls know that."

They nodded. Having gotten the weather update she wanted, Kristy changed the channel to a Saturday morning children's show.

Their apprehension swiftly forgotten, the girls began watching raptly. Kristy had just finished fixing their hair when a knock sounded on the door. Susie hopped up to get it.

"It's Connor!" she announced happily, as she ushered him in.

Connor was wearing another T-shirt, with the logo of a local charity emblazoned across the front, and jeans that fit just as well as the ones he'd had on the day before. He had the now paint-stained Carolina Storm cap she had given him looped through his belt, for wearing later. The enticing fragrance of soap clung to his skin. "I hope it's not too early," he said, flashing her an easy grin. "But Winnifred wanted you to know breakfast will be ready in about fifteen minutes."

Susie shifted her weight from foot to foot as she beamed up at him adoringly. "Can I show Connor our room?" she asked.

Aware that this was the first time he'd been granted entrée to her and the girls' private quarters, and that giving him the grand tour would further the intimacy between them, Kristy nodded, albeit somewhat reluctantly. She wasn't sure what a man to-the-manor-born would think about the Xena Warrior Princess bedspread that Susie had selected, or the Beauty and the Beast décor Sally had wanted for her side of the room they shared, but maybe it was time to find out.

Kristy could hear Susie's running commentary as she explained everything about their bedroom to Connor, while he lingered in the doorway, hands shoved in the pockets of his slacks and a sincerely interested expression on his face.

"Now it's my turn to show Connor my stuff!" Sally said. Excitedly, she detailed everything on her side of the room. "And here is our bathroom," she said, showing Connor their Little Mermaid shower curtain, bath mats and towels.

"And here's Mommy's room," the twins said in unison,

shoving the door to Kristy's room wide before she could stop them. She hadn't yet made her bed, and the pink-and-white-striped sheets and floral comforter were in a rumpled mess across the center.

"Nice," Connor said, his gaze lingering on her cozy brass bed, upholstered chaise and a closet overflowing with casual clothes. His eyes focused on the picture on the nightstand, of herself and her husband and the girls, taken shortly before Lance died. It was a happy photo, snapped during a rare family outing. As he noticed it, she caught the question in his eyes. Was she over Lance? Ready to move on? Or still holding tight?

A few days ago, Kristy knew she had still been clinging to the memories, good, bad and indifferent, rather than let go of her marriage and move on. But now, bit by bit, moment by moment, she could feel herself letting go of the past. Wanting, needing to move on.

She wasn't sure what that said about her as a person. She just knew it was how it was.

"Look, you can see all the cottages from our bedroom windows," Sally said, as she and Susie each grabbed one of Connor's arms and dragged him toward a window.

"And all the palmetto trees, too!" Susie added.

Trees, Kristy thought, that were looking sicker every day.

"And if you look out the sitting room windows, you can see the beach and the ocean." The girls showed Connor that, too.

"That's nice," he said. He looked around again, observing the kid-friendly blue denim sofa and patterned-denim armchairs, sturdy old-fashioned oak furniture and colorful red-blue-and-cream Persian rug. "So this is where you three live," he observed, approval shining in his eyes as he looked around at all the homey touches Kristy had added.

Susie nodded. "We don't have a kitchen, 'cause we have

the big one downstairs and we can use that one whenever we want.''

"Speaking of which," Connor said, abruptly remembering why he had come up in the first place. "I think we better head on down, if we don't want breakfast to get cold."

"I'D LIKE TO SPEND this evening and all day tomorrow baking all the sweet breads, cookies and cakes we're going to need for the conference next week, and then freeze them," Winnifred told Kristy over breakfast. "That will make things a little less hectic when the guests arrive. And Harry has agreed to help me."

Harry didn't look unhappy about that, Kristy noted. Which probably meant that he and Winnifred were making up. She smiled in approval of the plan. "Sounds good."

"Unfortunately, this poses a problem for me, since Harry and I were both supposed to be working at a fund-raiser this evening for the new teen shelter. So I was wondering, Kristy and Connor, if you two dears wouldn't do us a favor and take our places this evening. All you have to do— besides enjoy yourselves and participate in a very worthy cause—is get there an hour early, sit at the sign-in table outside the hotel ballroom and make sure everyone gets their name tags as they check in for the gala."

Kristy wasn't sure what to say to that. She didn't mind working for a worthy cause, but she was leery of being paired with Connor. She was having a hard enough time reminding herself they were on opposite sides of the fence, and keeping him at arm's length, without putting the two of them in a situation that would look very much like a date.

He, however, did not seem to mind being paired with her. "No problem—for me, anyway," Connor said, obviously delighted by the request. He looked at Winnifred. "What's the dress?"

"Black tie. Kristy will need a formal gown." Winnifred paused and turned to her. "Will that pose a problem, dear?"

Kristy shook her head. She already had a dress that was perfect for such an occasion. "Not at all. But it may not be easy for me to get a sitter for the twins on such short notice," she warned. And she couldn't expect Harry and Winnifred to supervise two eight-year-olds when they were working—and hopefully making up.

Winnifred waved off Kristy's concern. "I can ask my great-aunt Eleanor Deveraux to come out. She's lovely and she adores children. I'm sure she wouldn't mind watching over the twins if you don't mind putting her up in a cottage for the night, in return."

"It'd be my pleasure," Kristy said. It had been months since she had been blessed with a night out. It would be good to feel like a woman again, instead of just a mom.

Connor and Kristy spent the day cleaning all the windows in the north wing of the lodge, while Harry continued washing the bedspreads and draperies, and Winnifred worked in the kitchen, putting together casseroles that would be frozen, and then baked and added to the luncheon buffets. The twins had social studies projects due the following week, and they camped out in the dining hall, working on their reports and posters most of the day.

By dinnertime, Eleanor Deveraux had arrived. Kristy was pleased to discover the eighty-something woman was the epitome of Southern gentility and an era gone by. She was wearing a lace-trimmed, pastel-green dress, and her long white hair was caught in an elegant bun at the back of her neck. She had a delicate, aristocratic bone structure, a petite, slender frame. As Eleanor met Kristy, she clasped both of her work-worn hands in her exquisitely manicured fingers, and lifted her faded, sea-blue eyes. "Thank you kindly for inviting me out here this evening," she said.

"Thank you for coming," Kristy replied, knowing instinctively that her girls were going to get along famously with this lovely woman with the kind eyes and gentle air. "And offering to spend the evening with my girls."

"That will be my pleasure." Eleanor Deveraux smiled.

Winnifred swept out of the kitchen to give her aunt a hug, before she looked at Kristy. "Shouldn't you be going up to get ready, dear?" she said.

Kristy looked down at her dirt-stained work shirt and jeans. If that wasn't an understatement, she didn't know what was.

AN HOUR LATER, Kristy came down the stairs and into the dining hall, where everyone else was gathered, eating a casual Saturday evening supper of pizza and salad. "Oh, Mommy," Sally gasped.

"You look so beautiful!" Susie said.

"I clean up okay," Kristy murmured with a self-conscious wink as she turned, saw Connor walking across the lodge lobby toward her. He was dressed in a black tuxedo and snowy white shirt. He looked handsome and debonair, and he smelled wonderful, too—a wintry mix of musk, forest and man. She felt a thrill of excitement coupled with a tinge of alarm as he stopped in front of her, his eyes roving her upturned face, and gallantly offered her his arm. "Ready to go?" he asked softly.

Kristy nodded, her pulse kicking up another notch.

"Have fun, dears!" Winnifred said gaily.

Kristy said her goodbyes, then the two of them headed off across the lobby and out the door. As they circled around the building toward the parking lot, Connor leaned close to her ear and remarked, "The twins weren't kidding." His gaze roved the floor-length, champagne-colored, silk-chiffon sheath, taking in the glamorous swaths of beaded lace that started at one shoulder, swept across her breasts and continued in gorgeous serpentine patterns to the hem. "You look spectacular in that dress."

It was the most elegant dress Kristy had ever owned. She'd spent a great deal of time picking it out. Pleased to find someone else liked it as much as she did, she touched a hand to her upswept hair self-consciously. "Thanks."

Connor opened the door of his Mercedes and helped her into the passenger side. He bent to make sure the delicate fabric was safely tucked in, then closed the door and circled around to slip behind the wheel. "Is it new?"

"I've had it a couple of years." She had just never worn it.

Aware how much this felt like a date even though it was definitely not a date, per se, Kristy slid the end of her safety belt into the catch.

Looking as if his thoughts were drifting along the same lines as hers, Connor fit his key into the ignition. He shot her a curious glance. "Bought it for something special?"

Kristy nodded, replying, "A medical society dinner-dance."

Bittersweet light came into Connor's eyes. "Your husband must have loved the way you looked in it," he said.

The corners of Kristy's lips twisted into a rueful smile. Clasping the evening bag in her lap, she admitted sadly, "He never saw me wear it. He got called to do an emergency surgery."

Connor's brows knit together. "You didn't go?"

Kristy shrugged, remembering how hard it had been that night to hide her feelings. "I didn't want to attend alone."

Connor paused before turning his sedan onto Folly Beach Road. "How often did that happen?"

Kristy took a deep breath. Turning her eyes away, she admitted softly, "A lot."

"Sorry."

She shrugged and forced herself to forget about all the lonely nights and constant disappointments she'd endured during her marriage to Lance. "It was the way our life was." She'd known that, going in. And, had the two of them connected the way they should have as man and wife, Kristy knew she could easily have handled his frequent absences and enormous responsibilities. It was the feeling that she and Lance weren't really suited for each other, that he didn't really love her, not the way a husband should, that had made the disappointments so unbearable.

Oblivious to the reason for the brooding nature of her thoughts, Connor reached over and patted her knee companionably, through the silky fabric of her dress. "Well, you'll be glad to know I don't often get called out on emergency business meetings," he teased.

Warming to his efforts to inject a lighter mood into the conversation, Kristy turned toward him as far as her safety belt would allow. "You say that as if we're about to become a couple," she observed.

Connor met her eyes. "Aren't we?"

Kristy didn't know, wasn't sure she wanted to know. Fortunately, she didn't have to think about it, once they arrived at the downtown Charleston hotel where the event was being held. She and Connor were shown to the sign-in table, and were soon busy greeting guests and handing out name tags for them to wear. By the time they had finished taking "Winnifred and Harry's" shift, dinner was being served. And they found themselves going down the buffet line with Connor's recently divorced mother, Charlotte Templeton, and her escort for the evening, shipping executive Payton Heyward. Both were charming members of the old guard Charleston elite, and received Kristy with lovely gentility.

"So you two are dating now?" Charlotte asked, as they

sat down at a table decorated with linens embossed with blue and white stars. She wore a sequined, burgundy evening gown that went well with her slender figure and silver hair.

"I wouldn't call it that, exactly," Kristy said, noting that Connor had his mother's gray eyes.

Connor put a possessive hand on the back of her chair. "I would," he said. He leaned over to whisper in Kristy's ear, "Or we will be once the week is up."

While she blushed self-consciously and tried not to feel too thrilled by his declaration, Charlotte looked from one to the other, as if trying to size up what was really going on with her only son.

Before she could ask them anything else, Connor's sister Daisy and her husband, Jack Granger, sat down with them.

"I think I'd call it a date, too," Daisy remarked, as she joined in on the tail end of the conversation. "After all, Kristy and Connor are dressed up. They came in together, they worked at the check-in table side by side, and now, as the festivities begin in earnest, they're still together."

"Only as a favor to Winnifred Deveraux-Smith," Kristy declared.

Connor's widowed older sister, Iris, who had been happily talking business with another antique dealer, also came to join them. She looked at Connor and Kristy thoughtfully.

"Well, I think the two of you look as if you belong together," Daisy teased. Since she had fallen in love with Jack and become a happily married woman, she wanted everyone else to enjoy the same connection with someone wonderful.

"You really think we look like a couple?" Connor asked, pleased.

Jack Granger nodded slowly and thoughtfully. "I'd have to say your body language, the way you keep leaning toward each other instead of away, says so," he stated out loud.

Kristy didn't know about that, although Jack was right

about one thing—she and Connor did keep gravitating toward each other, physically and emotionally.

She did realize, however, that Connor looked every bit as at ease in this environment as he did strolling into Paradise Resort to see her. She couldn't say the same about herself.

While she didn't exactly feel ill at ease in the elegant ballroom, she did find herself feeling wary of the number of people Connor knew, and the long, complicated history he seemed to have with absolutely everyone at the elegant affair.

She felt out of the loop again, in the same way she always had with her family. It didn't seem to matter whether it was because she was the only nonmedical person, or the only one without deep Charleston roots.

At times like this she felt like an outcast, when what she secretly wanted was to belong at Connor's side.

Telling herself that she would eventually acclimate to her new town, Kristy forced herself to smile, then excused herself to go phone and check on things at home. To her relief, the girls were having a great time playing crazy eights with Eleanor. And she was going to have a great time here tonight, too, Kristy told herself firmly, as she started back toward the table where Connor and his family were sitting, laughing and talking.

She was halfway there when Skip Wakefield cut in front of her.

She had met him before several times, when he had come out to the resort to see about buying her property, and she'd always felt a little on edge whenever she was around him.

Maybe because to Skip Wakefield, business was business. Whereas to Connor, business was something to be accomplished while at the same time making everyone better off.

As Skip closed the distance between them smoothly, she found that nothing much had changed. She was still on edge around him, although for different reasons tonight.

She knew he mattered to Connor, and if she and Connor were ever going to be close friends as he wanted, then she and Skip would have to find common ground. Which wasn't going to be easy, given the way Kristy felt about what Skip was trying to do to Paradise Resort.

"You're looking lovely tonight," Skip told her kindly.

"Thank you," Kristy answered politely, noting that he and the Southern belle he had come in with earlier looked pretty good, too. "If you're hunting for Connor, he's over there with his family. In fact, I was just headed that way myself—"

"Actually, Kristy," Skip said, just as nicely, "I wanted to talk to you."

He waited until she turned her full attention to him before he continued easily, "I heard Winnifred Deveraux-Smith just took a position at your place as head chef. And that her butler, Harry, is working there, too."

Kristy nodded. "That's true."

Skip probed her face, as if trying to work out a particularly difficult puzzle. "I also heard that Connor had the interior of an entire wing of the lodge painted on very short notice."

"What's your point, Skip?" she asked, aware that people were beginning to notice the prolonged tête-à-tête.

He leaned a little closer to her ear. Abruptly Skip looked as protective of Connor as Connor was about Kristy. "What do you have on these people?"

Kristy blinked in surprise, sure she could not possibly have heard right. "Excuse me?"

He released an exasperated breath and pushed on in a low, frustrated voice. "Winnifred, Harry and Connor were never known to act irrationally. Until, that is, they became acquainted with you. Now, well, let's just say the actions of the three of them have tongues wagging all over the city."

Kristy's cheeks warmed self-consciously as she struggled to hold on to her cool. "I wouldn't term it that way," she countered stiffly. In fact, despite the long hours of hard work, they were having fun, all three of them! Just as she was.

"Well, I would," Skip stated bluntly. "How is Winnifred going to resume her position as the supreme doyenne among the social set, after working as a common laborer at a failing, run-down resort?" He shook his head at her in exasperation. "Don't you understand what you're doing here?"

Kristy folded her arms and studied the man. She wasn't sure what he wanted from her, save the sale of her property. "So you're saying what—that I should fire Winnifred?" she whispered right back.

Skip shook his head and continued regarding her as if she were completely clueless. "I'm saying, Kristy, that you should never have hired Winnifred or Harry Bowles. Not to mention whatever it is you've done to bewitch and bedazzle my friend Connor. Who, by the way, used to be known as the most levelheaded, up-and-coming business tycoon around. Before you had him cleaning toilets, anyway."

Kristy drew in a quick, shocked breath. Skip was right about one thing—she hadn't really given any thought at all to how any of this would look to others in elite Charleston society. "How do you know about that?" she demanded, aghast.

Kristy felt movement behind her, and then Connor was beside her, both his hands clamped reassuringly on her shoulders. "I'd like to know the answer to that myself," he said.

CONNOR HAD KNOWN Skip for years. They'd gone to school together and started a business that had grown beyond their wildest dreams, making them both very wealthy men in their own right. They'd seen each other through the best and worst of times. Connor relied on their friendship. And that made Skip's suspicious attitude toward Kristy all the harder to bear.

"Winnifred Deveraux-Smith said something about your crush on Kristy to my mother. Winnifred seemed to think your devotion to Kristy and her cause was adorable and that the two of you had some sort of bet going that might or might not culminate in some sort of date. My mother asked me for confirmation. I said I didn't know but would find out."

At that, it was all Connor could do not to groan. He should've realized word about his blossoming romance with Kristy would get back to Skip.

Skip's mother and Winnifred had been friends for many years, and as dedicated philanthropists, worked together for all the local charities on steering committees that also included Connor's mother.

He would have to talk to Winnifred, make her understand that what was going on between him and Kristy was private.

"Of course," Skip continued in a much more affable tone, "I really didn't think it could be true. If anything of that sort were going on, I would've figured it would be the reverse. Like tonight. With you taking Kristy out and showing her how elegantly she, too, could live if she'd only take us up on the very lucrative deal you and I have put together."

"If you two gentlemen will excuse me," Kristy said coolly, sweeping by them both with her head high, "I'm going to be heading home."

Chapter Ten

Kristy had just cleared the ballroom when Connor caught up with her. She had no idea what he had said to Skip after she left, and she assured herself she didn't want to know.

"Forgetting someone?" Connor quipped.

Kristy looked down at herself and replied with the same droll humor, "I seem to be all here."

He dipped his head in acknowledgment of her temper, all the while holding her gaze. "I meant me."

Kristy lifted her chin. "I can find my own way back to Folly Beach, Connor." She didn't mind helping out the charity or substituting, along with Connor, for Winnifred and Harry. Her mistake had been to try and make more of the evening than it was. There was no guarantee when their bet ended, however it ended, that the two of them would even remain friends. Especially when she still refused to sell her resort to him and Skip.

Like most self-made tycoons, Connor was used to getting his way. Kristy had to stop hoping that he would understand her, and her goals, once their week together had ended.

Because the simple truth was that, like Skip, he might not.

And if Connor couldn't do it, there was no hope whatsoever that the two of them would continue their romance.

"I totally understand if you don't want to talk about this

here," Connor said as they stepped through the electronic glass doors, under the portico.

All too aware of the heated glance he sifted over her from head to toe every time she turned her back, and sometimes even when she didn't, Kristy lifted her arm to signal the taxi parked at the hotel curb.

Connor stepped closer, bringing the tantalizing scent of his cologne with him and brushing her shoulder with his hard chest. He reached around behind her and drew her arm down as he handed the valet his ticket. "But we are going to talk about it."

Ignoring the jump in her nerves, Kristy pivoted to face him. Aware how good it felt being this close to him, even when she was ticked off, she smiled up at him and asked sweetly but deliberately, "Says who?"

Interest simmered in his smoky-gray eyes as he lowered his arm to her waist. His lips curled with a self-assured smile as he told her smugly, "Says me."

Kristy felt the hardness of his body and the swell of his biceps as a simmering silence fell between them.

"It can be back at the resort. Or we can go somewhere here in the city," Connor continued implacably. "Your choice."

Trying not to thrill at the possessiveness in his voice, Kristy folded her arms. "I'd prefer not to have this conversation at all." The last thing they needed was the girls, Harry, Winnifred and Eleanor overhearing any of this, she thought. And she could tell by the way Connor was looking at her that she might be able to put it off temporarily, but only temporarily. He was not going to rest until he'd had his say.

Connor shrugged and leaned toward her familiarly. "You want to go to a restaurant?"

Kristy shook her head. That wasn't much more private, in her view.

"Then how about my loft on Chalmers Street," he suggested, the warmth of his body, where it pressed against her, adding new heat to hers. Looking more enamored than ever, he persisted gently and persuasively. "It's quiet and nearby. Plus you haven't seen where I live, and I'd like to show you." He paused, looking deep into her eyes. "Since it's been renovated from an old wreck to a showplace, I think you might find it interesting."

He was right about that, Kristy thought. She was curious to see how—and where—he lived, when he wasn't out chasing business deals with Skip Wakefield. And they might as well get this set-to over with. Connor needed to understand how different they were. And decide if maybe they weren't too different. "Fine."

A parking attendant drove up with Connor's car. Kristy got in, wondering all the while how it was possible for an evening that had started out so wonderfully to be abruptly disintegrating so very badly. Connor still wanted her—and she still wanted him. That was apparent in the way she tingled every time he touched her.

But passion wasn't enough to sustain an intimate relationship. Nor was simple friendship. It took trust and shared goals and endless support of each other. It took all the things Kristy wanted, but had never had.

CONNOR'S CHALMERS STREET loft was located in a converted warehouse on a quiet street in the heart of Charleston. The exterior of the three-story, rectangular brick building had an elegant vintage style that carried over into the entryway. "There are three lofts in the building," Connor told Kristy as he took her hand and they stepped into the freight elevator. "Mine is on the third floor."

"How big is it?" she asked, focusing on everything but her growing feelings for him as he let them into his apartment.

"Twenty-two hundred square feet."

Looking handsome and at ease, Connor switched on lights while Kristy oriented herself to her surroundings. The space had distressed brick walls and concrete floors, and had only one walled-off area, the bathroom. Everything else—the bedroom, living room, kitchen and dining room—were completely open. There were no blinds on the plentiful multipane windows. The furniture was sleek and modern, in contrast to the classic design of the building. Expensive art decorated the walls. Beautiful rugs added interest to the concrete floor and delineated the separate living areas of the open space.

Kristy walked over to a window and looked out on the city, noting that Connor had a gorgeous view of the Cooper River, as well. "You have the entire floor?"

Connor nodded as he came to stand beside her. He loosened the first two buttons of his shirt, untying the tie, letting the ends lie flat on either side of his collar, then strolled over to the bar and opened a bottle of wine. He poured them both a glass of wine while Kristy slipped off her shoes and made herself comfortable, then he came back to sit beside her on the sofa. His expression concerned, he probed her eyes and cut straight to the chase. "What did Skip say that got you so upset?"

Kristy's nerves tightened as she thought back to the conversation she'd had with Connor's business partner. "In a nutshell, he thinks I am bad news, that I've lured you off whatever preordained path you were on, into a heap of trouble. That I've ruined your rep as one of Charleston's social elite in the bargain by enticing you to clean commodes with me. And he thinks Harry and Winnifred have fallen under my social-cachet-busting spell, too."

Connor looked her in the eye, his expression suddenly unbearably tender. "Nonsense. Harry and Winnifred might not have reconciled yet, but they are getting along much better since they're both out at the resort.''

Kristy sipped her wine, drawing a galvanizing breath as shimmers of awareness swept through her. ''Skip thinks that by giving them both jobs I've ruined their reputations.'' She needed to know. Did Connor feel the same way?

He frowned, shoving a hand through the neat layers of his dark blond hair. ''First off, it would be impossible to ruin Harry's rep, no matter what you said or did. He's the best darn butler around. And I'm sure he will be an equally successful and sought-after hotel concierge and assistant resort manager or whatever else he decides to do. As for Winnifred, she's a Deveraux, and has always been a woman who knows her own mind and lives by her own rules.''

Which meant, Kristy supposed, that when all was said and done, none of this would detract from the social doyenne in any way.

But that didn't mean Connor's family would approve of what he was up to at her behest, out at Paradise Resort, Kristy thought uncomfortably. And she did not want to be the cause of a rift between Connor and his family, any more than she wanted to be responsible for any downslide in his own reputation, business or otherwise. ''What about you?'' She tucked her legs beneath her and curled up in the corner of the sofa. ''You'd never cleaned a toilet in your life until you met me.''

He shifted so they were facing each other, his rock-hard thigh bumping against her bent knee. ''So?''

Kristy trembled at the contact. ''So now I've even got you making up beds!''

He flashed her a wolfish grin. ''That's a skill that could come in handy now and again, don't you think?''

Kristy stood and began to pace, aware that complications like this were something she had been striving darn hard to keep out of her already way-too-busy life, and that she had lost her starry-eyed naivete a long time ago. "According to Skip, I'm well on my way to ruining your image in the business community."

"If that's all it takes to ruin it," Connor drawled, "my image can't have been worth much to begin with."

She watched as he stood and strolled toward her, her gut telling her that he was not going to rest until he had proved his point. "This isn't a joke," she said miserably.

He lifted a censuring brow, the heat in his eyes telegraphing his intention to make her his, no matter what anyone else said or thought. "Believe me, I didn't take your walking out on me this evening as anywhere near amusing."

Kristy paused next to a particularly fetching painting that she was sure had cost an arm and a leg, and said, "Your partner thinks I must be blackmailing or somehow bewitching you."

Connor gave her a confident grin that turned her whole world upside down. His eyes darkened ardently. "Skip always was a little over the top."

"He thinks that if you had been thinking straight you never would've done what you've done," Kristy continued, aware that her heart was pounding in her throat and that he was suddenly very close to her. So close she could inhale the intoxicating fragrance of his skin and cologne.

"The only thing I want to do," he told her fervently, wrapping one strong arm around her and cuddling her close, "is this." He threaded his other hand through the hair at the nape of her neck and, angling her head, pressed a kiss to the top of it. Another on her cheek. The side of her neck.

"Connor…" Kristy warned, even as her face rested against the warmth of his close-shaven jaw. Had it ever felt so good to simply be held? she wondered, as she snuggled—albeit somewhat reluctantly—against his rock-solid body. Had she ever felt so safe, so protected, so revered, so absolutely and tenderly cared for? Not to mention the fact that he was generating tremors of heat and desire just holding her this way, and he hadn't even touched his lips to hers yet!

Connor lifted the veil of her hair and kissed his way down the exposed line of her throat to the U of her collarbone. "Forget what everyone else says or thinks, Kristy," he whispered in her ear. "And concentrate on what you feel...."

What Kristy *felt* was wanted and adored as he lowered his head and, taking advantage of the languid shivers of desire spreading through her, kissed her full on the mouth, until her toes curled and she surged toward him and a hot flush swept through her entire body.

"See?" he teased, dancing her backward, toward the bed at the other end of the loft. "You're feeling better already."

"Darn you," she murmured playfully, when he stopped at the foot of his bed and kissed her again, even more thoroughly this time.

"Want me to stop?" he whispered, deepening the kiss and cupping her breast through the fragile silk of her evening dress.

Kristy moaned when his fingertips closed over her nipple, caressing it to an aching point. "No," she said, as everything around her went soft and fuzzy except the hot, hard pressure of his mouth. It had been so long since she had let herself want. Too long. She was tired of being on her own, tired of feeling so alone and unprotected, of having all the responsibilities and none of the pleasures of an adult life. And though she knew all the practical reasons why they shouldn't consummate this relationship, she still had the urge to surrender completely to his sensuous touch and slow, tender kiss, damn the consequences. And judging by the ardent gleam she saw in his eyes, he felt exactly the same way. As if this was a risk, but one well worth taking.

"Good." He grinned, before kissing her again deeply, evocatively, with the reverence she deserved. "Because I don't, either."

Stepping behind her, he eased down the zipper of her dress and helped her step out of the fragile silk-chiffon confection. "Damn, but you are one gorgeous lady," he said, as he surveyed her in the lacy champagne-colored bustier and matching French-cut panties. He traced a finger along the top of one thigh-high stocking. "I had no idea what you had under that gown."

"I'm guessing you like it." Their eyes met and the air between them reverberated with excitement and escalating desire.

"Oh, yeah," he said hoarsely, putting his hands on her waist and drawing her intimately close once again. "I like it," he growled, lowering his head and reclaiming her lips. "You better believe I like it."

The kiss took on a life of its own. And once they were kissing again, there was no stopping. He stroked her tongue with his, he teased, he caressed, until she surged against him, threading her hands through his hair. Kristy might tell herself she didn't need to feel like a woman, but she did. She might tell herself that she didn't need to be taken, and made his woman, but she did. To have Connor suddenly appear in her life, become a part of it, was an unexpected, incredible gift. One she intended to enjoy to the fullest. Spirits rising, she rose up on tiptoe, giving back as good as she was getting, letting him know this was just the beginning, that the fire between them would only grow greater with time.

And he responded in kind. Kissing her even more deeply as he nimbly worked his way down the seemingly endless hooks and eyes holding her bustier closed. Cool air whispered over her back when the edges parted and the undergarment fell away.

Connor paused to look at her, his eyes taking in the creamy curves of her breasts, the pink, pouting nipples and the shadowy valley inbetween. ''Gorgeous,'' he whispered, his eyes warming her skin before returning to lock with hers. ''Absolutely gorgeous.''

He made her feel gorgeous, Kristy realized, and her heart took on a slow, heavy beat as he guided her down to sit on the edge of the bed. He knelt in front of her, like a knight before a queen. Still looking up at her adoringly, he cupped the weight of her breasts in his hands and with infinite slowness brushed his fingertips across the tips once, and then again, and again. Nothing had ever felt so wonderfully sensual, and Kristy moaned as her nipples budded tightly and an urgency swept through her middle, before pooling low.

Not content with just touching her, Connor laid her back gently on the bed. Taking both her wrists in one hand, he lifted them above her head and anchored them there. He smiled at the delicious way she trembled, looking as if he, too, had always known they would end up this way. Then his head lowered, and he circled the pale pink aureole with his tongue. Brushed it with his lips. Then suckled her tenderly again, until she felt deliciously aroused, delectably captive. ''And sweet.'' Connor continued his litany of compliments as he turned his attention to her other breast. ''Soft. Silky.''

''Connor…'' Kristy warned, able to see he wanted this and was quite prepared for it to take all night. Darn his mischievous soul.

He smiled at the way she trembled. Letting go of her wrists, he sat up, took off his shirt, tie, shoes, socks. By the time he got to his trousers, her mouth was dry.

He was beautiful, too. His shoulders were broad, his

chest nicely sculpted, with glowing, golden skin, well-defined pecs and washboard abs. A smattering of dark blond hair, a shade darker than that on his head, formed a line across his pecs and then arrowed sexily downward, to his waist. "You want to see more of me, too."

Knowing the only way she would get through this with her heart intact was to make light of it, Kristy grinned. "A lot more."

The pants came off.

"Black silk," Kristy murmured, appreciating the fit and quality of his boxers.

"That's all you get to see for now," Connor said, as he stretched out on the bed beside her.

"I guess that's fair," Kristy answered, trying—but failing—to keep her eyes from the imprint of his considerable arousal through the silk.

"Now where were we?" Connor teased. Thumbs slipping beneath the elastic of her French-cut panties, he kissed her nest of dark curls through the wispy champagne lace. Legs parting, she arched up off the bed restlessly. She was already wet, so wet...and they'd barely started yet.

Connor slid a hand between her legs, running his palm along her inner thigh down to her knees and back again. "You're right," he said, his smoky-gray eyes darkening, "this should come off, too." He dispensed with her panties, then moved between her knees. Grasping her hips, he slid her toward the edge of the bed. And then, kneeling once again, he found her with his lips, with his hands. Parting her delicate folds, stroking, making her blossom, tremble, sending her to the brink. And then his mouth was on her in the most intimate of kisses, and he sent her floating free into a bliss unlike anything she had ever experienced.

KRISTY CAME BACK to earth slowly, embarrassed to have let herself go, to have revealed the depth of her passion for him so completely, so soon. She opened her eyes, looked over at him. He was lounging beside her, a mixture of tenderness and sheer male appreciation on his face. "You're an amazingly sensual woman," he murmured hoarsely.

And suddenly, to Kristy, indulging her needs and living in the moment did not seem like such a dangerous thing, at least not tonight. "A woman who is only getting started," she murmured back, determined to give as good as she had gotten. She sent him a mischievous look that spoke volumes and tucked a hand in the waistband of his boxers. "These have to come off," she said.

Eyes sparkling playfully, Connor spread his hands wide before lying back and folding them behind his head. "If they must," he said.

Kneeling astride him, Kristy tugged off his boxers, brought them down over his knees and off. "For the record, you're amazing, too," she said. He wasn't just aroused, he was abundantly well-equipped. Suddenly, she wasn't quite sure she could pull this off, but she was willing to give it a try.

He looked at her, clearly ready, willing and able for anything she could dream up. "Ah. Before you have your way with me..." he drawled.

Kristy's heart slammed against her chest. "Yes?"

"Come here and kiss me," he ordered in a low, throaty tone.

Her heart racing, Kristy moved up onto the bed and sprawled carefully overtop of him. Aware that he was still waiting, she sank down on him, stretching out so they were length to length. He groaned. "Keep going, sweetheart."

Shifting her weight until they fit together as snugly as a catch and a lock, she lowered her lips to his. She used her tongue on him, delved deep into the silky cavern of his mouth. Her kisses were provocative, gentle, teasing and hot. She caressed his chest, let her fingers play down to his waist, beyond. She slid downward, almost to her quarry, aware of the need within her that seemed to grow even as it was met. Desire swept through her in powerful waves until she felt liquid and weightless. He was hard as a rock, throbbing, hot. And suddenly she wasn't the only one shuddering with pent-up need. The next thing she knew, she was on her back and underneath him once again. She looked up at him breathlessly, searching his eyes. "But I haven't—"

"Believe me," he said, his eyes filled with affection, his voice rough with the longing for more, "you've done quite enough."

And suddenly it was everything she could do to try and hold her soaring feelings in check. Then he was inside her. Filling her. Creating an urgent need only he could ease. Sensations ran riot, thrilling and enticing. Her body went soft and hot, and pleasure swept through her until she could barely breathe. She clasped him to her, surrendering herself, her heart, her soul. Needing him the way she had never needed any man, she arched upward to meet him, matching his movements, murmuring his name. They moved together, slowly at first, wonderingly, reverently, then more and more urgently. Passion and love, want and need, swirled together until their lovemaking was so strong and wonderful and right it didn't feel quite real. But it was, and heart brimming with tenderness and love, Kristy finally relinquished control, gave herself over to him completely as he guided her into ecstasy.

KRISTY WAS WRAPPED in Connor's arms, her head on his chest, when the clock chimed midnight. She moaned softly. Just like in the fairy tale, the wonderful evening was coming to an end. And like it or not, just like Cinderella after the ball, she had to rush back to her real life. She sat up reluctantly. "We have to go."

For the first time all week, Connor looked like the dedicated single guy he was, answerable to and accountable for no one but himself. "We could call," he suggested. "Let them know we'll be a little late."

For what? Kristy thought, discouraged, as the full impact of what they had just done came back to haunt her.

As wonderful as this moment had been, she realized sadly, that was all it was. A one-night stand, a fling. There'd been no talk of love, no thought to their futures. Nothing—besides the stunning nature of their passion—to indicate that this was anything but a momentary albeit very pleasurable diversion. And she was not the kind of woman who had flings. Which meant, like it or not, they had to be sensible. And that meant protecting her heart. And her feelings. And her reputation. "I really think I should get home," she repeated, even more resolutely. She needed to get it together, think about her future, her girls.

Abruptly, Connor looked as hurt as he was puzzled.

Another sign of how different they were, Kristy thought with a beleaguered sigh. He was a wealthy and successful man who rarely denied himself anything. Whereas she—a hotelier struggling to build a business and mother of eight-year-old twin daughters—rarely had five minutes to call her own. Never mind much opportunity to do exactly what she wanted, whenever, however, she pleased. "Why?" Connor asked.

Kristy sighed. "Look around you, Connor. Look how you live." His city loft was the epitome of a bachelor's lair. A place for seducing women. Not a place to entertain eight-year-old twin girls.

For a few hours, Kristy had let herself get caught up in the glamour of the evening, and forget that she was a woman with too many responsibilities and way too little time. But now, like it or not, the reality of her life was crowding in, making her realize how impossible this relationship with Connor really was. If they were to continue on, he would expect a lot more nights like tonight. Kristy would not be able to give them to him. Not if it meant neglecting her business or her daughters, and currently she did not have time for all three.

She didn't want to put them in a difficult position.

And yet, by acting so impulsively and giving in to her desire for him, she had.

Connor followed her gaze as she looked around his loft. "So I live in a loft. So what?"

"So Skip was right." Kristy struggled to be practical. "You're the consummate single, sophisticated man about town, and I'm a small-town, struggling businesswoman and mother of two. We were together tonight as a favor to Winnifred, but we exist in different universes, Connor."

He scowled. "Not for the past few days, we haven't."

"Oh, Connor." Kristy sighed, shook her head. "You don't want my life."

"I'll be the judge of what I want, Kristy," he said gruffly, "and what I want is you."

Whereas what Kristy wanted was to protect herself from hurt by not allowing herself to get involved with anyone again. Connor understood that because he had done it for years. But it didn't work. Avoiding emotional entanglements only made you lonelier and unhappier in the end.

"But you're right," Connor soothed, cupping her chin and lifting her face to his. He ran his thumb across her lower lip. "We do have to get back, because as much as I'd like to stay up all night making love to you, I have to get you home so we both can get some sleep. Otherwise…" he let her go with a reassuring squeeze "…we'll never have the energy to do everything we've got to do tomorrow to get ready for the conference."

Kristy stared at him, wide-eyed with amazement.

"You're not kidding!" she said. "You still plan to continue helping me."

Connor grinned. "Damn straight I do. Because—" he pressed a silencing kiss to her lips before she could interrupt "—I still want that date." *And*, he added silently to himself, *a heck of a lot more*.

But they wouldn't talk about that now.

They would wait until Kristy was ready.

Until she had accepted the fact that what had happened tonight had been more than a whim, on both their parts. It had been the gateway to their future.

Chapter Eleven

The girls didn't have school on Monday due to the Columbus Day holiday, so Kristy let them sleep late and play as much as they wanted under Eleanor Deveraux's supervision while she and Connor worked like crazy putting the twenty-five rooms together, and Harry and Winnifred knocked themselves out in the kitchen. By noon, all the rooms were ready for the conference guests to check in.

Daisy came over to take some digital photos of the newly renovated hotel interior and exterior. She brought her camera, computer and printer with her, and then set up in Kristy's office, printing off brochures. Connor helped Kristy search the resort records for previously loyal autumn customers and conference groups who might be persuaded to return, while Daisy's husband, an attorney, went over the fine print of an agreement Kristy was considering signing with an Internet-based travel agency.

"I think this contract is doable," Jack said cautiously, "but there are a few clauses I'd like to see changed in your favor before you sign anything, Kristy. How about I call their legal department for you tomorrow, and see what can be worked out?"

"I would really appreciate it." She smiled, confident that Jack would be able to negotiate a deal in her favor. He had been an attorney for Deveraux-Heyward Shipping Company. When Kristy had first met Jack the previous summer, he had still been doing that. Now he was married to Daisy and had hung up his own shingle. As had Daisy. His law office and her photo studio were in the same little shopping center. And the newlyweds looked blissfully content to be masters of their own destiny.

"No problem. Besides—" Jack winked at Kristy "—I can use the business."

"As can I," Daisy added as she sent her brother a teasing look. "Since my business is just getting off the ground, too."

"We all know you both are going to be very successful in your own right," Connor retorted. "You just have to give it time."

Which was what she needed, too, Kristy thought, happy that everything was falling into place so efficiently now. Just a little more time to get the place up and running.

As for her and Connor, well, time seemed to be working miracles there, too. Initially, she had felt awkward around him, after their passionate lovemaking Saturday night. But he hadn't pressured her, and his steady presence had been a balm to her nerves. She was beginning to see he wasn't just interested in her physically, or trying to win a bet. He wanted to get to know her and understand her and be her friend. Be more than a friend. And as time went on, and he remained helpful and kind and generous, Kristy felt her guard coming down, little by little. To the point that she could see them finding some common ground, some way to be with each other, either as lovers or friends or both, without worrying too much about either the ramifications of their actions or their futures.

After all, just because she had never been able to indulge in a no-strings-attached love affair didn't mean she had to either cut Connor out of her life or make demands on him that he might not ever be able to meet. She had a right to an intimate relationship, apart from her roles as mother and businesswoman. She had a right to a private life, apart from the family responsibilities she held so dear. And if Connor was willing to accept that, to conduct a relationship on her terms—in a way that totally shielded her daughters from hurt—there was no reason to deny either of them the pleasure and comfort of each other's company. At least not any that Kristy could see.

She looked up fondly as her twins came into the room. As usual, Sally was wearing a dress and carrying her dad's old beach towel. But her braid was a mess, she had smudges of what appeared to be vanilla frosting on her cheek, and tennis shoes—instead of T-strap dress shoes—on her feet. Susie, on the other hand, sported her usual shorts and T-shirt. But her hair was nicely combed and had a pretty ribbon running through it.

"What are you-all doing?" Sally asked.

Kristy smiled at her girls, aware of how much they had begun to relax and settle into their new environment in the past few days. "We're sending out more brochures to show how things have changed around here, so maybe people who used to stay here will want to come back again." She slid the photos across her desk so the twins could examine them, too.

To her delight, they looked as impressed as Kristy felt about what had been accomplished. "I wish we could write to Daddy and tell him how much this place has changed since we moved here," Susie lamented softly.

"And show him the pictures, too," Sally added, as she tapped a finger against one of the brochures.

Kristy wished they could talk to Lance. Maybe if they could have done so before he died, or at least known Lance had developed a heart problem that needed surgery and was facing hospitalization, they would have been a little more prepared. His death wouldn't have hit them so hard, and they would have had the closure they needed.

As it was, they were still having difficulty moving on, and Kristy wasn't sure how to help them. Except to do as their pediatrician and their school counselor had advised, and let the girls deal with the tragedy in their own way, in their own time.

"Can I have a brochure to show the kids at school?" Susie asked, already moving back to the original subject.

"Sure. You can each have one," Kristy said.

The twins smiled as Daisy handed them folded brochures of their very own.

Harry appeared in the doorway. "Dinner's on. Jack, you and Daisy stay, too, why don't you?"

Jack and Daisy exchanged looks and then nodded. "Thanks," Jack said. "We will."

"Splendid!" Harry looked at Kristy, "Your mother and brother telephoned. They won't be here until later. They've decided to wait out the traffic before they hit the road. Apparently, a lot of vacationers are cutting their losses and getting out of Hilton Head before the storm hits, or any forced evacuations are ordered."

Kristy knew that, as of that morning, Imogene had made a northward turn and was heading for the United States coastline. "What's the latest on the storm track?" she asked casually, doing her best to hide her anxiousness.

Harry smiled encouragingly. "As of half an hour ago, it was stalled off the coast of Florida."

"Well, that's good." Kristy was hoping Imogene would take another abrupt turn, as storms like it were wont to do, and head east and die out over the ocean.

Connor escorted Kristy to dinner.

Winnifred and Harry had surprised the group by putting dining tables out on the piazza that faced the ocean. Gingham cloths were fastened over the tabletops. Harry had set up one of the grills, and Winnifred was overseeing the grilling of hamburgers and hot dogs for the group. Bowls of potato salad, fresh fruit, baked beans and coleslaw garnished the table, along with big pitchers of lemonade and iced tea. As they sat down to eat, Susie pulled out her brochure to show Harry, Winnifred and Eleanor, who all oohed and ahhed over it.

"Susie and I wanted to send one to Daddy, too," Sally explained. "But mail can't be delivered in heaven, can it?"

The adults exchanged looks. No one knew quite what to say to that, including Kristy. "No honey, there's no U.S. Mail Service in heaven," she said gently.

"Well, then, how come you can send a letter to Santa Claus at the North Pole?" Sally asked, her lower lip shooting out petulantly.

"Well, the North Pole is here on earth," Kristy said. "Heaven isn't."

The girls looked crestfallen as they exchanged troubled glances. "Why is it so important you write a letter to your daddy now?" Kristy asked gently, aware that, beside her, Connor was looking just as concerned and empathetic as she felt.

"Well…" Susie looked at her twin. They elbowed each other back and forth, and finally Susie said, "Because we want a new daddy. And we want to ask him if it's all right."

THE PORCH WAS SO SILENT you could have heard a pin drop, Connor noted. Worse, Kristy looked as stunned and at a loss as to how to respond to that as the rest of them. Not that he could blame the twins for wanting a father. Theirs was the dream of every kid—to have two loving parents taking care of and bestowing love and attention on them.

"What made you realize this?" Kristy asked finally in a low, trembling voice.

Easy, Connor thought, as he reached beneath the table to take her hand in his and give it a reassuring squeeze. They were seeing their mom finally begin to shed her widow's weeds and move on, and they wanted to be able to get on with their lives, too. But because they were kids, and unsure of themselves, they needed permission to do so.

"Well," Sally explained practically, her eyes focused on Kristy's face, "there are some kids at school who have lost their parents, too. Our counselor let us have a group meeting with them, and they told us how hard it was for them, but then it gets better. And one of 'em, he got a new daddy when his mommy got married again. So Susie and I were talking and we decided that we think it's a good idea for you to get married again so we will have a daddy living with us. And we even know who we want," they said, looking straight at Connor.

He paused, feeling both stunned that Susie and Sally were bringing up something he had privately been thinking about, and touched that they had identified him as the daddy they yearned for.

Beside him, Kristy blushed to the roots of her hair as she struggled to regain her composure. "Girls, I understand how much you miss having a father in your lives," she replied gently, steadfastly avoiding Connor's eyes, "but it really doesn't work like that. You can't just pick someone out and say, 'I want you.'"

You have to fall in love with him first. The way I've fallen in love with you, Connor thought, as he turned and gave Kristy a look that spoke volumes about the way he felt.

To his disappointment, she ignored the feelings he was trying to convey to her, and looked helplessly over at the assembled adults. Her message was clear. She was asking them to help her out with this very delicate situation. Not him, as Connor would have preferred. Them.

"Then can Daddy pick someone out for us?" Susie persisted eagerly.

Just when you thought the questions couldn't get any more complicated, Connor mused.

"Well, we can't ask Daddy because Daddy is in heaven and we're here on earth," Kristy said, beginning to look a little exasperated as embarrassed color continued to stain her cheeks.

Sally frowned unhappily. "Can't we ask Daddy to come down from heaven and talk to us here on earth?"

"Yeah. There's such things as ghosts. And Daddy is a ghost now, right?" Susie said.

Again, all the adults, Connor included, were at a loss.

"And you can call up ghosts if you use a Ouija board." Sally hurried on persuasively, lifting her brows to emphasize her point. "'Cause one of my friends has one. And they said their Ouija board really works. So maybe we could ask Daddy that way."

Connor glanced over. Kristy looked as if she was either going to burst into tears or storm away from the table, he wasn't sure which. He did know she needed help. And that her girls needed some sort of closure to their father's passing, no matter how they got it. "Actually," he said gently, taking charge even though he knew Kristy didn't particularly want him to do so, "I have a better idea how you can talk to your daddy and tell him everything you want to know."

Kristy turned to him, a stunned look on her face.

"You can write him a letter and tell him everything that's in your heart, and then we'll tie it to a balloon, and send it up to him that way," Connor said. Several years before, he'd heard on the news about other kids who'd lost parents doing something similar. When interviewed, their parents had said that it had helped.

The girls glowed with a mixture of excitement and worry. "But what if the balloon accidentally goes somewhere else?" Susie questioned anxiously. "Like the ones we sent out at school in first grade. Some of them went to Florida and Colorado and New York. They ended up everywhere."

"But this would be addressed to Daddy in heaven, so I'm pretty sure it would find its way to him," Kristy said quietly. She shot Connor a grateful look, then continued seriously, "And you're right, girls. I think Daddy does need to hear from you. And Connor's idea is the best one to date, so…"

The girls jumped up from the table. "Can we get started on it right now, Mommy?" Sally asked.

Kristy nodded.

"We'll draw him pictures, too!" They raced inside the lodge to get their crayons, pencils and some paper, while the adults around the table breathed a collective sigh of relief.

"Sorry about that," Kristy said.

"I completely understand," Winnifred said empathetically.

"So do I," Harry agreed.

"I've never really stopped wanting to talk to my late husband," Winnifred stated candidly.

"Not that there are such things as ghosts," Connor interjected as he picked up his fork.

"I don't know about that," Eleanor said seriously, with an octogenarian's wisdom. "I've seen a ghostly apparition of my grandmother often over the years. Winnifred has seen her, too—in her attic and around her home in Charleston. And Chase and Bridgett swear they saw her image above the ocean, on their wedding night, from the bow of their yacht."

Connor took *that* claim seriously. Neither Bridgett nor Chase were inclined to suggestion. "Have you ever communicated with her?" he asked curiously.

"Not per se," Eleanor admitted with a shrug of her frail shoulders. "But she's left things for me from time to time—a handkerchief, a picture—to communicate what she wants me to know."

They were all silent, thinking about that.

Connor didn't know what to believe. Charleston was a city famous for its ghosts and apparition sightings. Where there was smoke, was there fire? Or were people just seeing and hearing and intuiting what they wanted to?

Susie and Sally came barreling back out of the lodge. Connor noted with relief that they didn't seem to have overheard anything the adults were saying.

"We have our letters and pictures ready," Susie said.

"Already?" Kristy blinked.

"We wrote real fast," Susie explained.

"And we already had some pictures drawed," Sally said. "So all we need is an envelope and a balloon!"

"That's something I can do," Connor said. He excused himself and, with Kristy's permission, went to the nearest market and returned in short order with two helium balloons.

ALL THE ADULTS went out to attend the letter sending ceremony at sunset.

Everyone linked hands and watched solemnly as the balloons headed toward the heavens and finally disappeared from sight. Then Jack and Daisy said their goodbyes. Winnifred and Harry also left, to drive Eleanor back into town, to the grand home where she and Winnifred lived. Kristy and Connor were about to start back inside when another car drove up. Kristy's mother and brother got out. Both hugged the girls and caught up on all the news, including the balloon messages that had just been sent.

"I'm sorry I missed that," Maude told her granddaughters sincerely. "But I'm sure your daddy will be glad to hear from you."

Susie and Sally nodded importantly. "We think so, too," Susie said for both of them.

"Can I get you two something to eat?" Kristy asked. The food from their holiday cookout had all been put away, but it would be easy to fix two plates.

"Thanks," Doug said, "but we're going to continue driving on back to North Carolina tonight."

Kristy couldn't hide her disappointment. She had been hoping to spend time with her family, show them all the improvements that had taken place since her brother and mother had been there. "You'll get in awfully late."

"I know it will be one or two in the morning, but with Hurricane Imogene possibly headed this way, we figure we'd better get on home to Raleigh."

"I understand," Kristy said. Both her mother and her brother had busy medical practices. Their patients would expect them back. If the storm continued on a northward trajectory, people would be cutting short vacations and leaving the coastal areas in droves, making the traffic along the I-95 and I-40 corridors slow to a crawl. A five-hour drive could easily take ten or twelve hours under those conditions. Besides, Kristy told herself, there would be other visits. Hopefully when the resort was completely renovated, and booked to the gills, her efforts a resounding success.

Oblivious to the nature of Kristy's thoughts, Maude looked around. "I worry about you, dear. If the hurricane hits here, all this work you've done could be for naught."

Not to mention, Kristy thought morosely, all the life savings and insurance money she had put into it, right down the drain. She forced herself to put on a cheerful face. "The chances of the hurricane hitting here are small, Mom." They always were.

"Still…" Maude frowned cautiously.

Kristy smiled and, putting aside her disappointment, leaned forward to give her mother a hug. "We'll be all right, Mom, I promise. Now, how about some cold drinks and sandwiches to take with you on your drive?"

"YOU'RE UPSET THAT your mother and brother didn't spend the night, aren't you?" Connor asked an hour later. The twins were asleep, and Harry and Winnifred had called to say they would not be back until later.

Kristy settled into one of the wooden Adirondack chairs on the piazza. "It showed, hmm?"

The night was blissfully warm and quiet. A brilliant moon shone against a velvety backdrop of stars and sky. Hurricane Imogene seemed very far away.

Connor dragged a chair close to hers and sank down into it, stretching his long legs out in front of him. "You've done a tremendous job here, Kristy, pulling this place together."

Kristy reveled in the pride in his voice and the respect in his eyes. "I wish the rest of my family could see that," she murmured, even though she knew simply yearning for something didn't make it happen.

Connor took the now paint-stained Carolina Storm cap she had given him off his head and let it rest on his knee. He smoothed his rumpled hair with the flat of his hand, then shot her a reassuring look. "They will, given a little time."

"And a lot of success," Kristy added. Unfortunately, that success was going to take time, maybe even years, and she needed the full support of her loved ones. Unfortunately, the only people she knew who were fully in her corner, besides her girls, were the friends she had made here—like Jack Granger and Connor's sister Daisy, and Winnifred and Harry. She reached over and touched Connor's hand. Looking into his eyes, she stated sincerely, ''Thanks for all the help you've given me this week.''

''Hey—'' he flashed her an easygoing grin and turned his palm up, so their fingers were now intricately meshed ''—we had a bet that I am still trying to win.''

Kristy melted at the soothing warmth of his touch. ''You know what I mean,'' she murmured, letting her head fall onto his shoulder and settling against him as closely as the arms of their chairs would allow. ''What you have done here the past few days has been way beyond the call of duty or the terms of any wager.''

Connor lifted their joined hands to his lips and tenderly kissed the inside of her wrist. ''It's been my pleasure.''

Tingles swept through Kristy as a poignant silence fell between them. She wished she could invite Connor up to her room, to her bed. She knew it was selfish of her, but she wanted and needed his arms around her. She yearned to feel as thoroughly wanted and loved as only Connor could make her feel, if only for a little while. But she couldn't do that, not with the twins underfoot. They had their eye on making Connor a member of the family already. And as much as he desired her, he really hadn't done anything to indicate that he was thinking about marrying again, ever. Never mind being a full-time father. In fact, his life, his home, seemed to be set up for just the opposite result. And she didn't want her girls hurt with expectations that might or might not come true in the long run. So, for now anyway, the intimate side of her relationship with Connor would have to be conducted outside the bounds of her family. There would be no hand-holding, kissing or snuggling when the girls were around to see.

"Well..." Kristy stood reluctantly, wishing, at least for the moment, that her life were a lot less complicated.

Connor rolled to his feet. "Headed to bed for the night?" he guessed as he tucked his hat into the belt of his jeans.

It was either that or make love with him right here, right now, Kristy thought wistfully. She nodded.

"Well, I guess I'll head off to bed, too," Connor said, moving forward until they stood toe to toe. He braced his hands on his waist and looked down at her with mock seriousness, cautioning, "But not before I get one more thing."

Kristy's heart began a slow, thudding beat. "What's that?"

He grinned and pulled her all the way into his arms. Locking both arms about her waist, he tugged her close, so they were pressed together from the waist down. And she had no choice but to feel the depth of his need for her, or hers for him. "My good-night kiss."

The sigh of longing in Kristy's throat was cut off as his lips covered hers once again. Groaning with a mixture of despair that this couldn't last, and exultation that they had found each other at all, she returned his searing embrace with all her heart and soul. And for the first time all day, she realized, she was exactly where she wanted to be, doing exactly what she wanted to be doing. Aware of how good, how right, they felt in each other's arms, Kristy moved even closer, surrendering as he increased the depth and torridness of the heated caress. And with every second that passed came the need to be much closer still.

They just needed the right time. The right place.

As if realizing this, too, Connor drew back, took in a rough, uneven breath, and looked deep into her eyes. And Kristy realized there was no longer any question about it. She wasn't *falling in love* with Connor Templeton. She was head over heels *in* love with him. The question was how did he feel about her? Kristy wondered as he pressed a brief kiss to her temple, turned and walked down the steps toward his cottage.

PRIOR TO THIS, Connor had never had a problem leaving a woman at the door with a good-night kiss. When the time wasn't right, it wasn't right. But tonight, even though all systems had not been go—in terms of the circumstances necessary for Kristy and him to be together again—he had still wanted to be with Kristy so badly it had been all he could do to let the evening end with one lengthy, passionate kiss.

He could tell, even though he'd be hard-pressed to get her to admit it, that Kristy was feeling the same way. And that made him work all the harder to clear the way for a very public romance between the two of them.

In the meantime, though, there were still some things he had to take care of for her. So the moment he got back to his cottage he telephoned the private investigator he had hired. To his disappointment, Harlan Decker had nothing substantive to report. "No one has been anywhere near those palmetto trees thus far, according to the surveillance videotape."

Connor frowned in frustration. "When did you last check it?"

"About an hour ago. It's possible something could happen tonight, of course, but…" Harlan's voice trailed off in a way that told Connor they were just going to have to wait and see what developed.

Which wouldn't have been so bad, had Kristy not had her first group of guests coming in thirty-six hours. Plus her palmetto trees were obviously dying, and Fitts was a loose canon, to say the least. Who knew what he might try and do to spoil Kristy's business? Connor bit back an oath as he sat down on the edge of the bed. "I was so sure Fitts was responsible for poisoning those trees with weed killer," he said.

"My guess is you're right," Harlan Decker stated bluntly. "Unless the guy owns some sort of lawn company, which he does not, there is no reason for him to have so much weed killer in his garage. And in fact, those plastic jugs could already be empty."

Connor paused. "That's true."

"If he has poisoned Kristy Neumeyer's palmetto trees, the arborist should be able to tell you that when the lab reports come back. In the meantime, we'll keep up the surveillance and just see what develops," Harlan said. "From what little I've noticed, that guy is a pretty nasty character. I doubt he'll stop his campaign to force Kristy out until either he gets caught doing something nefarious and is forced to stop, or she leaves. So chances are we will catch him at something eventually and be able to use it against him, to force him to leave Kristy and her property alone."

Connor sighed. "From your lips to God's ears."

"Yeah." Harlan chuckled. "Well, I'll work on that."

They said goodbye and hung up.

Connor spent the rest of the evening alternately reading his e-mails and getting caught up on business, and thinking about Kristy and her girls. The three of them were a package deal. Any man who loved Kristy had to be willing to love her daughters. Was he ready to be a father? Less than a week ago he would have said no both to marriage and fatherhood. He would have said it just wasn't his thing.

But a lot had changed in the past six days, Connor had to admit.

For one thing, he realized now what an insulated, pampered life he had always led. He didn't want to go back to it. It wasn't that he had a hankering to clean toilets; to be honest, he'd be happy if he never had to do that again. But he liked the physical part of restoring the lodge back to its former glory. Liked the instant gratification that came as they viewed the results of their hard labor. He liked being around to help take care of the twins, and the sense of multigenerational camaraderie he had enjoyed with Winnifred, Harry, Eleanor, Kristy and her girls as they gathered for dinner every evening in the hotel dining room. He had also enjoyed meeting her mother and brother and getting to know them a little.

There had been love in his own family, particularly from his mother. But there had also been a stiff formality, insisted upon by his father, that had really constrained them and left them feeling like strangers to each other in many ways, until very recently. Kristy felt that way with her own mother and brother now because of her own interests and outlook on life.

But the group at the resort had been different. Linked not by blood but by common purpose and congeniality. Connor didn't want to let go of that. He didn't want to let go of Kristy and her girls. Which could mean only one thing, he ruminated as he walked out to look at the beach. He was more of a family man—deep in his heart and soul—than he had ever dreamed.

KRISTY COULD TELL there was something different about Connor the moment she saw him the next morning. It was as if he had made peace within himself, come to some sort of conclusion or decision that satisfied him greatly. And in a way, she knew exactly how he felt. With every day, every hour, every minute that passed, she knew she had made the right decision to revitalize the resort, rather than sell it for destruction. She might have even made the right decision in getting close to Connor, Kristy realized, as she accompanied the girls to the dining room for breakfast. Certainly, he got on great with her daughters, and seemed to enjoy spending time with them as much as Susie and Sally liked being with him.

"Do you think we'll get an answer from Daddy today?" Sally asked, as she picked up her fork.

Kristy froze, her coffee cup halfway to her lips. Once again her girls had hit her with the unexpected. She sent a hesitant glance at Connor, letting him know he might have to help her out here, too. "What do you mean, honey?" she asked Sally gently.

"You know, is he going to send us a sign or something to let us know he got our letters?" Susie explained impatiently.

Kristy hitched in a breath, aware once again that she seemed to be fumbling along as a parent instead of automatically or instinctively knowing what to do or say. "It doesn't really work that way," she said with difficulty after a moment.

"At least," Connor interjected with a calm, reassuring look aimed at both Kristy and her daughters, "in the sense that you would get a letter back or something. Because as you know, that doesn't happen. We don't get letters from heaven."

Sally eyed Connor and Kristy thoughtfully. "Well, Mickey—our friend at school? When his mommy died, she wrote him a letter and his daddy read it to him after the funeral."

Kristy regarded them, gently explaining, "Mickey's mommy probably wrote that letter to him before she died because she was sick or something and knew that she wasn't going to be around anymore." Kristy reached across the table to squeeze their hands. "Daddy didn't know he was going to have a heart attack, so he didn't have time to do that for you girls. I'm sure, had he known he was going to have to leave us to go to heaven that day, that he would have written a letter to you girls first."

Susie and Sally nodded. They weren't sad, Kristy noted. They were just struggling to understand, to make sense and come to terms with their father's death. "Well, maybe he'll send us a sign, anyway," Sally murmured after a while. "Like, you know, a balloon or something on the beach that lets us know he got our letter and everything is okay with him, and that he doesn't mind if we play with his Frisbee with somebody else, like Connor."

Ah, so that was where this was coming from. Kristy began to relax. "Honey, I really think it would be okay if you girls wanted to play Frisbee with Connor," she said. "I think Daddy would be happy about that." *To see you running free. Full of love and joy, rather than continually haunted by the loss.*

"No. We have to ask him first," Sally said seriously.

Susie nodded. "You can't use things without permission."

Kristy gave up trying to reason with them on that one. Fortunately, they had finished their breakfast and the school bus was due shortly. Outside, it was partly cloudy and very humid. But there was no sign of rain as Kristy walked them out to wait for the bus. While they were standing there, she looked up at her palmetto trees. The leaves on top were definitely getting browner by the day, she thought. At this point, she doubted whether the trees could be saved, the damage to them reversed. She sighed, imagining how the lack of tall trees around the building would impact on the visual appeal of the historic lodge.

But, she thought, as the school bus rumbled toward them, she would deal with that bridge when she came to it. Right now, she had conference guests to prepare for.

"Girls get off okay?" Connor asked when Kristy came back into the kitchen to get another cup of coffee.

He and Harry were folding dozens of cloth napkins under Winnifred's direction.

Kristy nodded and looked at the television mounted near the ceiling of the lodge kitchen. "What's the latest on Imogene?"

"Not good," Harry said with an unhappy frown. "It's picking up speed again and heading for Jacksonville, Florida. They think, at the current rate, it will hit landfall early tomorrow morning."

Which was bad. The question was how bad. "Is it going to go north or west?" Kristy asked, as she went to sit next to Connor and lend a hand.

"North." Harry pushed a stack of cloth napkins in Kristy's direction. "They're expecting it to hit Charleston late Wednesday or early Thursday."

"But," Connor added quickly and cheerfully, as he finished his stack and started helping with hers, "they also think that by the time it gets here it will be downgraded to just a tropical storm."

"So the conference should be able to go on, no problem, even if activities for a day or so are indoors," Winnifred said.

Kristy breathed a sigh of relief.

"In the meantime, I still have a lot to do to get ready," Winnifred said.

"When are the food deliveries coming?" Kristy asked, forcing herself not to think about the possibility—or was it probability?—of Imogene changing speed, direction and intensity yet again as hurricanes were wont to do on an almost hourly basis.

Harry looked at the schedule Winnifred had tacked up on the bulletin board. "Seafood at nine, meat at ten-thirty, dairy at three and produce at five."

Connor looked at Kristy. "What would you like me to do this morning, when we get done here?"

Kristy made a face as she thought of the tedious but very necessary task ahead. "Help assemble welcome buckets."

A WELCOME BUCKET, Connor soon found out, was a big plastic sand pail filled with local maps, tourist information, flip-flops, candy, gum, tennis visors and T-shirts bearing the name of the resort.

They all had to be marked with the names of the couples checking in, and it took the entire morning to do all twenty-five buckets, plus a couple extra just in case. By then Connor and Kristy were needed in the kitchen, and they spent the rest of the afternoon there, stopping long enough to walk out and make sure that Susie and Sally got safely off their school bus.

The girls brought their books into the kitchen and did their homework on a corner of the table while work continued. Connor could only marvel at how quickly and efficiently Kristy and Harry were able to help assemble the many food dishes that Winnifred was preparing for guests who would be arriving at noon the next day. He was a little less skilled, although no less enthusiastic. And they had accomplished a lot by five that evening when they turned on the news and weather and learned that Imogene was now headed straight for Jacksonville. A powerful category-three hurricane, it had sustained winds of nearly a hundred twenty-five miles per hour. And looked to reach category-four status, with winds of up to a hundred and thirty, by the time it hit landfall at midnight.

Chapter Twelve

"What do you think? Should we board up the windows?" Connor asked late Tuesday afternoon as they slid the low-country chicken casseroles into one of the big commercial refrigerators, where they would stay until they were baked at noon the following day.

Kristy shook her head as she carried several big plastic containers of cut-up vegetables over to the fridge and slid them in beside the prepared sour cream ranch and onion dips. "Not unless or until the state issues an evacuation order. Right now, there's still a chance the storm will go east or west of us, or will have diminished considerably by the time it gets here." There were at least a dozen hurricanes every year. Very few of them actually hit the Charleston area, and most of them had been downgraded to tropical storms when they did. Kristy was hoping for the same here. But she could see that Connor was less confident of her decision.

"How long will it take if we do have to board up the windows?" he asked, as Harry ladled homemade shrimp bisque and vegetarian chili into plastic containers.

"Five or six hours," Kristy said. She carried some of the pots over to the big, stainless steel sink for washing. "We already have all the supplies—they're in the storage shed with the mowers."

Susie and Sally continued on with their language arts homework, unconcerned. They, too, had weathered too many storm alerts to become upset.

Sally looked up. "Our teachers said we might not have school tomorrow, if the weather is really bad."

"Yeah, but we have to do our homework anyway, just in case," Susie said.

Kristy smiled. "That sounds like good advice."

UNFORTUNATELY, THE PREDICTIONS were correct, and Imogene roared onto Jacksonville Beach at four-fifteen the following morning, a category-three hurricane. Winds of nearly a hundred twenty-four miles per hour knocked out power lines, toppled buildings and inflicted property damage in the millions for the state of Florida.

Airports all along the east coast were closed as the storm turned and continued slowly but steadily northward, and hundreds of flights were cancelled.

Kristy heard from the conference organizer at eight-thirty that morning. "I suppose you already know the Charleston airport has been closed, our flight from Chicago cancelled," she said.

Kristy and the others had been gathered in the kitchen watching the weather forecasts and morning news shows since dawn. All were focused solely on the hurricane. "By the time Imogene gets here later this evening, it's going to be a tropical storm," she soothed the anxious organizer. "That means a lot of rain and some high winds, but Imogene will be out of here by tomorrow morning. That still leaves the rest of the weekend."

"I'm sorry, but the airline has already told us there is no way they can get us all there tomorrow morning. They're busy moving planes out of the area and away from any potential storm damage even as we speak, and we have to hold this sales meeting this weekend. So we've decided to stay here in the city. Truly am sorry." She paused. "I understand we're out our deposit, but owe nothing else, given the extreme circumstances."

"That's right," Kristy said, well aware of the terms of the reservations agreement that provided an out in case of hurricanes or other severe weather. She paused in turn, aware she hadn't felt this deeply disappointed in a very along time. "You're sure we can't reschedule your visit here? We could apply the full deposit to another date."

"No. I'm sorry. Maybe next year. Thanks, anyway."

Kristy hung up to find all eyes turned to her. "The conference has been moved to another site," she reported in the most even tone she could manage. She caught a glimpse of the compassion in Connor's eyes as he searched her face, and then went on to sum up the conversation she'd had with the event organizer.

"Oh, Kristy, I'm so sorry," Winnifred said, splaying a hand across her chest.

Harry nodded. "Dreadful turn of events," he said in his clipped English accent.

The twins, who were just happy that their school had been cancelled for the day, looked at Kristy. "Does this mean you don't have to work today?" they asked eagerly.

Doing her best to hide her quickly mounting worry about how she was going to make up for this financial loss, now that she had salaries to pay and Connor to reimburse, Kristy nodded.

All this did was make Connor—and others—right about the unfeasibility of her staying here, trying to make a go of it.

"I don't get it. How come we don't have school today if it's not even raining?" Susie asked.

"Because they think the storm will have reached us by around three o'clock today, and they want to make sure everyone is home from school when the rain starts," Kristy said simply. "So it just makes sense for the district to use one of your bad-weather days today."

In the meantime, it was gray and gloomy outside, and the wind was picking up. But there was no reason to panic; they still had a while to get ready for Imogene. "The question is what are we going to do with all this food?" Kristy asked Winnifred. "Some of it can be frozen for later use, but the rest of it really should be eaten." And they had enough to feed fifty and then some!

Winnifred smiled thoughtfully. "We could always have a hurricane party," she suggested, like the inveterate social hostess she was. "Invite family and friends to come and ride out the storm here."

Harry jumped on the bandwagon. "Who knows, maybe we could even talk them into renting a few rooms for the night."

"Now you're thinking!" Connor nodded.

"I don't know about that." Kristy frowned. "I don't want to twist anyone's arm or put them on the spot. If we invite them, I think they should just come as our guests, period."

Everyone looked at her. "You sure you have the toughness needed to be a business person?" Connor teased gently.

"Connor's right," Harry warned soberly. "You'll never turn a profit that way."

"I'll worry about profit later," Kristy said, waving off their concern. "I'd rather just have fun tonight and celebrate what we've done here thus far."

Connor regarded Kristy thoughtfully. "You could still turn this to your advantage."

No wonder he was a business tycoon, Kristy thought. He just wouldn't let go of any opportunity to come out ahead. She folded her arms and lounged against the stainless steel kitchen counter. "How?"

"By turning this into a publicity-generating event, and writing off the costs for entertaining everyone. That way you don't have to charge anyone, and yet you can still make use of all the hard work, by having my sister Daisy document through pictures what it's like to ride out a tropical storm at Paradise Resort. You can put that in your brochures, maybe get a mention and a photo op in a local paper, or travel agency newsletters."

Kristy had to admit it was a good idea. "Who could we get to come, do you think?"

"The entire Deveraux family," Winnifred said.

Connor grinned. "The Templetons, too."

Winnifred simultaneously made phone calls, issuing invitations, and watched over the kids while Kristy and Connor and Harry went outside to gather up anything and everything that could get blown away in fierce winds.

They carried it all to the storage shed. "Sure you don't want to board up any windows?" Connor asked, with a worried glance at the lodge.

Kristy shook her head, vetoing his suggestion "It's not necessary for a tropical storm. Only hurricanes." And with Imogene steadily losing strength as it moved across land, it would be nothing more that when it finally passed over the Charleston area later that day.

Chapter Thirteen

It had just started to drizzle when the guests arrived at three o'clock that afternoon. By the time they sat down for dinner at six-thirty, rain was falling in sheets, while fierce gusts of wind blew it around. They were able to watch the storm surge out the dining room windows. The wind was blowing around forty miles per hour and the waves crashing onto shore were six to ten feet high. No longer a hurricane, Imogene had been downgraded to a diminishing tropical storm. Nevertheless, they knew the torrential rain and wind would continue through the night. And talk during dinner was of other storms they had all weathered, many of them much worse than the one currently pounding the entire eastern half of South Carolina.

By eight-thirty that evening, the twins were all tuckered out from the excitement of the day. Kristy took them up to her suite on the second floor. While the palmetto trees bent in the wind, and rain pounded upon the roof and the eaves, she tucked them into bed.

"I had fun today, Mommy," Sally said.

"Yeah. Me, too," Susie confessed around a yawn.

'I'm glad.'' Kristy kissed and hugged each of her girls.

"Think we'll have school tomorrow?" Sally asked.

"They'll let us know at 6:00 a.m. tomorrow, but I'm guessing not," Kristy said. With a good six inches of rain predicted, a lot of streets would be flooded, and school would not be held unless the buses could get out to collect students county-wide.

Kristy turned out the lights in their room and went back down to her guests, who were gathered in the comfortable chairs around the big stone fireplace. "How are the twins adjusting to your move here?" Grace Deveraux asked.

"Better now that they've finally started dealing with the enormity of their loss." Kristy began telling the popular television show host and matriarch of the Deveraux clan about the girls' struggle to understand the finality of their father's death, the letters they had written to their dad and the balloons they had sent up to heaven earlier in the week. By the time she finished, everyone was listening and nodding compassionately. "Unfortunately," Kristy concluded, "I know they're still waiting for an answer from Lance, some sort of permission to go on with their lives."

Winnifred smiled wanly. "I know how that feels. Sometimes I think if I could only have talked to my husband before he died, or found a way to be released from the promises we made to each other at the time we married, I might have been able to move on years ago. And start over again, instead of deciding then and there never to remarry."

"So do it now," Great-aunt Eleanor suggested, her thin voice sounding stronger, more determined than it had all evening.

"How?" Winnifred asked, her elegantly shaped brows knitting together.

Eleanor shrugged. "We could have a séance."

At that, every man in the room groaned loudly.

Gabe Deveraux, a critical care physician, rolled his eyes. "Tell me we're not going to spend the evening trying to communicate with ghosts!" he insisted with a humorous look.

"I think it would be fun," Amy Deveraux declared, as

she fit her hand into her husband's. "I've never been at a séance before."

"Neither have I," said Daisy, looking as if she, too, was amenable.

Mitch Deveraux's wife, Lauren, a Realtor who specialized in historic properties, said, "Charleston is supposed to be haunted by all sorts of ghosts."

"Only for the sake of tourism," Mitch pointed out, ever the practical shipping executive.

"That's the way Bridgett and I felt," Chase said, looking like the sexy magazine publisher he was. "Until we saw the apparition of a woman in white on our wedding night."

Tom Deveraux turned and looked at his eldest son, blinking. "You really think you saw a ghost that night?"

Chase shrugged. "We were standing on the deck of the yacht, and we both saw what looked like a woman from another era hovering above the water for a couple of minutes, before she disappeared into the mists. And in fact, Aunt Eleanor, she looked a lot like you. Only younger."

"That might have been my grandmother," Eleanor said. She turned to the group. "I told you-all I've seen her off and on through the years."

Connor's mother clapped her hands together. "So let's see if we can conjure up one!" she said. She turned to her escort, Payton Heyward. "Are you game?"

Payton nodded. "I've never been to a séance, either."

As they all headed into the dining room to light candles and pull some tables together, Kristy insisted, "You all have to promise me that not one single word of this will be breathed to the twins."

Everyone concurred as they settled into their chairs.

Kristy dimmed the lights in the dining hall. As she took a seat beside Connor, a chill swept through her, and she reached over and took his hand, and on her other side, the hand of the grande dame of them all, Eleanor.

The elderly woman turned to Kristy. "When I was very young, I fell in love with a sea captain named Douglas Nyquist. He had been promised to Dolly Lancaster by his family, but the two of them weren't in love, and he did not want to marry her. When he tried to break it off, she grew very angry and had someone familiar with witchcraft put a curse on him and the entire Deveraux family. She swore he would never have a chance to love me or make me his wife—and sure enough, his ship went down in a storm off the coast of Charleston shortly thereafter, killing him and everyone on it."

"Oh, dear," Kristy said, able to see how much that had hurt the elegant Southern lady.

"She also promised that the entire Deveraux family would suffer for my actions, and that no love would ever last. But I'm happy to say that curse has at last been broken, and now everyone in the Deveraux family has found the love they've been wanting."

Even Winnifred, Kristy thought, realizing—as did everyone else in the room—that she and Harry Bowles were meant to be together.

"Amen to that," Chase exclaimed.

Enthusiastic cheers were heard around the table.

"Anyway, I'd like to be the first to talk to the spirits, if I may," Eleanor continued as they all linked hands and closed their eyes. A murmur of assent rippled around the table, and then, as they all focused on their surroundings, an eerie stillness swept through the room.

Kristy kept telling herself this wouldn't, couldn't work, that there were no such things as ghosts, but she found herself mesmerized by the darkness and the flickering candlelight, and the relentless sounds of the storm outside.

In a low, tranquil voice, Eleanor summoned the heavens and the attention of her beloved, Douglas. "I want to tell you I'm back with my family, after so many years away.

And I'm happy now. I still want to be with you, Douglas, and I will be, one day, I promise. But not until it is my time, too."

They all waited, barely breathing, for some reply, but there was nothing. No sign that anyone in the spirit world had heard. No sign they hadn't. Kristy's hand trembled slightly, as across from her, Harry Bowles cleared his throat. "I have something I want to say, too, to Winnifred's late husband, Lieutenant Smith," Harry stated seriously. "And it's simply that I love Winnifred. And I promise I will always take care of her whether she ever decides to marry me or not."

A hushed gasp swept around the table. No one was surprised by the feelings, just the bold declaration of them.

Winnifred opened her eyes, looked at Harry and smiled. Then she closed her eyes again, and the mood grew solemn as she, too, spoke to her deceased husband. "I would marry Harry. But I'm bound by the promises I made. I can't unless you give me a sign."

Without warning, the lights in the adjacent lobby flickered off and then on again.

"I don't know about the rest of you but that felt like a sign to me," Tom Deveraux said, nonplussed.

It felt eerie as all heck to Kristy. And judging by the way Connor was suddenly gripping her hand, he felt the same. A candle in the center of the table went out, then another—for no reason that anyone could see. Another eerie chill swept across the back of Kristy's neck.

"Mommy?" Susie and Sally were suddenly standing in the entrance of the dining room.

Without warning, Kristy was suddenly shivering. Her skin was ice cold and her teeth were chattering.

"We saw Daddy," Sally declared.

Looking stunned and disbelieving, but more comforted than frightened, Susie added, "*And* a lady with hair like that—'' she pointed to Great-aunt Eleanor ''—in a long white dress.''

The storm howled outside as the girls walked across the wide-planked floor in their cartoon-decorated nightgowns and bare feet. ''Yeah, they waked us,'' Susie confided as she slid onto one side of Kristy's lap, Sally the other. Kristy held them close, grateful for their warmth. Beside her, Connor moved in protectively, too.

''Daddy wanted us to come down here,'' Sally declared.

Kristy buried her face in the fragrant softness of her daughter's just-shampooed hair. ''You were dreaming, honey.''

''No,'' Susie insisted stubbornly, as she pressed her head against Kristy's shoulder and wrapped her arm around her waist. ''He and the lady led us all the way down here before they disappeared.''

Kristy swallowed, aware that the room had grown utterly silent even as Tom Deveraux got up and calmly went over and hit the lights, bathing the dining hall in a warm glow. ''What do you mean, disappeared?'' Kristy asked, her adrenaline only increasing. How much of what they had just been saying and doing had the girls witnessed?

''Like magic,'' Sally explained.

Only there was no magic.

Just as there were no ghosts. Or any way to really communicate with those in heaven. Not here on earth, anyway. Kristy held her daughters tighter. She was about to tell them it was just the storm when there was another burst of wind, a loud, slow, crackling noise and a huge, horrible crash.

CONNOR AND THE REST of the men there spent the next few hours dealing with the huge palmetto tree that had smashed through the windows of the bedroom where the twins had been sleeping, just minutes before they had awakened and vacated their beds.

The only casualty, it seemed, was the Carolina Storm cap he had put on before going out into the rain to the storage shed, in search of plywood panels to board up the broken windows, and a chainsaw. The cap Kristy had given him was torn off his head and whipped away before he could attempt to catch it.

Connor lamented that for a number of reasons. It was the first gift Kristy had ever given him. It bore the paint stains of all the hard work he had personally put in on the lodge. And it was a symbol of the different kind of life he would have if he and Kristy made their relationship permanent. The kind of life where everything was possible and nothing, from the most mundane to the most magnificent, was off-limits to him.

Hoping the hat would turn up somewhere on the beach the following day, Connor went back to work, and the rest of their mission went fine.

By midnight, he and Harry and the Deveraux men had managed to saw off the part of the thirty-foot tree sticking through the window, clean up most of the broken glass and board up the opening, to protect the interior from further damage. But the floor of the girls' bedroom was drenched with rainwater blown in by the wind, and everything in the room was a soggy mess. Connor knew there would be damage to the ceiling of the guest rooms situated directly below them, as well.

The twins had been kept downstairs, where there was no shortage of adults to comfort them and assure them everything was going to be all right, and put them to bed—this time on mattresses that had been pulled to the protected sitting area in the lobby.

Susie and Sally were delighted—it was like a giant slumber party with adults—and no one else seemed to mind.

But Kristy was shaken to her core, and the first moment

he got her alone, Connor took her into his arms to reassure her, too.

"I don't understand why that tree fell over like that," she said.

But Connor knew, and the next morning, when dawn broke and Imogene had moved up the coast, and they surveyed the half dozen other trees that had also been toppled during the storm, he made a surreptitious phone call to Harlan Decker and asked the private investigator to meet him as soon as possible.

"I want to talk to you, too," Harlan said. "I've got something to show you."

"Proof?"

"And it's all on videotape. Where and when do you want to meet?"

Connor knew something had to be done before the insurance investigators came out to look at the situation. Kristy had already put in a call to them. "How about half an hour? Can you make it out to Folly Beach?"

"Yeah. I'm just a few miles away from Paradise Resort now. Do you want me to come there?" Harlan Decker asked.

"No." Connor wanted to know what they were dealing with before he presented Kristy with the facts. "There's a coffee shop half a mile up the road. I don't know if it's open or not, but we could meet there in the parking lot."

Meanwhile, as the rainwater receded, the guests all began heading off to their respective homes, and Tom and Grace Deveraux took the eighty-six-year-old Eleanor home with them.

The resort and many of the other homes along Folly Beach had lost power during the night, but Kristy had backup generators that powered the lodge refrigerators and freezers, so she turned those on. Charleston was fine, so Harry and Winnifred offered to take the girls to Winnifred's historic-district home, to stay until services at Paradise Resort were restored and they again had electricity to power their lights and hot water heaters.

Kristy agreed with the plan. First, though, she wanted to survey the fallen trees, and she had promised the twins they could take a walk along the beach before they left. They knew, as did Kristy, that after a storm of that magnitude, there would be lots of interesting things deposited onto the sand. That was okay with Harry and Winnifred. They had some things to talk about, and wanted to take a private walk along the beach, too.

Connor wasn't surprised. In fact, he was betting, from the way the two were looking at each other, that they'd be either dating or married soon.

"You want to come with us, Connor?" the twins asked him eagerly as they prepared to set off with their mom. Kristy looked as if she wanted him to join them, too.

Reluctantly, Connor had to decline. "Actually, I've got an errand to run—some pending business with a property I'm involved with that I need to check on," he said, promising himself he would tell her the whole story as soon as he could.

He saw a brief flash of hurt in Kristy's eyes. The girls looked surprised and disappointed, too, that he would be running off to do something work-related instead of spending time with the three of them. But it couldn't be helped. And soon Kristy would understand why, Connor vowed silently. "It should only take an hour," he continued easily. "Then I promise I'll be back to help you get squared away here."

Kristy pulled herself together even as she stepped away from him. "Take your time," she said in the polite tone she usually reserved for potential customers. "I realize you have responsibilities, too."

None, Connor thought fiercely, *more important than the three of you.*

HARLAN DECKER WAS WAITING when Connor pulled into the parking lot. The coffee shop was still closed, due to lack of power, so Harlan left his car and got into Connor's. He had a compact video camera in his hand and several videotapes. "I want you to take a look at this," he said, turning on the camera and handing it over.

Connor viewed the picture on the playback screen—and saw Bruce Fitts carrying jugs of weed killer from tree to tree, dousing the roots liberally with the poison.

Connor scowled. "That son of a..."

"My feelings exactly," Harlan said.

Connor handed the tape back to the detective. "Did you see what happened last night at the resort?"

Harlan nodded. "Looked like half a dozen palmetto trees toppled over."

"One of them crashed through a window in the twins' bedroom. They could have been seriously hurt."

"What do you want to do?" Harlan asked, sharing Connor's concern.

What he had been wanting to do, Connor thought. "Talk to Bruce Fitts." He paused, aware that the ex-cop was in a position to be very helpful. "You want to come with me?"

Harlan nodded. "It'd be my pleasure."

Connor drove to Fitts's place. As he turned his Mercedes into the driveway, he saw the man standing in the garage. Bruce was wearing a bathing suit, gold chains and flip-flops. He had a cloth in his hand and was polishing his car. Fitts smirked as he watched Connor get out, then turned curious eyes toward Harlan. "Well, well, well, if it isn't the turncoat," he said nastily. "Sleeping with Beauty yet? Or still just making out with her every chance you get?"

Wondering if Fitts had been spying on him and Kristy on Tuesday evening, as they'd kissed good-night, Connor held on to his temper with effort. It was all he could do not to punch the smarmy neighbor in the face. "The palmetto trees at Paradise Resort have been poisoned. Do you know anything about that?"

"Do I look like a tree specialist?" Fitts asked sarcastically.

Harlan pointed at the jugs of weed killer lined up in the garage. "You don't have to be a genius to know that large doses of weed killer can kill a tree. And that dead trees topple a lot faster than healthy ones."

Fitts shrugged uncomfortably. "I had nothing to do with that."

"The surveillance videos at the resort say differently," Harlan stated impassively, looking at that moment every bit the ex–law enforcement official he was.

"So here's the deal," Connor said, picking up where Harlan left off. "You've got twenty-four hours to figure out what kind of reparation you're going to make to Kristy for the property damage you've done. You're going to apologize to her, and then you're going to leave her and her property alone."

"And if I don't?" Fitts countered with an ugly smile.

"Then," Harlan explained, just as smoothly, "I telephone my friend the district attorney. We show him what we've got, and encourage him to prosecute to the full extent of the law. For property damage, as well as the potential health threat posed."

Bruce Fitts glared at them silently. For once he had no smart-alecky comeback.

"Twenty-four hours," Connor warned silkily. "And Bruce?" he added, narrowing his eyes. "Be generous."

KRISTY TOLD HERSELF the fact that Connor had been behaving oddly since the previous evening had more to do with the storm and the tree crashing through the window than anything she had said or done.

As for him going off alone, to make secret phone calls on his cell phone that morning...well, they probably had to do with the pending business he said he had elsewhere. He dealt with commercial properties. He probably had something on the market that might also have been damaged in the storm.

It was perfectly logical that he would want to go take a look. She just wished he had been more up front with her about what he had been going off to do. She didn't like being left out of the loop that way. It reminded her too much of the way Lance had always patted her on the head and told her not to worry about family finances, or the problems and challenges he encountered in his medical practice. It had seemed as if Lance didn't really think she could handle things, so felt he'd had to protect her.

Kristy didn't want to be protected. She wanted to be respected.

Until now, she felt she'd been getting that from Connor.

Now...now she had the oddest feeling he was shutting her out, the way her late husband had.

Kristy sighed wearily and swept her hand through her hair as the girls raced ahead of her up the beach, shouting out happily as they discovered curiosities here and there. Maybe she was just tired. Imagining things. Lord knew it had been a very long and emotional night, what with everything that had happened. And she still had so much ahead of her to do. Trying to deal with the insurance people, and getting the fallen palmetto trees cut up and carted away. The landscaping around the lodge restored...

"Mommy, you are not paying attention!" Sally scolded, as she doubled back to take Kristy's hand.

Susie raced back and took her other one. "You have to enjoy yourself, Mommy!"

"Yeah," Sally chimed in, "we want you to have fun with us this morning!"

"'Cause there's no school!" Susie said.

Tugged out of her troubled reverie by her daughters, Kristy grinned. They were right. The sun was shining. They had dodged a bullet with Imogene; the damage had been minimal, compared to what people in north Florida were dealing with, where the storm had first come ashore. It was a beautiful day. And her daughters, after grieving for so long, were finally looking happy and excited, and yes, almost carefree again.

"All right. I'm concentrating now," Kristy said. "So let's see what we can find."

As it turned out, they found quite a lot. There were oars, part of what looked like a trashed sea kayak, lots of colorful seashells and chunks of driftwood, a plastic soda bottle and a cooler. And near their favorite place in the dunes, the spot where they used to sit with their daddy and study the ocean, they all saw a sliver of something bright orange sticking out of the sand. As they got closer, Kristy realized what it was. "Look, it's Daddy's Frisbee!" Susie said, tugging it free. She inspected it curiously. "How did it get here?"

"It must've been picked up by the wind and blown out of the window when the tree came crashing in," Kristy murmured. Strange, though, that it would have ended up here, of all places.

"And here's his old beach towel!" Susie pulled and tugged until it came up out of the sand, where it, too, had been buried.

And beside that was something else they had been on the lookout for all morning—Connor's missing hat.

Chapter Fourteen

Connor had just gotten out of his car and was walking across the hotel lawn when the twins came racing across the dunes to his side. Kristy was right behind them. "Look, Connor! We found your hat and Daddy's Frisbee and his beach towel!"

"And they were all together."

"Yeah! Half-buried in the sand."

Connor looked at Kristy, wondering if this was some sort of hoax. "It's true," she said quietly. He could tell by the cautious way she was looking at him that she wanted to know if he'd had anything to do with it.

He let her know with a return look that he hadn't.

"Do you want to play Frisbee with us on the beach, Connor?" Sally asked happily, as she handed over his sand-encrusted Carolina Storm hat.

Connor knew how they'd felt about that before. They'd wanted to receive some sort of permission from their father first. "You're sure it's okay?" he asked, looking at the two little girls, then their beautiful mother. Kristy seemed just as stunned by the request as he was.

Sally nodded and continued enthusiastically, "We think it would be okay, now that we've seen Daddy again."

"Yeah, we're pretty sure this is what he wants us to do.

Otherwise he wouldn't have left his stuff out there for us to find," Susie said.

"You two go ahead and I'll catch up with you. I want to talk to your mommy a minute," Connor said. He and Kristy watched as Susie and Sally raced off, both of them looking equally messy and exuberant.

"They really think they saw Lance last night," Kristy murmured, stepping close to his side.

Connor wrapped his arm around her shoulders. "Maybe they did," he said softly, glad they finally had time and opportunity to have a heart-to-heart talk about this. "Something—or someone—got them out of that bedroom in the nick of time last night. If they think that angel of mercy was their father, then maybe it was."

"And he wants us all to move on," Kristy murmured back.

"I have to admit," Connor said as his arms tightened around her, "I want that for you, too." He wanted it for all of them.

CONNOR, KRISTY AND the girls spent the next half hour playing Frisbee on the beach. They were still enjoying themselves immensely, romping around in the sand, when Harry and Winnifred walked up hand in hand.

"I've got to go to Charleston and check on my home there," Winnifred told them with a contented smile. "Harry is going to go with me. We thought the girls might like to spend the rest of the day with us, and you could pick them up later—say this evening after supper?"

"That sounds wonderful, if you're sure it wouldn't be too much trouble," Kristy replied. That was a long time. Longer than she had planned on.

"Not at all," Winnifred said sincerely. "We really enjoy their company." She cast a look over her shoulder at the lodge. "And I know you still have a lot to do here."

That was true. Although they had removed most of the broken glass the evening before, Kristy still had the storm-soaked linens, and rugs and other furnishings to deal with. She wanted to get the twins' room put back together as soon as possible, but because of the tiny shards of broken glass that still remained scattered about, it wasn't a task that her eight-year-old daughters could assist with. "That would be a big help, thanks," she said, giving Winnifred a hug. The last thing they needed was a trip to the pediatric minor emergency center.

As soon as Winnifred, Harry and the girls left for Charleston, Kristy turned back to Connor. As much as she wanted his company, she knew she had taken advantage of his generosity. She didn't want to wear out her welcome, so to speak. "I know you have business to attend to, so…you don't have to stay and help." She could manage the work on her own.

"Are you kidding? I want to! Although," he added with a perplexed frown, "without electricity we won't be able to do the linens."

Kristy sighed as they walked back into the lodge, hand in hand. "I was hoping it would have been turned back on by now," she lamented.

"I heard on the car radio that a substation out here was knocked out, so it could be late this evening before they get it up and running again," Connor warned, as they headed for the staircase leading to the second floor.

"Well, we can at least bring the mattresses and toys downstairs and put them on the porch to air out."

When they went to pick up the mattresses, however, they realized just how wet and heavy they were. "I'm not sure these are going to be salvageable," Connor said as, between them, they carried a twin-size mattress downstairs.

Kristy had been thinking the same thing. As she contemplated the price of replacing all that, she flashed him a weak grin that was a lot more cheerful than she felt. "You know what they say," she said, as they laid the mattress near the end of the piazza, to begin drying out. "If it weren't for bad luck, I've have no luck at all."

Connor walked upstairs with her to get the other mattress.

"Will your insurance pay for it?" he asked, as they moved carefully around the shards of glass still glittering here and there.

Kristy grabbed the broom and swept all the glass she could see into a pile in the corner.

"After I pay the deductible."

"Which is…?"

"One thousand dollars."

"Ouch." Connor regarded her sympathetically.

"Yeah. I know." Kristy felt a self-conscious flush warm her cheeks as she picked up one end of the second mattress and Connor got the other. "I opted for lower premiums and a higher deductible, figuring nothing would happen. I figured wrong."

They turned the mattress on end, and he took the lead—as well as the bulk of the weight. Backing out the door, he gave her a concerned glance. "If you want to borrow money…" he offered generously.

"Thanks," Kristy said, feeling even more embarrassed by yet another poor decision on her part. She should have let him board up those windows yesterday the way he wanted! "But I've got it covered," she continued resolutely. "When my house in North Carolina sells, I should have a nice sum to add to my bank account."

"Have you had any offers on it?"

Kristy shrugged as they headed down the stairs, being careful not to scrape the just-painted walls. "One, a few months ago, that I refused because it was so low." Now out of sheer necessity Kristy was thinking about revisiting it, to help her cash flow problems caused by the cancelled conference and the storm damage. It was twenty percent less than what she had hoped to make off the sale, but it would also rid her of the mortgage payments on that property. And that would help her a great deal. She could only hope the architect and his wife who had made the offer were still interested.

"That's the downside of owning real estate," Connor replied easily. "Since it's in a constant state of flux, you never know what the value will be when you decide to sell."

Kristy caught his glance as they set the mattress down and walked back in, side by side. It wasn't hard to imagine what Connor must be thinking she should do. What he— and Skip and her family—had thought all along. "I think," she commented dryly, feeling so discouraged she could barely look him in the eye, "that this is the point where you encourage me to cut my losses and sell out to you and Skip."

Connor paused at the foot of the stairs as if he didn't know what to say. "I thought you wanted to bring the resort back to its former glory," he stated carefully, after a moment.

Kristy sighed with a weariness that came straight from her soul. Suddenly she couldn't hold back her feelings anymore, and the words came pouring out of her. "That," she said, her voice breaking, "was before Imogene. And the palmettos coming down with some mysterious malady and the tree crashing through the window. And the cancelled conference. And extra food. And people I hired that I don't know if I'm going to be able to pay very much longer. And the lack of electricity and hot water today." Her smile wavered and then, to the distress of both of them, she burst into tears.

Horrified to be breaking down in front of Connor like

this, Kristy turned and rushed away, her hand pressed to her mouth. He rushed right after her, catching her as she reached the reservations desk, where he turned her to face him and wrapped his arms around her. "Come on now, Kristy," he soothed. "It's not that bad."

"It is!" She cried all the harder. She had been kidding herself. Kidding him. "I can't do this!"

"Yes," Connor told her sternly, "you can."

"N-n-no, I can't!" Kristy sobbed, her whole body shaking. "Don't you understand, Connor? I'm broke. *Broke!* This conference would have given me operating costs through the end of the year, but to do any more than that, I need a *lot* more guests coming in. I need to be full over the holidays. And I just don't see how that is going to happen with that mess out there—" she waved her hands at the sick and fallen palmetto trees "—this mess upstairs in our suite…"

Connor wasn't sure whether this was the time to tell her about Bruce Fitts and his part in the sabotage or not. Particularly since he didn't know if Fitts was going to do the honorable thing, ante up and pay for the damages, or continue to be a jerk, make it unnecessarily hard on all of them and force them to go to the district attorney or file a civil lawsuit. Both would take time and money. And an emotional strength and energy Kristy seemed to be lacking right now.

"Look," Connor said, wrapping his arms around her tightly, "you have insurance on this place, and it should pick up a lot of the costs."

"You're missing the point. It will take several weeks, at the very least, to get the outside looking good again. And until the outside looks good again, I can't book rooms here. If I can't book rooms, I go further and further into the red. It's a downward spiral that never seems to end!"

"Are you telling me," Connor asked evenly, searching

her face, "that you are ready to flat-out give up and throw in the towel and sell Paradise Resort to me and Skip?"

Kristy bit her lip, looking for the first time as if she was ready and willing to lean on him completely. "Tell me the truth, Connor. Is that what you think I should do?"

"I'm asking you what you want to do," he replied, just as seriously, willing to do not what would serve him and his partner and the consortium they'd put together, but Kristy and her girls. Willing, for the first time, to forget the bottom line and the task of making everybody involved in a deal happy, and focusing only on one. Only Kristy. Even though that was going to tick off and disappoint a lot of people who had been counting on him.

But he had to make a choice here, Connor knew. And as far as he was concerned, he had made it.

A tense silence fell between them. Kristy gulped. Finally, she said in a very small voice. "I don't know what I want to do, Connor. I just…don't…know." She shook her head, her body slumping in defeat.

CONNOR CALLED WINNIFRED from the car, en route to Charleston. "Hey, Winnifred, it's Connor. Kristy's exhausted. Yeah. I don't think the twins should see her like this. Could you? Just for this evening? And don't tell them—I don't want them to worry…. I think with some sleep… Absolutely. All right. We'll see you tomorrow morning, first thing."

Connor turned to Kristy. "Winnifred and Harry are going to keep the girls at her place tonight."

Kristy nodded as tears of defeat and exhaustion continued to roll down her face. His expression determined, he continued authoritatively, "So you've got a choice. A hotel…"

She laughed shakily at the irony of that, wiping the tears

from her face. Her spirits rose, crashed and rose again. "Didn't I just leave a hotel?"

"Or my loft on Chalmers Street," he offered, even more deliberately.

Kristy felt a lump the size of a walnut gathering in her throat. "You don't want me there," she murmured wearily. Not when she was such a basket case.

"Au contraire, babe." Connor flashed her a sexy, single-man-about-town grin completely at odds with her disheveled state. He took one hand off the wheel, reached over and squeezed her knee. "Besides, don't you owe me a date? After all—" he slanted her an even sexier glance "—I did win our bet, did I not?"

Stubbornly, Kristy ignored the tingles of desire he was creating. "You did. And to be honest, I'm in no condition tonight for a date." Even if the selfish part of her wanted nothing more than to spend the entire night wrapped in his arms, alternately pouring out her troubles and crying her eyes out, and making love with him.

Connor parked in front of his building. He looked at her the way he had the night they had been all dressed up, attending the benefit for the teen shelter—as if she were the most beautiful woman in the world. Heck, the only woman for him. "Then I get a rain check?" he asked softly, taking her in his arms.

Kristy sniffed and rested her forehead on his strong shoulder. She supposed a bet was a bet. "If you want one," she allowed, ashamed that she still couldn't seem to get hold of herself, or stop the tears that kept leaking from the corners of her eyes, no matter how hard she tried.

"I insist," Connor said gently, pressing a light, loving kiss to her temple.

"I'm not going to be very good company," she warned as he held the door for her and they took the freight elevator up to his place.

"You don't have to be any company at all," Connor said, wrapping a strong, comforting arm about her waist. "You just have to shower and sleep, and later eat."

She'd forgotten to bring clothes, so after she'd had a long, hot shower, he lent her a V-necked T-shirt and a pair of his pajama pants to sleep in. Then he led her over to his bed, tucked her in and stayed beside her until she fell asleep.

When she finally stirred, the digital clock beside the bed said 7:30. Confused, she looked at the dusky light outside the windows of the loft and, yawning, struggled to sit up. "Is it morning?"

Connor came out of the chair he had been sitting in and sauntered over to his bed. "Night."

Kristy blinked the sleep from eyes that still felt puffy from her crying jag. Not that Connor seemed to mind. He was still looking at her as if she were the most beautiful woman in the world. She pushed herself up on her elbows. "How long was I asleep?"

"About four hours."

Kristy groaned and stretched. It felt like too long, and not long enough. He had showered, too. And changed into casual slacks, a crew-neck knit shirt and deck shoes.

He perched beside her on the edge of the bed, favoring her with a sexy smile that did funny things to her insides. "Hungry?"

Kristy had to think about that. "Maybe. A little," she allowed, as she regarded him with the same measure of satisfaction he was giving her. Her heart was suddenly thumping so hard she could hear it in her ears. "How about you?" she asked breathlessly.

His eyes still holding hers, Connor inclined his head slightly to one side. "For just one thing," he admitted, smiling. Then he slid over next to her, took her in his arms and captured her mouth in a soft kiss that made her heart soar and had her senses spinning. Realizing all over again how much she loved the warmth and strength of him, Kristy wrapped her arms around Connor's neck and kissed him again and again, savoring the taste of him, even as she inhaled the faint fragrance of shampoo and soap and shaving cream.

Without breaking the kiss, he slipped off his shoes, lifted the covers and slid in beside her, taking her fully into his arms. He was warm and solid, the best reality in her problem-laced world, and she moved against him, needing his quiet strength and the safe harbor of his strong arms.

He kissed her again, until passion swept through her and her body arched and her hands clung. He kissed her until she lost what was left of her restraint and was inundated in the pleasure and the wonder of the moment.

Kristy hadn't meant to fall in love with Connor. Hadn't wanted to fall in love ever again. Because that meant being vulnerable, meant she could get hurt again. But Connor wasn't going to hurt her, shut her out or deceive her, she realized as he eased the T-shirt over her ribs, past her breasts.

Her pulse jumped as he bent and brushed light, butterfly kisses across her skin. A soft moan—or was it a sigh of surrender?—shuddered through her as he palmed her breasts and stroked his thumbs across the pearling tips.

"Oh, Connor…" Kristy murmured, already feeling the dampness between her legs and the restlessness building inside her. "I want you so much."

He looked into her eyes, and she saw an answering tenderness and need that surprised her. "I know," he murmured back, divesting her of the T-shirt and then the pajama pants. "I want you, too."

She watched as he stood beside the bed and began to remove his clothes, his eyes never leaving hers. Shirt, slacks, boxers fell away. The soft light on the other side of the loft clearly illuminated the hard ridges and masculine contours of his body. His desire for her apparent, he climbed back into the bed. For a moment, he let his gaze trail over her. "You are so beautiful," he whispered.

She reached for him, smiling, letting her hand trace the ridged muscles of his abdomen and the silky hair covering his well-defined pecs and shoulders. There was a time when she would have felt this was a mistake, Kristy knew. But the events of the last week had shown her it was inevitable. The two of them were meant to be together. She didn't know for how long, or in precisely what way. She just knew she needed and wanted him with every fiber of her being. "I love the way you look and feel, too," she said, almost shyly.

He bent to kiss her throat, pausing to trace a lazy circle where her pulse throbbed. Kristy let her head fall back as her heart took up a steady, mesmerizing beat. Sliding a hand beneath her hair, he brought her lips to his again. He kissed her gently, his tongue mating with hers. His lips traced the shell of her ear, the slope of her neck, leaving her feeling deliciously distraught, and then his mouth moved even lower, to the slope and curve and jutting ends of her breasts, kissing and caressing, sending her into a frenzy of yearning. She arched against him, burying her hands in his hair.

Groaning, Connor shifted his weight, settling between her thighs, his hips nudging them apart. She drew in a shaky breath as he slid ever lower. She gripped his shoulders hard, arching up to meet him as he touched her languidly, knowingly, taking her to heights and depths, teaching her every nuance of desire. Only when the excitement inside her had subsided to a gentle tremor did he find his way back up her body, pulling her knees to his waist, pushing his erection into her silky, trembling wetness.

He moved with tantalizing slowness, filling and retreating, going ever deeper, encouraging her to give back everything, even as she, too, demanded more. She wanted everything—passion, pleasure, tenderness, surrender. She wanted Connor, Kristy thought as the two of them went spiraling over the edge. Heart and soul.

WORRIED THAT HIS WEIGHT was too much for her, Connor eased away from Kristy and onto his side the moment he caught his breath. Wrapping his arms around her, he brought her close, and with a shuddering sigh of what sounded like utter contentment, she went willingly into his arms, placing her head on his chest, an arm on his shoulder, a leg draped across his waist.

Connor had never been much for cuddling, but the feel of Kristy beside him, all pliant, giving woman, combined with the wild, wanton pleasure of their lovemaking and the clean, sexy fragrance of her hair and skin, made him never want to let her go.

He knew he could make love to her every night for the rest of his life and it still wouldn't be enough, would never be enough. He didn't know how or why she had become such a huge part of his life, he just knew she had. And that being with her completed him in some fundamental, essential way.

Kristy pressed her lips to his chest. His body responded. She kissed the curve of his shoulder. He felt himself throb like a nineteen-year-old kid. She stretched out overtop of him and began to kiss him again in a way that was reckless and relentless. There was no denying her passion, no denying the feelings swirling around in him.

Their relationship might have started out as a battle of wills, but it had evolved into so much more. Connor wanted her, needed her, needed this. He moaned as she kissed her way downward, settling between his thighs. Her lips and hands moved over his skin, touching and caressing and loving, as if she couldn't get enough of him. Whatever shyness and reservations she'd had initially were gone now. She cradled him with one hand, while stroking him with the other. Aware that he'd never experienced anything sexier in his life, he watched as her head lowered, her hair spilling across his stomach like ribbons of silk. Her lips moved over the rigidness of his erection to the base, and lower still to the part of him that sheathed his seed, before moving ever closer, once again, to the sensitive crest.

With a mixture of eroticism and tenderness he could only have imagined, she traced every inch of the ridgelike seam. Connor hadn't known that he, too, could be seduced into surrendering, but that was exactly what he did as she continued tantalizing and arousing. Loving him with her fingertips, palms, lips, before finally drawing him into her mouth. Over and over she lashed him with her tongue, teeth, lips and kissing and caressing, working her tender magic until he shuddered uncontrollably and beads of lubricating moisture appeared on the tip of his shaft. Knowing that if he didn't change gears it would all be over way too soon, he started to move, to shift her so she was beneath him and he was in charge once again.

Her eyes dark and imploring, she caught his forearm. She wasn't ready to give up control. "Let me," she demanded, her lips curving into a soft, seductive smile.

Shifting upward so she was on top of him, her thighs straddling his hips, she slowly, provocatively lowered herself onto him. Hardly able to bear it, he sucked in a breath, wanting everything she had to give. And she wanted him, too. He could see it in her eyes as she arched and bucked, and tightened her body around him. Taking him into her, taking him deep, giving him everything he had ever wanted from a woman, everything he had ever needed.

"Like this?" Connor whispered, wanting to please her as much as she was pleasuring him.

''Exactly like this,'' she agreed sexily, as she lowered her mouth to his.

Lips locked together in a fierce, primal kiss, they continued merging bodies, merging souls, until for the first time Connor knew what it was to give—and take—without restraint. To love boldly. Proudly. He hadn't known he could want a woman like this, he realized in amazement. Hadn't known he could want Kristy so fiercely and completely. But he did, and those feelings, he knew, weren't ever going to go away.

REALIZING THEY WERE ravenous, they ordered in, feasted on Chinese food, made love again. By dawn, Kristy knew what she had only guessed at before. She wanted to spend the rest of her life with Connor Templeton because she was head over heels, irrevocably, wonderfully, impossibly in love with him. She wanted to marry him someday, be his wife. And he was...well, she wasn't sure exactly what he felt about her. Enamored? Attracted to? Was this going to lead to marriage? Was he even the marrying kind? Should she even be speculating about it at this point in their relationship? Or should she be doing what he was apparently doing—just enjoying the moment?

''You're worrying again,'' Connor said, as the two of them lounged about, she in his pajama pants and T-shirt, he a robe, eating a breakfast of croissants and fruit they had ordered in. His glance drifted to her breasts before returning to her face. ''Are you still thinking about giving up the resort?''

Kristy swallowed around the sudden tightness of her throat. ''That was yesterday.''

''I know.'' Still eyeing her with a depth of male speculation Kristy found very disturbing, he shifted toward her. ''I'm asking about today.''

''To be honest—'' Kristy put down her napkin and

picked up her coffee cup "—I still feel pretty tired and defeated, but I also know it's too early to be throwing in the towel. That there are other business approaches I could try." With effort, she met his gaze.

Connor sat back in his chair, the successful self-made tycoon again. "Want to discuss them with me?"

Abruptly feeling every bit as inept and useless as she had the day before, Kristy replied as evenly as possible, "Nope."

Ignoring the flip note in her low voice, he asked seriously, "Why not?"

Noting that he didn't like being shut out by a significant other any more than she did, Kristy hesitated. She wasn't sure Connor was going to understand her need to succeed or fail entirely on her own, for once in her life, but she had to try and make him understand nevertheless, because it was the only way she *could* succeed. She took a bracing breath as she fumbled with her mug. "Because I don't know if any of my other ideas will work, and until I have time to figure out if they will or not, I don't want to talk about them."

He looked so hurt that Kristy felt compelled to rush on, "I know you're a very successful business person and you might have valuable input for me, Connor. And I know I more or less tried to get you to advise me yesterday, and somehow take responsibility for the decisions that need to be made now. So if it turned out to be the wrong decision in the end it wouldn't really be my failure but yours. But I also know I started out determined to do this on my own or not at all, and I have to forge on despite the difficulties facing me, and keep to that."

Connor regarded her with respect. To her relief, he seemed to understand why she needed to do this her way, come what may. "Is that the only thing on your mind?" he asked softly.

No, Kristy thought. *I'm wondering if you really love me as much as you act as if you do.* But unable and unwilling to put him on the spot about the exact nature of his feelings for her, she lifted her shoulders casually and said with an inner confidence she couldn't begin to feel, "What else, beside the business problems facing me, could be?"

KRISTY HAD JUST GONE into the bathroom to finish getting ready to go pick up the girls when a knock sounded at the door. Wondering who could possibly be coming by so early—it was barely nine o'clock—Connor went to get it and found Skip Wakefield standing in the hallway. He looked upset.

"Where have you been?" Skip demanded, charging inside. "I've been calling you since yesterday on your cell, and out at the resort."

Connor stared at his business partner irritably. "I haven't checked any of my messages." Kristy had her cell phone on, in case the girls needed her, but Connor hadn't been interested in getting any calls, and had turned his off and let his voice mail take them.

"Why didn't you pick up the phone here?" Skip demanded, looking even more aggravated.

"Because I was busy," Connor warned in a hushed voice. Not wanting to disturb Kristy, he took Skip by the arm and pushed him toward the door.

Skip saw the pair of woman's sneakers on the floor next to a handbag. Scowling, he glanced back at Connor. "Thanks to you, Bruce Fitts is threatening to sue us."

Connor kept his voice deliberately low. "What the hell are you talking about?"

Skip's face tensed. "He says he didn't have anything to do with those trees being uprooted on Paradise Resort."

"Oh, he does, does he?" Connor replied in a voice dripping with sarcasm. The lout obviously knew no bounds, if he was trying to pull this off! Especially in light of all the man had already done.

"He said the storm did it," Skip continued, in an upset tone. "And furthermore, he resents the heck out of you and Harlan Decker for going over there yesterday and trying to put the lock on him to pay for the damage."

"Obviously, he didn't tell you the whole story," Connor said with a sigh.

"He didn't have to." Skip looked back at Kristy's sneakers and handbag. "It's obvious you've gotten way off track here. Or need I remind you of your original mission?"

"I know what I was supposed to do," Connor retorted gruffly. What he was always supposed to—and did—accomplish. Get everyone on the same page, and feeling good about it.

"Then why don't we have a signed agreement yet?" Skip demanded impatiently, looking as if he wanted to understand his best friend, but didn't.

"Because Kristy Neumeyer doesn't want to sell," Connor explained, dropping his voice to a hushed whisper and hoping Skip would do the same. The bathroom was on the other side of the loft. Normal voices would be muted, unintelligible, but shouting was something else....

"Yeah, well, she *might*," Skip pointed out, exasperated, "if you hadn't been out there all week helping her out, free of charge."

Aware they were about to cross a line that shouldn't be crossed, Connor scowled. "That was between her and me, Skip."

"Yeah?" Skip slammed his hands on his hips, pushing back his blazer. "Well, what about what's between you and me and the rest of the consortium we put together?" His brows knit in a frown. "It's a great opportunity, Connor, but it's not going to be there forever unless we can get her signature on the dotted line. Darn it all, for all the time you spent schmoozing her, she should have agreed days ago!''

The bathroom door opened. A fully dressed Kristy walked out. It was clear from the expression on her face that she had heard most, if not absolutely everything, the two men had said.

So much for sound not carrying across the loft, Connor thought, swearing inwardly.

She smiled at both of them tightly. ''Unfortunately, I'm a stubborn cuss. Aren't I, Connor?''

Connor glared at Skip again, then looked at Kristy and lifted an imploring hand. ''You weren't meant to hear any of this,'' he said quietly.

Kristy plucked up her sneakers and handbag. ''Gee. Now that's a surprise.'' She looked at Connor's partner as if she had expected this all along. ''Hello, Skip.''

''Kristy.'' Skip nodded at her politely. ''Sorry for barging in,'' he said sincerely, letting her know his quarrel was not with her, but with Connor.

Connor tensed all the more as Skip turned toward the portal and Kristy held up a cautioning hand, stating icily, ''Don't leave on my account, Skip. We were all just getting to know each other.''

Connor didn't like that tone in her voice. The one that said she had already tried and convicted him. ''I can explain.'' He pushed the words through tightly gritted teeth.

She released a derisive breath. ''Oh, I'll bet you can.''

Another silence fell between them.

''And you can start with your threatening Bruce Fitts,'' Kristy continued calmly as she sat down on the sofa to put on her shoes.

Connor swallowed, aware that about this much she might possibly have very good reason to be angry with him. ''You heard that?''

Kristy shrugged as she stood and squared off with them.

"Fortunately or unfortunately, depending on how you look at it."

Connor shifted his weight so he was standing with his legs braced apart, arms folded in front of him. "He's been poisoning your palmetto trees with big jugs of weed killer. Harlan Decker, the private investigator I hired to look into it, is also an ex-cop. He and I visited Fitts yesterday morning and I gave Fitts twenty-four hours to make it right, or we go to the district attorney."

Skip blinked in total surprise. Kristy looked equally stunned by the revelation, though not nearly as surprised.

"You're sure about this?" Skip said.

Connor nodded. "I have videotape to prove it."

"Geez." Skip swore. He shoved a hand through his hair and began to pace. "I had no idea. I mean, the guy is a jerk, but that's sick." He turned to Kristy. "That's not the way Connor and I operate," he said firmly.

"But you do double-team people," Kristy said, elegant brow arching.

Skip shrugged his shoulders indifferently, not about to apologize for his and Connor's success. "I go in with the business pitch, the hard line, and get people thinking about what we want to do. Connor smoothes the way and mediates between both parties until we have an agreement."

"Which is what he was supposed to do with me," Kristy ascertained dryly.

Skip nodded. He turned to Connor. "But somehow he got off track this time, and started working on your behalf, instead of everyone else's."

"Well, I can see how that would be a problem," Kristy said, even more coolly. "Me being so hardheaded and all."

Connor turned to Skip. "I need to talk to Kristy alone."

"All right. I'll catch you later. Kristy—sorry about your trees."

She nodded, accepting his apology, and Skip let himself out.

Connor turned back to her. He wanted this to work with all his heart and soul. He had thought Kristy did, too. It hurt to realize she was ready to both think the worst of him and run at the first sign of difficulty. "I'm sorry I didn't tell you," he apologized calmly as he closed the distance between them. Only now did he see what a big mistake that had been.

"Why didn't you?" she asked quietly, the hint of tears adding a luminous quality to her dark brown eyes.

Connor looked down at her. He knew she was upset. He didn't blame her. He was upset, too. "I was trying to protect you," he explained gently.

She dragged a hand through her hair, pushing the dark, silky strands from her face. "Like I haven't heard that one before." She sighed wearily.

Connor tensed, irritated that she insisted on thinking the worst. "If you're comparing me to your late husband..." he began.

Chin up, she slanted him a reproachful look. "One and the same."

"Our situation is entirely different," Connor continued flatly.

"Is it?" She folded her arms and turned tormented eyes to his. "Obviously, you didn't trust me with your suspicions about Bruce Fitts."

Connor placed his hands on her shoulders. "You had enough on your plate."

Kristy blinked. "So you think I'm, what? Fragile and weak, or just incompetent?" she demanded irascibly, flattening both hands on his chest and shoving him away.

His own temper flaring, Connor retorted, "Neither."

"Of course, I can see how you'd think I was a ninny." Kristy paced back and forth. "I wasn't exactly Superwoman yesterday afternoon, was I? Falling apart like that. Crying in your arms. Being so distraught you had to put me to bed." She shook her head in disgust at her own vulnerability.

Connor saw nothing to feel ashamed of and everything to be proud of in the way she had allowed herself to finally lower her guard and turn to him. "You were exhausted," he reminded her gently. "You'd been working nonstop. You hadn't had any sleep." She had needed him to be there for her, and he had been glad to do so.

Kristy scoffed and grimaced self-effacingly. "I could say the same about you, yet you coped just fine, Connor. Hell, you were even able to slip in a secret visit to threaten Bruce Fitts, without me or the girls knowing about it." She paused and tilted her head consideringly. "When did you do that, by the way? Oh, I know!" She snapped her fingers. "It was yesterday morning, when you went out on that mysterious errand—to check on some pending business with a property, wasn't it? Not that it matters in any case," she continued, giving him no chance to reply.

But it did matter, Connor thought. Just as they mattered and her dream mattered. And somehow he had to get her to realize that. "I was trying to help you."

"Why?"

"Because you put your whole heart into resurrecting Paradise Resort and making it all it could be," Connor told her simply. And somehow, someway, in the process of him trying to understand her and see things from her viewpoint, her dreams had become his dreams.

But Kristy obviously didn't see it that way. Eyes flashing, jaw set, she continued accusingly, "Tell me something, Connor. What were you going to do if I was actually *able* to make a go of the place? Hmm? You must have been really happy when I told you I was ready to throw in the towel yesterday, that I just couldn't do it anymore."

"On the contrary," Connor retorted tightly, taking her into his arms once again. "I didn't want to see you go down in defeat."

Tears filled her eyes as she looked at him. "Because that would have robbed you of the chance to mediate a solution in some clever, sunny fashion?" She swallowed hard and pushed on in a low, trembling voice. "Or was sleeping with me supposed to smooth away the rough edges and accomplish that?"

Now she had crossed the line, Connor thought. He released his hold on her abruptly. "You can't honestly think I made love with you to work out the fine points of a business deal."

But that, he realized sadly, was exactly what she did presume. "Romancing got you close to me." She spoke as if he weren't even there. "I guess I'm just a sucker, because those kisses felt so real—"

"They were real!" Connor interrupted.

"—that I began to trust you. So much that I confided everything to you." She drew in another shaky breath, shook her head in obvious regret. "You know my financial situation, exactly how much longer I can hang on."

"Damn it, Kristy, I never asked you for that information!"

She laughed bitterly. "That's what makes it all so sweet! I volunteered it. Willingly. Stupidly! Naively. And now you have everything you and Skip need to take me down. With or without the nefarious Bruce Fitts's help. All you have to do is wait a few months, and hell—I'll be begging you two to make me a deal. You might even be able to shave a mil or two off the purchase price."

Connor regarded her stonily. "You really think I'm that low?"

"What I think," Kristy said, tears blinding her as she

grabbed her shoulder bag and rushed for the door, ''is that I've been a fool.''

Connor moved to block her way. He'd lived a life of bitter accusations and no resolutions before, and he wasn't doing it again. Wasn't going to be with a woman who didn't believe in his capacity to love. ''Damn it, Kristy, if you leave like this, if you refuse to stay here with me and find a way to work things out, it's over,'' he warned roughly. ''Do you understand that?''

''Oh, Connor,'' Kristy said wearily, ''it's been over from the moment Skip walked in that door.''

Chapter Fifteen

Connor spent the rest of Thursday alternately moping around and trying—and failing—to be cavalier about the whole thing. It wasn't as if he had ever expected to fall in love with and marry Kristy Neumeyer, after all. He had been there to simply mediate a solution and bring her around to his and Skip's way of thinking, so Paradise Resort could be sold, torn down, an exclusive condominium built.

By Friday he had tired of both approaches, and moved on to meeting with Skip and coming up with solutions to their current myriad of business problems.

The entire time, he stayed close to the phone, thinking, hoping that Kristy would realize the error of her ways and call him or come to see him. She didn't. And by Saturday morning, he had to admit to himself what he supposed the practical side of him—the side used to cutting his losses and moving on—had already known. That his time with her and her two girls had been like a dream. One that, however pleasant and inspiring, was bound to end.

That didn't mean, however, that he could stop dwelling on their failed romance. And he was still mulling over his myriad experiences at Paradise Resort when his mother and two sisters came to see him Saturday at noon. They wanted him to go to lunch with them.

He wasn't interested.

There was one thing, however, he wanted to know. Connor picked up the sand-encrusted cotton cap he had laid on a pile of old newspapers, for lack of a better place, and looked at all three woman. Surely, one of them would have the answer. "Do you know how you're supposed to clean hats like this? Do you send them to the dry cleaner or…?"

Iris shrugged before he could even finish his question and, as beautifully dressed as always, in a pencil-slim gray skirt and white cardigan set, said, "Honestly, Connor, why bother with that? Why not just get a new one?"

Because this one is special, Connor thought.

"I agree with your sister. That looks like something you picked up off the beach," Charlotte said with a perplexed frown. And since Connor had always been a sophisticated man about town, his mother really didn't understand what he was even doing with a red-and-gray Carolina Storm cap. Since the hockey team was located in North—not South—Carolina.

"It's actually pretty new," Connor said. Less than a week old, in fact.

"Could have fooled us," Daisy teased.

"Yeah, well, it was left out in the storm the other night," he told her.

"I've never known you to form an attachment to caps like that," Charlotte continued with a puzzled look. "Especially one with paint splattered on it."

Daisy folded her arms and regarded him speculatively. "Maybe this one has special significance."

She was right. It did. It was the hat he'd worn the entire week he had been out at Paradise Resort with Kristy. It was the hat he'd worn in an attempt to fit in with her and her girls, the hat that had made him feel less like a wealthy scion and self-made tycoon, and more like a regular guy who had real husband and father potential.

"In fact," Daisy continued, tilting her head to study it from another vantage point, "I think I might even recognize it—"

Connor cut her off before she could make the connection out loud. He knew Daisy had seen him wearing it at the resort the day she'd come out to take pictures for Kristy's brochures. "All I want to know is how to get it clean enough to wear again," he said in exasperation.

"Oh, well, that's easy," Daisy said, with an airy wave of her hand. The only one of the Templetons to reject their blue-blooded lifestyle out of hand, she had long worn casual gear. "You just put it in the top rack of your dishwasher and run it through the wash cycle. Then take it out and let it air dry on your counter, so it doesn't lose its shape. Although I have to tell you I don't think the paint is going to come out."

"That's okay," Connor said. He didn't mind the specks of green, blue and white paint on the cap, as those brought back happy memories, too. The fact that he had been a part of the transformation of one wing of the lodge.

Charlotte and Iris turned to Daisy in stunned amazement. "How do you know how to wash a cap?" they asked in unison.

Daisy shrugged and ran a hand through her wavy blond hair. "What can I say? I married a talented guy who taught me all sorts of things."

"And you're happy, aren't you?" Connor observed. In fact, she was the only one in the family who'd been blessed with the kind of man-woman love that was so strong and real it was palpable.

"Really happy," Daisy confirmed.

"What's this all about, Connor?" Charlotte asked with motherly concern.

He held back a sigh of aggravation. He had never confided anything about his love life to the women in his family and he wasn't about to start now. Fortunately, he was saved from replying by a knock at his loft door.

He went to answer it. Skip Wakefield breezed in, papers in hand. Catching sight of the three Templeton women, Skip stopped in midstride. Sent Connor a hesitant look. "Obviously, this is a bad time. I can come back."

Connor halted Skip abruptly. "It's fine," he said briskly. "How did it go?"

"The deal is done. The property and everything in it is yours, as of—" Skip consulted his watch "—thirty minutes ago."

"When can I take possession?" Connor asked.

Skip handed over the title. "Immediately."

"What about the other problem?" Connor rifled through the rest of the documents, making sure everything was in order. It was.

"Also taken care of," Skip said.

Connor took the papers over to his desk and inserted them in a manila business file. "You're sure?"

Skip shot a cautious look at the three women, then looked back at Connor. As carefully as if speaking in a code only they could decipher, he said, "He understands that if word of what he has done gets out, he will have no friends in this community. So he's going to set things right, and then move on. He said something about Hilton Head, or Kiawah. I think he's already made arrangements to look at properties in both places."

"Thanks," Connor said sincerely.

"Hey." Skip held up both hands apologetically. "I owe you for not realizing what a mess that was going to end up being."

"Anyone want to clue us in?" Daisy interjected dryly. Never one to bear being shut out of a family situation, she stepped forward, propped both her hands on her hips. "Or would you rather just continue talking as if we aren't here?'' She glared at her brother.

"Sorry," he murmured. He hadn't really meant to be rude, but he had been waiting all morning for the outcome of the negotiations and needed to know those things. "I just bought a house on the beach."

Daisy brightened at the thought. She had been after Connor to give up his city life for a while now. "Near me and Jack?" she asked excitedly.

"No," Connor admitted reluctantly, knowing it wasn't going to take his nosy little sister long to put it all together. Not that he could keep it a secret, anyway. "On Folly Beach."

"Near Kristy," his mother murmured, already jumping to conclusions.

"Right next to Kristy," Skip interjected, like the concerned friend he was. He regarded Connor protectively, once again speaking more to Connor than anyone else in the room. "Although that may not be the smartest move your big brother has ever made, Daisy, since Kristy is not currently speaking to him."

Charlotte touched a hand to her pearls as she, too, struggled to take it all in. "But darling, the two of you were getting on beautifully the other night at the hurricane party!"

Iris, never one to dwell on anyone's love life, nevertheless looked rather intrigued, too. "What did you do to tick her off?" she asked with an amused grin.

Connor sighed. Leave it to the three women in his family to assume the breakup was somehow either temporary or all his doing. "It's a long story."

Daisy beamed and sat down on the edge of the sofa. "We have time."

Briefly, reluctantly, Connor explained how he had kept

Kristy in the dark regarding his suspicions about her obnoxious neighbor, Bruce Fitts.

"She shouldn't be angry at you for trying to protect and
help her," Charlotte said with maternal indignation, immediately taking Connor's side.

"She most certainly should," Iris disagreed, just as
hotly. "Connor had no call to treat Kristy like an imbecile!
She's a businesswoman, for heaven's sake!"

"Who cares whether he should have protected her or
not?" Daisy said. She looked straight at her brother and
commanded, like Patton addressing the troops, "Apologize
to her immediately, Connor."

As far as Connor was concerned, he had already said
what had to be said and done what needed to be done—
for either Kristy and her resort, or the consortium and any
new construction that might go there, if it ever came to
that—by purchasing the adjacent property and getting rid
of any potential trouble from Bruce Fitts. As for the rest of
it, Connor felt it was up to Kristy to cool down and come
to him. Tell him she had made a huge mistake. Because he
was not going to be with anyone he had made as unhappy
as he had made his late wife, or be with someone who
doubted his love. He had no intention of ever living that
way again. "I shouldn't have to prove myself to her," Connor retorted, ticked off. If Kristy didn't know who he was,
after the week they had spent together, if she didn't know
he was decent and caring and gallantly motivated, she
would never know!

Daisy snorted in exasperation. She regarded him as if he
was the one who was a total idiot. "Then prepare yourself
for one long and lonely life," she said.

"GOSH, THEY LOOK HAPPY, don't they?" Harry Bowles
murmured on Saturday morning as he and Kristy finished
putting all the furniture back on the lodge veranda. Kristy

sank down on one of the white Adirondack chairs and watched as Susie and Sally raced back and forth on the sand, playing with their daddy's old Frisbee. For the first time she could remember in a very long while, both girls were in shorts and T-shirts. Susie's hair was in braids, Sally's a ponytail, but both wore colorful ribbons. They were equally disheveled and out of breath, both giggling wildly.

"It's nice to see them just be themselves," Kristy murmured. The way she had always wanted to be when she was growing up, instead of being forced into the serious, superstudent mold.

"I wish I could say the same about you," Harry continued, sitting down, too.

Winnifred came out the door, pushing a serving cart. Harry jumped up to help her. Soon all three of them were sipping ice-cold lemonade and eating ginger cookies, meant for the resort-saving conference that hadn't happened. Kristy could tell by the way Harry and Winnifred were looking at each other that they had something to say to her.

"You may as well fess up," she said eventually, "because I doubt it's going to get any easier."

Winnifred nodded. "I'm giving you my notice today, Kristy."

Kristy had hoped that wouldn't be the case, but... "I figured it was coming," she said. Winnifred was a wealthy woman who had a very full life, aside from the work she had done at Paradise Resort.

"As much as I've enjoyed being here the last week and a half, I realize Harry is right." Winnifred reached over to briefly and lovingly touch his hand. She looked into his eyes a long moment, before turning back to Kristy and continuing, "I was never cut out to hold down a regular job. It's true I love to cook and entertain—so much that I once attended the Culinary Institute. But it's still merely my avocation, done primarily for family, on a whim. The work I do for charity is my career. And the past ten days I've been sorely neglecting that,'' Winnifred concluded seriously.

"I appreciate all your help,'' Kristy said. She rose gracefully. "I'll cut you a check for all the hours you've put in.''

"When you do, please make it out to the Charleston Children's Fund, on my behalf,'' Winnifred said.

"Will do,'' Kristy said. She turned to Harry, hoping he wasn't going to tell her the same thing, but understanding if he was. It was clearer than ever just how much Winnifred meant to him, and vice versa. "Are you leaving, too?'' she asked, trying hard to respect his wishes, whatever they were, and not influence his decision either way.

He smiled at Kristy fondly. "Not if you're going to keep trying to turn this place around.''

"I am.'' In fact, Kristy had been thinking hard and had come up with a number of ideas about how to accomplish just that. "I have to warn you, though, it's going to continue to be an uphill battle,'' she said.

Harry tilted his head in a devil-may-care way. "I'm up for it.''

Footsteps sounded on the cement walk. Kristy and the others turned in time to see Bruce Fitts marching around the side of the lodge toward them. For once her florid-faced, overweight neighbor was clad in a yachting jacket, white trousers, shirt and shoes instead of his usual too-small swimsuit and gold chains. He stomped up the steps, his face set and angry, and thrust an envelope at her. "I believe you've been waiting for this,'' he said nastily.

Kristy had no earthly idea what he was talking about, but she took the large sealed envelope, anyway.

Bruce adjusted the navy-and-white yachting cap he wore on his head. "It's a check for the damage done to your palmetto trees, your house and your car, as well as a formal letter of apology."

Kristy regarded him evenly. He owed her this much and more. It was obvious he wasn't making reparation because he felt a duty to. Nevertheless, there was a lot of damage that he had caused, so she would take his money. "Thank you," she said, with as much grace and class as she could muster, knowing that even if he was a horse's behind, it didn't mean she had to act like one.

"Don't thank me." Bruce Fitts hitched a thumb in the direction of the luxury beach house to the south of Paradise Resort. "Thank your new neighbor."

Kristy blinked as the meaning of his words sank in. "You sold your place?" For politeness, she didn't want to act as elated as she felt.

"Yesterday," he growled. "To Connor Templeton! As if you didn't know!" With a last indignant sniff, Fitts stomped off as cantankerously as he had arrived.

"Hmm," Harry said.

"How lovely that Connor will be right next door!" Winnifred observed happily.

Kristy wasn't sure about that. What did it mean? Was Connor simply doing something nice for her out of guilt or obligation? Or was he paving the way for a trouble-free building project for his and Skip's consortium, in the event that Kristy did decide, or was forced, to sell Paradise, after all?

Curious to examine what Fitts had brought her, Kristy opened the envelope. Inside was a certified bank check that would more than cover the removal of the dead and dying palmetto trees and the cost of new landscaping, plus the damage done to the girls' room. The letter had been written by Fitts's attorney and was full of legal language, but the upshot was that if Kristy accepted the check as reparation, the matter was closed. No legal action would be taken by either party in the future. Which was fine with her.

Briefly, she explained the contents to Harry and Winnifred. "Connor did this."

"Then you definitely owe him a word of gratitude," Harry said.

Kristy sighed and pushed a hand through her hair. "I don't think Connor wants to talk to me."

"Since when?" Winnifred demanded.

Recalling just how angrily they had last parted company, Kristy clamped her lips together. "Since we agreed it would be best if we never saw each other again."

"I can't believe he meant that," Winnifred stated firmly.

Kristy had seen Connor's face. She'd participated in the exchange of harsh words. She looked down at the porch. "He meant it, all right." In fact, he had been as hurt, angry and disillusioned by the breakup as she was.

Silence fell on the porch, as out on the sand, the twins continued to play.

"So in other words," Harry stated bluntly, as he stood and squared off with Kristy, "that means you're not going to tell Connor Templeton how you really feel about him and want him to feel about you."

Kristy tensed. How was it possible they knew what no one else did—that despite the way Connor had shut her out and failed to believe in her, the way she wanted and needed to be believed in, that she was still in love with him and always would be? "What do you mean?" she asked warily.

"Trust us on this," Winnifred said as she laced a gentle arm about Kristy's shoulders. "Harry and I wasted most of the past twenty years because we were too stubborn and foolish to put our pride aside and be completely truthful with ourselves and each other. And although we've made a pledge to stop doing that, we can't get back the time we wasted. Don't you and Connor make the same mistake,

Kristy. Don't stick with less than what you want, just because you're afraid to upset the status quo.''

Harry nodded determinedly. "If it's worth having, it's worth the risk.''

WAS IT WORTH THE RISK? Kristy wondered. She could have her heart broken all over again. On the other hand, her heart was already broken, so what was one more loss? One more dent to her already wounded pride, when absolutely everything she had ever wanted and dreamed about was at stake? Kristy turned in the direction of the luxurious beach house south of her resort and saw a familiar black sedan pull into the driveway.

Kristy saw Connor get out of the car and go toward the front door, without so much as a glance at the resort. She looked down at her jeans and the oversize blue denim work shirt she had on. She should go inside, change clothes, get cleaned up. But if she took the time to do that, she might lose her nerve. She turned to Winnifred and Harry.

"Go," Winnifred said with a gentle smile. "And take as long as you need to take. Harry and I can watch the kids.''

Kristy swallowed around the knot of apprehension in her throat. "You're sure?" she asked hoarsely.

Harry and Winnifred both nodded.

On legs that shook, Kristy walked across the porch, down the beach, past the property line and across the dunes to the beach house. Connor was standing on the deck, his hands clasping the railing in front of him. He was wearing khaki slacks and an open-collared blue shirt. His dark blond hair was windblown, and aviator sunglasses shaded his eyes.

Without turning his glance from the waves rolling gently onto the sand, he informed her matter-of-factly, "I bought the place.''

Was that the only reason he was here? To check out his new property before he did whatever he planned to do with it? Not to live here, as she hoped? "I know," Kristy murmured quietly. "Fitts told me when he came to see me to make reparation."

With an effort, she ignored the sudden pounding of her heart. Taking a deep breath and doing her best to look as cool, calm and collected as he did, she walked up the steps, across the wooden deck to his side. He had never looked better, and a tingle of awareness swept through her as she asked, "Are you going to put it on the market?"

Connor turned his head toward her, took off his sunglasses and slid them into the pocket of his shirt. His gaze roved her face, her flushed cheeks, her dark tousled hair, before returning ever so deliberately to her eyes. Immediately she was inundated with memories of their brief, passionate affair. "Do you want me to put it on the market?" he queried.

Kristy looked behind her at the zebra-stripe theme of the living room, visible through the large floor to ceiling windows. "It doesn't really seem like you." In fact, it was tacky.

"It isn't. Right now. But it could be if I made it my home."

A second of silence stretched between them. Kristy looked at him. Connor looked back at her. There was no denying it. This was the moment of truth. And there was so much to say, so much to repair, that she hardly knew where to begin. "Did you buy this place to protect me?" she asked quietly, hoping like heck that was indeed the case. Not because she needed the protection. She didn't. But because it meant that, deep down, he still cared for her, just as she cared for him.

"Partly," Connor allowed with a dip of his head.

Kristy took a step closer, hope beginning to rise within

her, like a buoyant balloon, to the sky. "And the rest of the reason?" she asked, still holding his eyes.

A grin appearing on his face, he ambled closer. He placed both hands on her shoulders, cupping them with a gentle possessiveness that robbed her of breath. "Because I want to live out here at the beach, where I can see you—and your girls—every day."

Forcing herself not to get too excited—this could mean, after all, that he just wanted them to be friends—she rested her hand on his chest. "So you can continue to keep an eye on us?"

Connor cuffed an arm about her waist and hauled her against him. Breathing deeply, he buried his face in the fragrant softness of her hair. "So I can make you mine." He kissed her thoroughly, then drew back to look into her eyes. "I love you, Kristy," he said hoarsely. "I don't think I told you that yet, but I do, with all my heart and soul. I know I've made mistakes."

So had she. But she knew that now.

"I initially showed up on your doorstep for all the wrong reasons." Connor paused, shook his head ruefully. "I was trying to smooth the way for a business deal that would have benefited us all greatly. Not that it's any excuse—"

Kristy caught the past tense. "Wait a minute. What do you mean, would have—?" she interrupted. Had he given up on trying to buy Paradise Resort from her?

Still holding her close, Connor continued, "Skip and I have talked to the members of the consortium. They understand you're not interested in selling, and have agreed to let us look for another site for the project we want to build."

Kristy studied him. She knew what a successful businessman Connor was, that he had never been one to take failure—in anything—lightly. "And you're not upset about that?" she asked cautiously.

Connor's arms tightened around her. He held her as if he never wanted to let her go. "It's a setback, no doubt about it, but compared to having you walk out of my life, it's a very tiny one. Because I mean it when I say I love you, Kristy."

Her eyes filled with tears at the words she had longed to hear, and say. Contentment sizzled through her and was mirrored in the expression on his face. "Oh, Connor, I love you, too." Kristy went up on tiptoe, wreathed her arms about his neck and kissed him fiercely. She drew back slightly. Knowing that before they went forward, they had to go back, she confessed soberly, "But you aren't the only one who's made mistakes. I've made my share of them, too. Starting with the way I treated you."

He looked down at her and she continued miserably, "I gave you such a hard time when you first came to see me."

Conner grinned, then quipped wryly, "One I think I richly deserved, given my motives."

Kristy made a face. "But I really put you to the test."

His dark eyes hopeful, he asked, "Did I pass?"

"Oh, yes. Absolutely. More than that, you believed in me, in what I was trying to do," Kristy continued seriously, remembering all he had done to help her. "We were so busy getting ready for the conference that ultimately didn't happen, that I don't think I realized just how much faith you had in me."

"And I do," Connor said seriously.

"Or how much you trusted every business decision I made."

He took one of her hands and lifted it to his lips. He kissed the underside of her wrist, and then the back of it, too. "I want you to realize your dream."

"And I will," Kristy vowed softly as her heart took on a staccato beat. She looked deep into his eyes. "But I know now I don't have to do it all at once. I can take my time, renovating the resort, building up a clientele, to the point I can turn a profit. I just need a better business model from which to work, and I think I have one now."

Connor grinned proudly. He backed up to a deck chair, sank down into it and pulled her onto his lap. "I'd like to hear about it," he said, as they both settled comfortably in the chair.

"I'll show you, in great detail," Kristy promised. Then she continued happily, "But I think if I spend most of my time trying to generate bookings for the twelve cottages and the north wing of the lodge, and make sure we have really good service for the guests that are at the resort, that I'll be in the black, with money to not only continue renovation on the other three wings, but to pay you back by the end of next year."

He held up a hand to silence her. "I told you I'd wait as long as you needed."

"I know. And it's generous of you," Kristy said with a grateful smile. For the first time in her life she was determined to lay all her cards on the table and say everything that was in her heart and on her mind. "But it's important to me to stand on my own, to do this by myself." She searched his face. "Can you understand that?"

Connor nodded compassionately. "That's why I went into business with Skip, instead of becoming part of the family antique business—because I needed to do my own thing, be my own person."

"Then you do understand," Kristy said softly, relief flowing through her in great waves.

"Yes." He stroked a hand through her hair. His low, husky voice was filled with emotion. "I'm just sorry I didn't make that clear to you earlier."

"There were a lot of things we didn't make clear," Kristy confessed, her voice catching at the thought of all they had very nearly lost. The look of love in his eyes giving her more courage than she had ever known she could possess, she said, "But that's something we can easily fix. All we have to do is talk to each other, openly and honestly."

"I'm all for that," Connor murmured as he drew her to him for another, lengthier kiss that filled them with warmth and love. They didn't stop until they were both trembling and breathless. "I promise you no more secrets."

"None," Kristy agreed. "But there's one more thing." She leaned back and looked into his face. She was wearing her heart on her sleeve, but that was okay, since her heart was now his for the taking. "I still owe you a date for winning that bet," she said.

Interest flared in his smoky-gray eyes. He placed a palm on his chest. "I'm ready, willing and able."

Kristy grinned. Unable to contain her euphoria, she asked, "Tonight okay with you?"

"Tonight, and every other night the rest of my life," Connor confirmed, before he indulged in another long, leisurely kiss that left them both glowing with happiness.

Epilogue

One year later…

"Columbus Day isn't exactly a traditional day for a wedding," Winnifred Deveraux-Smith commented as she looked around at the beautifully decorated Paradise Resort. "But I have to admit, it really is shaping up to be lovely."

"Thanks," Kristy murmured, pleased, as she studied their surroundings. The furniture had been moved out of the club room, and white folding chairs had been set up for their guests, in two sections, with an aisle between. Arrangements of white roses and baby's breath were nestled amidst delicate greenery. White satin bows and ribbon adorned the end of each row, and an antique silver candelabra gave the room a simple but elegant ambience. A trellis covered with fresh flowers would serve as their altar. "I think so, too."

"But, as the bride, are you sure you should be out here overseeing the reception decorations, instead of upstairs getting dressed?" Winnifred—who had just become engaged to Harry Bowles and was planning a June wedding—asked.

"I just wanted to make sure everything was perfect," Kristy murmured, touching a hand to her carefully upswept hair. And as far as she could see, it was. And not just for her and Connor's wedding.

Thanks to heavy advertising on the Internet and complimentary weekend stays for travel agents, so the agents could see and experience the rustic old-fashioned beauty and ambience of the resort firsthand, bookings were now running close to one hundred percent. Harry ran the resort with the same aplomb he had once run Winnifred's Charleston mansion, while Kristy concentrated on bringing in new business and continuing the renovations, which were almost complete.

And it wasn't just for Kristy that things were going well. Daisy and Jack were expecting a baby. Connor's sister Iris was as deeply into the antiques business as ever. His mother had decided she would not marry again, but she and retired shipping executive Payton Heyward spent many wonderful hours together and seemed to enjoy each other's company tremendously.

Grace and Tom's second marriage was flourishing, and so was Grace's new cable television show, as well as the Deveraux-Heyward Shipping Company. As for the Deveraux offspring, Amy Deveraux and her husband, Nick, had had a little girl. Gabe and Maggie had had twin boys. Bridgett and Chase were so enamored of their niece and nephews, they were thinking about starting a family, and so were Mitch and Lauren.

Kristy's own family had finally accepted that she was meant to be an innkeeper, that the beach was and would always be where her heart—and home—was. Kristy accepted the fact that they would always privately be disappointed that she hadn't become a doctor like everyone else in the family, but they were keeping those feelings to themselves these days, and that made for much happier get-togethers.

As for Connor, he and Skip were still in business and

had finally found a site for the luxury beachfront condominium project they wanted to build, on nearby Seabrook Island. Connor loved the twins, and had become the father they needed and wanted. And they adored Connor as much as he did them. They were doing well in school now, and at age nine, were a good mix of tomboy and princess. They still wrote letters to their daddy in heaven and sent them off to him via balloon. Kristy encouraged the communication for several reasons. One, you could never have too much love or family in your life. And two, who was to say Lance wasn't receiving them?

But Winnifred was right, Kristy thought, as she dashed up the service stairs to her own private suite in the lodge. It was time to get dressed.

The girls were there to help her into her wedding gown, a tea-length, ivory satin sheath with a beautiful beaded jacket. And so was Kristy's mother.

"Are you nervous, Mommy?" Sally asked, as the short veil was attached to the floral wreath already in Kristy's upswept hair.

"No," she said, as she knelt to help her twin daughters put wreaths of flowers in their hair, too. And it was true. She had never been more certain of anything in her life than she was of her love for Connor, and his for her.

And she saw the same sentiment in Connor's eyes when they stood before the minister on that perfect afternoon and said their wedding vows.

"I, Kristy, pledge to you, Connor, my love and devotion...."

"...and forsaking all others," Connor promised, "keep you only onto me, to have and to hold, for as long as we both shall live...."

"For inasmuch as you, Connor and Kristy, have made these vows and plighted your troth before God and these witnesses, by the authority vested in me by the state of

South Carolina—'' the minister beamed ''—I now pronounce you man and wife.''

Connor drew Kristy to him and kissed her tenderly. She kissed him back. A cheer went up from the guests gathered around them, and then the whole group moved outside, beneath the clear blue South Carolina sky, and a whole slew of wedding balloons were let go, flying high, toward the heavens.

The reception was every bit as joyous as the sweet and simple ceremony had been. At last, Kristy thought, she had everything she had ever wanted. Her twins, however, weren't so easily satisfied. She could tell by the way they approached her and Connor as the reception drew to an end that they had something very definite on their minds.

''Mommy and Connor,'' Sally announced importantly, as the girls sat down at the bride and groom's table. She plucked at the fabric of her pink chiffon flower-girl dress. ''We have a very serious question to ask you.''

Connor smiled at Kristy and took her hand. He looked at the twins like the loving dad he already was to them. ''Okay, girls, we're ready.''

Susie, who had spent a good part of the reception enjoying the company of the babies in attendance, smoothed the skirt of her own pink chiffon dress and, with a look at her twin, drew a deep breath and said, ''We want to have a baby in our family, too!''

Their request made, Susie and Sally looked up hopefully.

Unbeknownst to the girls, Kristy thought, smiling, that issue had already been decided. Connor kissed her tenderly and drew her near. ''I think that can be arranged,'' he murmured.

Eyes shining with happiness, Susie and Sally looked at Kristy.

She grinned. ''I promise you two kiddos we'll get right on it.''

And hours later, in the cozy comfort of their honeymoon cottage on the beach, she and Connor did.

HARLEQUIN®

AMERICAN *Romance*®

celebrates its 20ᵗʰ Anniversary

This June, we have a distinctive lineup that features
another wonderful title in

The Deveraux Legacy

series from bestselling author

CATHY GILLEN THACKER

Taking Over the Tycoon

(HAR #973)

Sexy millionaire Connor Templeton is used to
getting whatever—whomever—he wants!
But has he finally met his match in
one beguiling single mother?

And on sale in July 2003,
Harlequin American Romance premieres
a brand-new miniseries,
Cowboys by the Dozen,
from **Tina Leonard.**

Available at your favorite retail outlet.

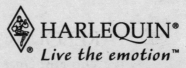

HARLEQUIN®
Live the emotion™

Visit us at www.eHarlequin.com

HAR20CGT

HARLEQUIN®

AMERICAN *Romance*®

prescribes three exciting doses
of heart-stopping romance in
a brand-new miniseries by

Jacqueline Diamond

Special deliveries straight to the heart!

Don't miss any of these heartwarming titles:

DIAGNOSIS: EXPECTING BOSS'S BABY
March 2003

PRESCRIPTION: MARRY HER IMMEDIATELY
May 2003

PROGNOSIS: A BABY? MAYBE
July 2003

Available at your favorite retail outlet.

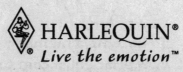
HARLEQUIN®
® *Live the emotion*™

Visit us at www.eHarlequin.com

HARBDC

eHARLEQUIN.com

Becoming an eHarlequin.com member is easy,
fun and **FREE!** Join today to enjoy great benefits:

- **Super savings** on all our books, including
  members-only discounts and offers!

- Enjoy **exclusive online reads**—FREE!

- Info, tips and **expert advice** on writing
  your own romance novel.

- FREE romance **newsletters,**
  customized by you!

- Find out the latest on your
  favorite authors.

- Enter to win exciting **contests
  and promotions!**

- Chat with other members in our
  community message boards!

**Plus, we'll send you 2 FREE Internet-exclusive
eHarlequin.com books (no strings!)
just to say thanks for joining us online.**

**——— To become a member, ———
visit www.eHarlequin.com today!**

INTMEMB

If you enjoyed what you just read,
then we've got an offer you can't resist!

Take 2 bestselling
love stories FREE!
Plus get a FREE surprise gift!

Clip this page and mail it to Harlequin Reader Service®

IN U.S.A.
3010 Walden Ave.
P.O. Box 1867
Buffalo, N.Y. 14240-1867

IN CANADA
P.O. Box 609
Fort Erie, Ontario
L2A 5X3

YES! Please send me 2 free Harlequin American Romance® novels and my free surprise gift. After receiving them, if I don't wish to receive anymore, I can return the shipping statement marked cancel. If I don't cancel, I will receive 4 brand-new novels every month, before they're available in stores! In the U.S.A., bill me at the bargain price of $3.99 plus 25¢ shipping & handling per book and applicable sales tax, if any*. In Canada, bill me at the bargain price of $4.74 plus 25¢ shipping & handling per book and applicable taxes**. That's the complete price and a savings of at least 10% off the cover prices—what a great deal! I understand that accepting the 2 free books and gift places me under no obligation ever to buy any books. I can always return a shipment and cancel at any time. Even if I never buy another book from Harlequin, the 2 free books and gift are mine to keep forever.

154 HDN DNT7
354 HDN DNT9

Name	(PLEASE PRINT)	
Address	Apt.#	
City	State/Prov.	Zip/Postal Code

* Terms and prices subject to change without notice. Sales tax applicable in N.Y.
** Canadian residents will be charged applicable provincial taxes and GST.
   All orders subject to approval. Offer limited to one per household and not valid to current Harlequin American Romance® subscribers.
   ® are registered trademarks of Harlequin Enterprises Limited.

AMER02   ©2001 Harlequin Enterprises Limited

HARLEQUIN®

AMERICAN *Romance*®

The Hartwell Hope Chests

RITA HERRON

returns with her heartwarming series.

Something old, something new, something borrowed, something blue. Inside each Hartwell hope chest is a dream come true!

Sisters Rebecca and Suzanne are as different as night and day, but they have one thing in common: a hope chest from Grammy Rose is certain to have them hearing wedding bells!

Have Bouquet, Need Boyfriend
On sale June 2003

Have Cowboy, Need Cupid
On sale July 2003

Available at your favorite retail outlet.

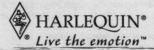

HARLEQUIN®
Live the emotion™

Visit us at www.eHarlequin.com

HARTHHC